D0194808

A Crime in the Neighborhood

A CRIME
in the
Neighborhood

a novel by
Suzanne Berne

Algonquin Books of Chapel Hill • 1997

Published by
ALGONQUIN BOOKS OF CHAPEL HILL
Post Office Box 2225
Chapel Hill, North Carolina 27515-2225

a division of
WORKMAN PUBLISHING
708 Broadway
New York, New York 10003

Grateful acknowledgment is made to *Agni*, where an excerpt from this
novel first appeared in slightly different form.

Library of Congress Cataloging-in-Publication Data
Berne, Suzanne.
    A crime in the neighborhood : a novel / by Suzanne Berne.
        p.   cm.
    ISBN 1-56512-165-1 (hardcover)
    I.   Title.
  PS3552.E73114C75   1997
  813'.54—dc21
                                                96-47654
                                                    CIP

10   9   8   7   6   5   4   3   2   1
First Edition

For Ken

One

In 1972 Spring Hill was as safe a neighborhood as you could find near an East Coast city, one of those instant subdivisions where brick split-levels and two-car garages had been planted like cabbages on squares of quiet green lawn. Occasionally somebody's Schwinn bicycle was stolen, or a dog was hit by a car that kept on going. Once in a while we heard about a shoplifter at the Spring Hill Mall, six blocks away. But otherwise both the mall and the neighborhood always struck everyone as the most ordinary of places.

Then one summer evening around five-thirty, just as business at the mall had finished for the day, a florist named Miss Evelyn Crespo carried a box of orchid corsages out to her car for a wedding that night. She had parked far back behind the mall in a row of spaces reserved for employees, below a two-acre wooded rise. That time of day, the mall's triangular shadow cut upward across the hill like a wedge. As Miss Crespo slid the corsages into her back seat, she heard what she thought was a cat mewing from the shaded half of the hillside.

The sun was in her eyes when she backed away from the car to look around. After a moment, the mewing came again, or something like it, a small, weak sound. Although she was a heavy woman, and the day was hot, she climbed partway up the rise toward where it flattened out, wading through the broken bottles, locust husks, and tangled creeper vines to see if the source of the mewing might be somebody's lost kitten. When she didn't find anything, she carefully edged back down toward the parking lot, once grabbing the branch of a laurel bush for support. Then she went inside the mall, locked up her shop for the night, waved to the hairdressers in the Klip 'n' Kurl hair salon, came out through the automatic glass doors to her car carrying the bridal bouquet, and drove off to Bethesda to deliver her wedding flowers. The whole experience lasted no more than ten minutes.

As it turned out, Miss Crespo was to recount the details of those ten minutes over and over in the next few weeks, first to the Montgomery County police officers who came to question her, then to a police detective, then to three newspaper reporters, later to her family and neighbors, and finally to her customers, who came into the shop to lean against her refrigerated display case of long-stemmed roses, tiger lilies, and baby's breath.

She described those ten minutes so frequently she grew sick of the sound of her own voice. She also ceased believing that the details she recounted were true, which happens when you tell a story about yourself so often the words are memorized. Because what Miss Crespo had heard that mid-July evening was not a kitten mewing, but a young boy groaning behind a clump of laurel bushes, where not twenty minutes before he had been raped by a man who had also tried to choke him to death.

In her police report, part of which was published in the *Post*, Miss Crespo said she had seen nothing unusual at the mall that afternoon. To her knowledge, none of the other store owners had seen anything unusual, either; most of them reported serving regular customers that day. However, an elderly woman walking her dog on Ridge Road near the big brick U.S. Defense facility did testify to seeing a boy talking to a man in a car just before five o'clock; the man, she thought, was balding, but she couldn't recall the color or make of the car. A bag boy at the Safeway, who was breaking down cardboard boxes outside by the Dumpster, heard a car skid out of the parking lot around five-thirty and looked up to see the taillights of a brown coupe, possibly a Dodge, or so he thought when presented with drawings of different car silhouettes. Neither the florist nor anyone else saw a man with a boy, and no one had seen anyone on the hillside that day.

It was Thursday, the 20th of July. The child's name was Boyd Arthur Ellison. He had just turned twelve years old. He couldn't help the police by describing his attacker because by the time he was found very early the next morning, his attacker had come back and finished what he'd started.

As the *Post*'s reporter later reconstructed events, the man who killed Boyd Ellison had seen the florist when she came out to her car with the box of flowers. Ducking and scrambling, he fled to a bushy stand of white pine farther behind the mall. From a distance, he must have watched her place the box on the back seat, watched her stiffen as she heard a noise. He must have watched her back away from the car, shade her eyes, and look up the hill, then make her slow way over the curb and up through the creeper, her broad face perspiring in the late-afternoon sunlight as she paused to listen again. She had run her nylon stockings in her search; she kept them to show the police. He must have seen her bend down with an irritated exclamation and lift her skirt hem to look at the pale ladder widening on her calf.

According to the police report, she had stepped within five yards of the boy; if she had turned slightly left, if she had looked carefully, she might have seen one of his bare shins, his foot in a white gym sock, half buried in leaves. But Miss Crespo was nearsighted. One of her small vanities was to avoid wearing her glasses in public. Even if she had turned left, even if she had looked, she might still have missed seeing the boy's bruised leg. What she should not have missed seeing, although perhaps she never brought herself to admit it to the police, was a boy's black basketball sneaker, unlaced, which had tumbled down the hill and lay in the gutter under the curb, only a few inches from the front tires of her car.

At the inquest, Boyd's parents, Walter and Sylvia Ellison, both testified that the morning of their son's death imitated every summer morning of his life. His mother woke him at seven so that he could have breakfast with his father before Walter left for work at eight. According to what I remember, it was a bright, hot morning. According to what I imagine, the family had breakfast on their screened porch, as most of our neighbors liked to do in the summer. Like most fathers, Walter Ellison would have skimmed the newspaper while he ate his grapefruit. Boyd drank a glass of orange juice, ate an English muffin with raspberry jam and a soft-boiled egg from a china eggcup designed to look like a chick with an eggshell on its head. While he waited for his egg, he told his father about the book he was reading, *The Call of the Wild*, which my brother had read the summer before. Walter finished his toast, drank a glass of milk, kissed Boyd good-bye, and told his wife he would be home at the usual time. Then he kissed her good-bye, too, and left for work.

At six-fifteen, just as he was about to leave his office at the Federal Reserve, Walter Ellison got a call from his wife saying that she couldn't find Boyd. He hadn't come home after she'd sent him to the mall at four for a packet of straight pins and a carton of sherbet. Walter told her to phone the police and said he would be there as soon as he could.

It was Walter who found him. With over fifty men from the neighborhood, Walter had searched all night, swinging a flashlight under people's hedges, behind garages, through backyards, calling and calling and calling. The neighborhood men divided up into search parties of three or four, and each group sent runners periodically to find out if the other groups had discovered anything. Walter's group had picked across the mall's parking lot and found the black sneaker, but twice went right up the hillside past where the boy lay. Only the third time, as the sun was coming up, did they see him—did his father see him. He got down on his knees and tried to cover the boy with himself while another man ran down to the parking lot to call an ambulance from the pay phone beside the mall.

Walter told the man who stayed with him that he thought he felt his son's heartbeat. But that was impossible, the coroner said later; the boy had been dead more than eleven hours by then. When the ambulance shrieked into the parking lot to take Boyd's body down MacArthur Boulevard to Sibley Hospital, no one had yet discovered the three-pound, conical piece of limestone, lying a few feet away under a laurel bush, that had been used to smash in the back of his skull. All his father knew, as he pressed his son against his chest and imagined the beating of his heart, was that he had been found.

Two

Why I recall that particular grisly incident so exactly has something to do with my age at the time, and something more to do with what my family was going through that summer, and also with the fact that I knew, very slightly, the boy who had been murdered. But mostly it has to do with a kind of fanatic vigilance I practiced back then.

If you ask my mother what I was like as a child, she'll tell you that I was one of those little girls who never said much but who was always *there*, especially during fights. At every spat, every loud argument, every disagreement in the grocery store check-out line, there you'd find me, looking on. Though small for my age, I was the first one to push inside the circle during playground brawls, just out of range of the kicking and flailing, but right up close so that I could see everything. Later on in my bedroom I'd replay the scene, repeating bits of dialogue in front of my mirror, examining each insult and shove to figure out why it had happened.

I always wanted a reason. "Why?" I asked my mother, my father, anyone who would listen. "Why did it happen?" I was fascinated by how people managed to hurt one another, by what could make them want to do it. Not sentimentally fascinated; my interest in those days was mechanistic: I wanted the mainspring, the wheels and teeth.

So it's not surprising that although Boyd Ellison's killer has never been found—one of those unfinished stories that sometimes happen in life—as a child I was so anxious to discover him that for a while I almost believed I knew who he was.

But to tell that story I need to tell this one, which is less sensational, except perhaps to those who have lived through something like it.

One cold February evening, as we were all sitting at the dinner table eating pork chops and mashed potatoes and speculating on whether it would snow, and whether if it did snow it would snow enough that the Maryland schools would close the next day, my mother suddenly turned to my father, who had been staring out the window, and said in a conversational tone, "I know you know I know."

She might have opened her mouth to ask him to pass the butter, but another sentence had come out instead. A very strange sentence, I thought at the time. Without understanding what my mother was talking about, I recognized a clutch of implications. What did she know? And how could my father know she "knew" something and yet have to be reminded he had such information?

As the youngest of three children, I was used to being un-enlightened during dinner-table conversations. I went on eat-ing my pork chop. But it was impossible to ignore what hap-pened next. My mother picked up her plate and, with a snap of her wrist, sailed it like a Frisbee straight across the dining room. China shattered. Mashed potatoes and gravy splattered against the wall and onto the blue carpet and sprayed my father's white shirt with grease spots. One half-eaten pork chop landed on top of the china cabinet.

It was an absurd and terrible moment, and in the way of such moments, also cinematic—with that pork chop bal-anced on top of the china cabinet and my family staring up at it with open mouths, which made me want to laugh. Even my mother looked as if she wanted to laugh. Her eyelids crinkled and the corner of her mouth jerked up. But the next instant she reached over and one after another sent my brother's, my sister's, and my own plate spinning.

"I won't pretend I don't know," she said. Then she stood up and left the room. We watched the kitchen's swinging door swing behind her. My father was still holding his fork.

Of course, for many people who grew up in the '70s, child-hood was spent between parents, rather than with them. If parents didn't actually divorce, they certainly thought about it, often out loud, and sometimes requested their children's advice. I've heard horror stories about Christmases spent in airports, scenes at high school graduations, photo albums with one parent or the other scissored out. I've heard so many of these stories that they're no longer remarkable—in fact, they have stopped being stories at all and have turned into clichés, and the more predictable the worse they are: the father remarries a witch who dislikes his children and turns him against them; the mother remarries a brute who likes her daughters too much. But any cliché has a fact for a heart, and the fact is that marriages, like political alliances, broke up all over this country in the 1970s, which in the latter case at least had never happened before.

The cause of my own parents' divorce was predictable enough. My father began seeing another woman. What spins their story in a slightly different direction is that the other woman happened to be my mother's younger sister, her favorite sister, Ada.

My mother never much trusted men. In her opinion, they lacked character. When she was seven her own father died of pneumonia after falling asleep drunk on a Baltimore park bench in the snow, leaving his wife with four little girls and no life insurance. They moved in with my mother's grandparents, who were well-to-do, but six months later her grandfather had a stroke and spent his last three years in bed, rattling the brass headboard with his good hand. It was soon revealed that he, too, had neglected to prepare for anyone's future, and after paying off the night nurses and the funeral bills, six females found themselves close to broke just as World War II was ending.

They managed. The two women took in sewing, did some typing, ate corn flakes for dinner, and, with a loan from a great-aunt, finally moved to Bethesda and opened a gift shop that specialized in Hummel china figurines. My mother says she and her sisters grew up tough and sober, qualities they believed their male forebears had lacked. While they dusted those porcelain shepherd boys and goose girls, they planned how to be unbreakable.

"Always pay for your own movie on a date," they told one another sternly. "Never say thank you unless you mean it. Get respect."

Their loyalties lay strictly with one another, especially when it came to men. They knew how fragile men could be, how easily they succumbed to a cough, to a palpitation. Hadn't they seen it? Males, they confided, carried diseases. Sitting cross-legged on their beds at night, they demonstrated for one another how to kiss boys with lips sealed shut. Wear an undershirt *and* a bra, the older ones instructed the younger ones. Be prepared.

My grandmother used to say she had given birth to one daughter with four heads, an uncomfortable image that seems unlikely coming from the plump old lady I remember dozing by the radiator in her brown wool slacks and pink fur house slippers. But the image was true enough in its way. My mother and her sisters liked to exact unified vengeance when one of them was mistreated, usually by way of carefully orchestrated, malicious jokes. In one story my mother liked to tell, her sister Claire dated a boy who then lied to his friends about having sex with her in the back of his father's car. Two days later, the results of this boy's yearly physical examination, signed by the school nurse, were "stolen" from the school infirmary and appeared on a bulletin board. The report graphically detailed the boy's unfortunate condition as a hermaphrodite and recommended surgical intervention. I have forgotten which sister forged this document, but apparently the forgery was so excellent that no one believed it was a fake until the school nurse stood up during an assembly and declared she'd had nothing to do with it.

My mother and her sisters always figured in these stories as a hilarious, vindictive sorority: Fran, Claire, Lois, and Ada, the fabulous Mayhew girls—funny, brazen, compassionate, and ruthless, a private female army. The Mayhew Girls, that's how I thought of them. Like the title of a book.

My mother and her sisters were all very tall, which may be why the fast put-down happened to be their particular talent. "This big," they would say, holding a thumb and forefinger two inches apart when some miscreant boy passed by. It was left to him to decide if they meant a specific part of his anatomy or only his general character.

As I still imagine them in these stories, the Mayhew Girls are always dressed in nunnish black ankle-length skirts, white blouses, and seductive, shiny patent-leather pumps. They wear red lipstick, but their underwear is sewn by their mother out of old linen pillowcases. They smoke cigarettes and toss around slangy phrases like "Hey, Daddy-o" and "Catch you on the flip side"; yet they perform brilliantly in Latin, shouting lines from Virgil in the bathtub, writing *"panis"* instead of "bread" on grocery lists, quizzing one another on verb conjugations while they pluck their eyebrows. Like my grandmother, I had a hard time as a child separating one aunt from another. In my mother's stories, virtually no separation existed.

Of course, that was my mother's story. The true story, if there is such a thing, must hover somewhere closer to misery. The fifties weren't a time to be odd, and four lumbering girls with no father and pillowcase underwear must have felt unbearably unusual in suburban Maryland. Most likely they stuck together because they felt left out of any other group they tried to join. Their devotion to one another was defensive, reflexive, parochial. Us/them.

Which is probably why they exaggerated so cruelly about one another. "Claire called the other day," my mother might tell Ada as they sat at the kitchen table stirring their coffee. "I had to listen for two hours while she complained about how much the dog sheds. 'Why don't you just *harvest* the damn thing,' I said. 'Make it into an afghan.' Well, you know Claire—"

Or she might hang up the phone from talking to Aunt Fran and immediately dial Ada's number to say, "Listen to this, I just talked to Frannie. She's bought a new Sears dishwasher—well, you know her, you'd think she'd bought the Waldorf-Astoria. 'Why don't you just move into it,' I said. 'It sounds a lot fancier than your house—'"

Naturally my mother never said any of the things she reported herself as saying. Maybe Aunt Claire had complained briefly about the dog's shedding; maybe Aunt Fran boasted for a moment about her dishwasher. But for my mother to render these details realistically would be to miss a chance of celebrating her latticelike relationship to her sisters. She loved to talk about one sister with derogatory intimacy to another. And whatever self-criticism she was likely to entertain she also leveled at them, so that she was continually admiring her own flaws in the others. "We're all touchy," she might say proudly. "You know us."

The only one who sometimes escaped this X-ray attention was Ada. Ada was the baby of the family, even several inches shorter than the other three. As a child she had been unusually self-absorbed and was therefore considered artistic. She spent hours in her room with scissors and a pile of magazines, cutting out movie stars and pasting them into little booklets she made out of stapled construction paper. The movie stars were then given bits of dialogue in balloons, most of which concerned Ada herself. "Isn't Ada the cat's pajamas?" Rita Hayworth asks David Niven in the one booklet that survives. "Isn't she the bee's knees?"

In keeping with her artistic nature, Ada seemed more

exotic to me than my mother or my other aunts. She had grown her hair long, when most women her age wore bubble cuts and shags. Her hair was a bright auburn and she liked to sweep it back from her forehead with her hands and bunch it between her fists. She had a fondness for silver bangle bracelets that clinked whenever she swept back her hair, and when she laughed her eyes disappeared. Privately, I believed, or hoped, that I resembled her; in fact, my hair is the same color, although curlier.

But Ada was always different from the rest of the family, and it wasn't simply that she was more attractive. She not only looked soft, ripe, and pliant, and seemed to feel that way, but she appeared to consider this quality enough to recommend her to anybody. Her laugh was slow and full; her gestures were languid, even when she meant to be in a hurry. Her arms plumped near her shoulders, and under her flimsy embroidered peasant blouses, her full breasts swayed, braless. My mother and aunts could be self-critical to the point of paralysis, but not Ada. Ada *liked* how she looked. I've known a few women like that since, who truly think they are beautiful or sexy and become so, even if they're plain, and I've always been a little afraid of them, as my mother and her older sisters sometimes seemed a little afraid of Ada. Sexual preoccupation is an imperious thing, and when it's in full color, it makes all other preoccupations look slightly beside the point.

Oddly enough, my mother felt protective about Ada. "Oh,

she's had a lot on her mind," she would argue if Fran or Claire accused Ada of laziness when she failed to send Christmas presents or forgot their birthdays. My mother had a certain admiration for vanity, for its vividness, the way scrupulous people can admire hucksters. "You know Ada," she would say with a laugh. "She's a little distracted by herself."

And until the year Boyd Ellison was murdered, the sight of Aunt Ada in our kitchen, long hair curling loose down her back, sitting at the Formica table doodling on a paper napkin while my mother made dinner, was as familiar to me as the sight of my own brother or sister. Ada had accepted her role as the family artist and, with financial help from her older sisters, had gone to art school for a year before dropping out to marry Uncle Roger, who managed a steakhouse in Bethesda called The Flaming Pit.

Ada taught art classes at an elementary school in Rockville. She had no children of her own.

"It's Little Miss Marsha, the Martian Girl," she always said when I came home from school; then she asked me what was "new." She listened seriously to whatever I told her and often drew a picture of what I described. When I was finished talking, she'd hand me the napkin. If I had done well on a quiz, she drew a crown. If another child had hurt my feelings, she drew a picture of that child being pierced by arrows or getting run over by a truck.

"Come on, Ada," my mother sometimes said. "That's not nice."

"Come on yourself," Ada would laugh, sweeping back her hair.

But most of all I remember her smell, a disturbing smell, provocative, fruity—I can smell it now just thinking about it —a smell something like moist apricots. Sometimes when she spoke she would hood her upper lip like a horse trying to nibble a carrot. Of all the sisters, she had married first, at eighteen.

"Well, you know Ada," said my mother, when anyone asked why.

I mention all this history as a roundabout way of saying that despite the natural resentment any timid woman holds for a bold one, I believe my mother loved her sister Ada more than she loved my father. Simply, she trusted her. She trusted her as one trusts someone fully comprehended, which may not be a good idea as there is no such thing. Ada was a safeguard, an ally, part of my mother's future plan, which she had learned early to prepare and maintain. Her betrayal was far more shocking to my mother than my father's betrayal, which she had always more or less expected. In all the cruel, elaborate jokes they crafted together, my mother never imagined a sister would play one on her.

Two days after that cold February evening when my mother sailed our plates through the air, Aunt Fran and Aunt Claire arrived for a visit.

They appeared at the front door clad in nearly identical outfits of pastel blouses and tweedy slacks, and Aunt Fran was wearing desert boots. They were leggy, stoop-shouldered women, edging past forty, with short toast-colored hair and worried brown eyes, more angular versions of my mother. Aunt Fran was the tallest, with a big jaw and a skinny neck. Aunt Claire had kindly, popped eyes, which made her look like a Boston terrier.

Every time my mother told one of her Mayhew Girls stories, I always pictured Fran and Claire as elegantly insouciant, the sort of women who made wisecracks and wore scarlet lipstick, who drank martinis and didn't eat the olive, who could sprint in high-heeled shoes. Every time I saw them, I had to remember all over again how ordinary they looked; but this time their ordinariness seemed deliberate. Aunt Fran carried both of their plaid suitcases, while Aunt Claire toted along an enormous half-finished needlepoint of the Eiffel Tower with a leftward tilt. As they strode toward the house from the car, they looked like a matched set of army nurses. "Hi, kids," they shouted as they stepped through the door, in rough sweet voices that might have demanded hospital corners and sterilized gauze.

When Aunt Fran bent to kiss me, a sharp whisker prickled my cheek. She smelled of peanuts and wintergreen Life Savers. "For you," she murmured, slipping into my pocket a bag of sourballs.

That night my sister and I slept in sleeping bags on the floor of my brother's room to free up enough beds. Suddenly our house filled with raspy whispering female voices, a sibilant, maddening sound to a child who is afraid to know why her father drives off to work red-eyed every morning, while her mother spends her mornings vacuuming ferociously, up and down the stairs, through every room, her mouth set like a gladiator's.

My father had confessed. Why or how I do not know; my mother has never said, and she is not easy to question. But apparently during this time an attempt was made "to work things out." Ada stayed banished in her brick townhouse in Bethesda, painting watercolors of fleshy peaches and pears, while her two eldest sisters drove back and forth in our Oldsmobile station wagon bearing messages, conferring, theorizing, solemn as a pair of generals. A hectic excitement surrounded them both: Aunt Fran had left her husband and son in Milwaukee, and Aunt Claire had left her two daughters and her husband in Detroit. As difficult an occasion as it must have been for them, it was still a vacation. They bought packs of Kools as soon as they arrived, though both had quit smoking, and drank white wine before dinner. After dinner they draped their long legs across the sofa, displaying at last a hint of insouciance, and blew perfect smoke rings at the ceiling.

The rest of the time Aunt Claire stitched at her pillow while Aunt Fran hunkered onto the floor to do stretching exercises, their hoarse voices hoarsening as time went on, and during the day they persuaded my mother to go shopping for shoes. At least, I remember her, during that period, wearing several pairs of new platform shoes, which looked like hooves.

My aunts took turns corralling the twins and me into the station wagon as soon as we got home from school to herd us off to the mall. Trailing whichever aunt had accompanied us, we would buy chewing gum and jawbreakers from the drugstore, then wander past shop windows, stepping on the heels of one another's sneakers, snickering at the negligees in the window of the Coy Boutique, always ending up at the pet shop to watch the tropical fish avoid each other in their aquariums. This diversion was to give my mother more time to "talk" to the aunt who had remained behind. But when we returned, she would be sitting silently on a kitchen stool, staring at the gold flecks in the Formica tabletop.

Perhaps the twins and I talked about our parents among ourselves that week. Perhaps one night I cornered my sister, Julie, and asked her what she thought was happening. But I don't think I ever did. She and Steven had each other for confidantes—they were twins after all, and at fourteen plunged into intrigues with each other and their friends that I found unfathomable until I got to be fourteen myself.

Also Julie despised me. Whenever I asked her anything she mimicked my questions back at me in a lisping voice. She had a passion for British novels in those days and had adopted an affected Oxford tone straight out of Evelyn Waugh, which made every nasty thing she said sound even nastier. "The Child," she and Steven called me, "Marsha the Swamp," or simply "Swamp."

My aunts spent hours talking to my mother. Their voices sailed out from the living room, swooping back to a whisper if my mother reminded them we might be listening, only to rise again, flapping upward like shorebirds. When she arrived, Aunt Claire had given me a conch shell from Bermuda. I remember being embarrassed by the shell's glossy pink interior, which looked to me like an exaggerated version of my mother's broad upper lip. My mother had never had what you could properly call a harelip, but her lip was wide and gently peaked at the top. "Go on," said Aunt Claire, when I hesitated to press my ear next to the shell's opening. "Hear the ocean talking." From then on the cloistral roar of the conch shell was what I always imagined when I passed the living room and heard my aunts' voices.

They both thought my mother should give my father time, that he needed to get "it" out of his system. "Not that we're excusing *her*," they often said, sometimes in unison. "Don't think that for a minute. You know us." Vigorously they nodded their cropped, delicate-looking heads.

Who knows why my father decided to stay in the house during that week. Perhaps he thought it was a show of strength or, more likely, an act of atonement. In the early mornings before he left for work, and in the evenings after he got home, my father drifted through the house like smoke from my aunts' cigarettes. He played "As Time Goes By" and the easier parts of "Moonlight Sonata" before dinner on our upright piano in the living room; but now he didn't ask me to turn the pages of his music books, and he made more mistakes than usual. In the evenings after dinner he mixed Scotch and milk in a Flintstones glass and drank it standing up by the refrigerator.

Sometimes he paced back and forth on our screened porch. More often he disappeared. I began hunting him through the house even after I was supposed to be in bed, finding him in odd places like the basement near the boiler or in the kitchen hovering by the back door. Late one night I found him standing outside his own bedroom.

"Hi there," he said. He looked like someone waiting to be called into the dentist's office.

We stood a few moments together, examining the hallway's orange carpet with its rushing pattern that always reminded me of goldfish swimming upstream. Here and there the carpet had worn thin in places; some of the goldfish had nearly vanished.

"You know," my father murmured, looking at the carpet and twisting a button on his cuff. "You know a lot's been happening around here. A lot of changes. Not about you, though. None of this is about you, sweetheart." He smiled at me sadly. "So you just keep on with what you were doing, Marsha honey. Do whatever you need to do."

"But I wasn't doing anything," I said.

"That's all right." He seemed anxious to reassure me, but uncertain about the direction this reassurance should take.

That night, cross-legged on my bed in my pink nightgown, I wrote him a note on a strip of notebook paper. "Hi, Dad. This is from your daughter Marsha. Bet you're surprised to find a note in your pocket. I just wanted to say you do whatever you need to do, too!" This last bit didn't sound quite right, but I couldn't think how to change it and I was suddenly very tired, so I stumbled downstairs and slipped the note into his overcoat.

A night or two later, I sat watching *Laugh-In* on television in the living room with my father and the twins. I had been sitting close to my father's armchair, holding his hand by the wrist, when halfway through the show I suddenly felt I had to see my mother. I wanted her in that way of very young children, a muddled, weepy kind of lust.

I searched first in the kitchen, then in the basement, finding traces of her everywhere—a coffee cup with lipstick prints, a crumpled tissue. Finally, as I padded into the dark upstairs hallway in my stocking feet, I heard first her voice and then my aunts' as they talked in her bedroom.

From what I could hear, they were getting ready to trim one another's hair, and Aunt Claire was proposing to give my mother a henna rinse in the bathroom.

"Take off your blouse," one of them ordered. My parents'

bedroom door had been hung backward, so that it opened into the hallway; it stood partly ajar, and almost without thinking, I stepped behind it.

"You know, you're going to have to face up to the situation," Aunt Claire was saying. "Confront it. Then you have to go on."

"That's easy for you to say," said my mother.

"Of course it is," said Aunt Claire. "But it's still true."

"What you have to do," Aunt Fran said, "is forget about dignity."

"Believe me," said my mother. "Dignity is about the last thing on my mind these days."

I edged around so that I could squint through the crack between the hinges and the doorjamb, hoping, and fearing, but hoping more intensely, that my aunts would take off their clothes. I believed they would still be wearing that pillowcase underwear I had heard about, and I wanted to see what it looked like—I even pulled my glasses out of my pocket and put them on in anticipation of this possibility. I was also interested in seeing their breasts, which I imagined as fleshy megaphones topped with glowing red doorknobs. That's what breasts looked like in Steven's drawings, which he hid under his bed. He called them "tooties." Why I assumed my mother's breasts, glimpsed occasionally in her bedroom or in the women's changing room of our community pool, were not "tooties," I'm not sure, except that nothing belonging to my mother seemed unusual to me then, or seemed to belong to anyone but her.

My mother and my aunts abruptly stopped talking, and for an instant I thought they had seen me behind the door. But then they began again, talking now with the stiff casualness of people who are forced off a subject that interests them.

"It'll give you a lift," Aunt Claire told my mother, standing close behind her. She ran her fingers slowly up the back of my mother's hair while they both stared at themselves in the mirror over the dresser. "Auburn highlights. That's all it is."

"I don't know," said my mother in a querulous voice.

Aunt Fran sat down on the edge of the bed and pulled off her sneakers. "You have the cutest figure, Lois," she said, smiling at my mother's back. "Really. What a nice little package." She leaned over and gave my mother a swat on the bottom.

Staring gravely at herself in the mirror, my mother turned her head from side to side, Aunt Claire's fingers still sifting her hair. "You don't think I'll look silly?"

Aunt Claire slid her hand out of my mother's hair and let it rest loosely on her shoulder. "You'll look beautiful. You look beautiful now."

"Ha," said my mother.

"Oh, you don't know." Aunt Fran pushed her green tweed slacks down around her hips. She stood up to wriggle them down to her knees, then stepped out of them and left them crumpled on the floor. She wore plain white underwear, a fringe of dark hair curling tightly out from under the white fabric at the top of each of her legs. As she unbuttoned her blouse, I could see the front of her brassiere, a bit of lacy panel. She let her blouse hang open and sat back down on the bed, crossing her legs. "You've always been the beautiful one."

"I am not," said my mother, but she smiled a little into the mirror, one corner of her broad lip lifting.

"Much more beautiful than Ada," said Aunt Claire.

"Ada's getting fat," said Aunt Fran, gazing again at her own long, muscular legs.

"I don't want to talk about Ada." My mother moved away from Aunt Claire and headed toward the bathroom, out of my sight. Aunt Claire raised her eyebrows at Aunt Fran, who shrugged.

"Take off your blouse and skirt," Aunt Claire called after my mother. "And bring out the scissors. We'll trim your hair first while the henna dissolves." She sat down with a bounce on the bed next to Aunt Fran and began unbuttoning her own blouse. "All I want is about an inch off the ends. How much do you want?"

"Oh I don't care. I had my hair cut last week. I'm just doing it to be part of things."

Aunt Claire smiled as she pulled off her blouse. She wasn't wearing a brassiere at all. Instead of the two cones I'd been expecting, a pair of small, flattened-looking eyes confronted me, oatmeal-colored save for the brown, protruding, button iris—bizarre, almost horrible, plain human flesh.

Aunt Fran had now taken off her blouse and was standing

by the bed in her bra and white underpants. She looked like a giraffe, she was so tall and sinewy, so unnaturally unencumbered as she shifted from one leg to another, flexing her leg muscles, her smallish, sleek head lifting suddenly, blinking at the sight of herself in the mirror. On the bed, Aunt Claire leaned over to pull off her penny loafers and then her knee-high nylon stockings. Her pale back was spattered like a dog's belly with large brownish freckles.

She sat up again and fluffed the back of her hair with one hand, yawning, then looked toward the bathroom. "Lo?" she called. "Are you ready?"

Both of my aunts sighed as my mother came suddenly back into view. She was wearing a green towel around her head; otherwise she was completely naked. It was a surprisingly sad thing to see my mother naked. I had seen her naked before, but not, it seemed to me, for a long time, and certainly not in this way. She looked diminished and ribby and white—and unexpectedly hairy. She also looked on display, like a store mannequin waiting to be dressed. A thin, pinkish scar I remembered but had forgotten sliced along her lower belly, ending in a grim bristle of hair.

Was this what my father saw when he looked at her at night in their bedroom? I imagined my mother demanding that he touch it, touch her scar. He would be afraid; he would curl his fingers back at the last moment. And I guessed that this scar must be the root of their trouble, their fighting, their silence, that my mother's body should have been perfect, as mine was perfect. She put one hand on her hip, one on the doorjamb, and waited.

"Why look at you," cried Aunt Fran. "Venus on the half shell."

My mother smiled blankly. The lenses of my glasses fogged up. I closed my eyes and counted twice to one hundred by tens. When I stopped counting, my mother had gone back into the bathroom.

The very next night I was sitting on my mother's bed with her and Aunt Claire, when my mother abruptly got up and flung open the bedroom closet where my father's suits hung neatly on the rod. "I guess we should think about giving these old clothes away," she said. Perhaps I imagined it, but the creak on the stairs seemed to be my father, shifting back down to the kitchen.

"Lo," said Aunt Claire. "This isn't the way to handle it."

"Tell me another way," said my mother, tightening her lips.

By then she was already referring to my father in the past tense. "Larry used to like that show," she might say if we were all in the living room trying to watch television.

He would look up and lightly shudder.

"Larry always ate his grapefruit after he finished his coffee," she might tell my aunts at the breakfast table, "because if he had them together he said they left a moldy aftertaste." And there my father would be, holding his coffee cup, his grape-fruit untouched in front of him.

Once she got going, she couldn't stop. The fast put-down. The cruel, humorous revenge. Having the Mayhew Girls in the house inspired her.

"It can't be sex she wants him for," she said loudly to Aunt Fran on the last morning of my aunts' visit, just as my father was leaving for his office. "That thing hasn't had batteries for years."

The twins smirked nervously at each other.

"Lois." Aunt Fran pointed her big chin at me over the cereal boxes.

"Oh, they don't even know what sex is," said my mother.

"*Lois*," said Aunt Claire.

But my mother had already added: "They're his kids, after all."

And then from the doorway, my father said, "That's *enough*."

We all looked up. He was standing in his dark blue over-coat, his hat in his hand lifted halfway to his head so that it looked as though he were doffing his hat to my mother. My note must still have been in the pocket of that coat; as soon as he put his hand in his pocket, he would feel it rustle against his fingers, slender as a fortune from a fortune cookie.

As I recall that moment now, the pause thickens, grows greenish and dense; a shadow blows across the kitchen windows, darkening the room. From a street away, a dog begins to bark. In the flat chill of that morning, sound carries acutely; the dog could be barking in our own kitchen. Someone yells at the dog to shut up. The dog barks louder. My father continues to stand in the doorway, still in his attitude either of leave-taking or congratulation, or perhaps supplication, his hat cradled in his hand.

The shadow blows past; sunlight washes back through the windows; the dog stops barking. My father stares at my mother, and she stares back.

"That's enough," he says.

And in a reasonable, almost pleasant voice my mother says, "I agree."

Three

My father and Aunt Ada betrayed themselves with the sort of small, deliberate indiscretion people always seem to make when they have done something they're ashamed of. My father had a birthmark the size of a plum on his right hip, just above his groin. It was dark red and tender-looking, shaped like a rabbit with one ear. I recall noticing it one day when I caught him stepping out of the shower. It was a very innocent-looking birthmark.

One Sunday evening my mother, my father, Ada, and Uncle Roger were sitting in our living room drinking beer and watching a news broadcast about President Nixon's trip to China.

This trip marks a new era, my mother said. The world is finally coming together.

"Hope Nixon's not turning commie on us," said Uncle Roger, who hated Communists the way people these days hate smog.

"Roger thinks Communists should be branded with a scarlet C," said Ada, flicking his thigh with her fingernail.

"I've heard," said Uncle Roger, "that real Communists all have a little tattoo they can show each other to prove party loyalty. They make them show it at the door before they can go into meetings."

And my father said: "Rog, I bet you think everybody with a birthmark is a Communist."

It was, naturally, only logical that at this moment Ada would giggle and say: "Like you, Comrade Larry."

"Comrade Larry," repeated my mother, her mouth extremely small.

But I'm not satisfied with this story, although it's the only one my mother ever told me about my father and Ada, and she told it only once. Despite her usual truthfulness, my mother has exaggerated. She is too stock in her role as the naive idealist, along with Uncle Roger as the red-faced McCarthyite, my father as the flawed social critic, and Ada as the tipsy adulteress who forgets to keep her mouth shut. While I do believe the four of them sat in the living room and watched Nixon wave from the Great Wall of China, and I do believe this was the day my mother realized her husband and her sister were having an affair, I don't believe my mother's realization happened as crudely as she has chosen to characterize it. Perhaps she liked this story because it's just complicated enough to sound true, and because Ada and my father look sordid; especially Ada seems sloppy, thoughtless, a woman no one would miss having as a sister. Anyone hearing my mother's version gets Ada with her stocking feet on the coffee table. The living room flickers with blue light. My father hulks in his armchair, the top buttons of his shirt undone, displaying the collar of his undershirt. Uncle Roger chews pretzels on the sofa, occasionally elbowing Ada to get him another beer. My mother, through all, sits primly in the bentwood rocker; if she knitted, she would be knitting.

None of these people bears much resemblance to the people I knew. Like cartoons, a few features remain recognizable in magnified form. Otherwise, my mother's story seems received, a narrative she picked up, like the new shoes she kept buying, because it fit and because it made her feel a little better.

However she found out, she found out. As I imagine it, my mother glanced up from the television set and saw my father looking at Ada. My version of the story has its received side, too: because I see in that look the sort of frank, sensual absorption I've glimpsed in the movies, once in a great while, between an actor and an actress who want each other and can't have each other and never, in the movie at least, get each other. I think my father was looking at Ada like a man stirred by something he found beautiful. His stare was appreciative, alive with a current of desire. Desire on a man's face can be ugly, but my father's face that night looked almost pure. There he sat, a settled-looking man of forty-two, with a small chin, aviator-style glasses, thick, longish ginger-colored sideburns, and a broad, pale forehead—gladly subsumed. He wanted Ada, and his want concentrated his whole face into an unaccustomed severity, so that my mother could see bones where his face had grown fleshy, could see the outline of his skull, as if the force of his longing had begun to waste him away.

What told my mother everything was not that my father had never looked at her like that. She knew the look, although she hadn't seen it for some time. She knew where it came from, which was not from a fantasy experience but from the anticipation of a real one.

Nixon waved from the Great Wall. Uncle Roger drank his beer. My mother rocked in the rocking chair. Finally she glanced at Ada. Ada was not looking at my father. She was examining her smooth fingernails, painted that night the moon color of pearls.

I imagine my mother got through the rest of that February evening in the living room by paying careful attention to everything said on the news about Nixon's visit to China. She leaned forward, her eyes fixed on the television screen as TV commentators speculated on how trade with China might alter domestic affairs. It became her passion for the next few weeks: Nixon's visit to China and how the world had changed.

The twins and I were also in the living room that evening, lying on the rug with our chins in our hands, watching the TV set, though I doubt we were paying much attention since we thought news happened to other people. In a moment, in a glance, life for us was changed forever, and we never saw a thing.

"This is history," my mother said again and again that year as she read aloud articles from the *Post* or reported what she'd heard on the *CBS Evening News with Walter Cronkite*. Governor Wallace shot in Laurel, half an hour from our house; the Watergate break-in; the murder of eleven Israeli athletes at the Olympic games. I hardly listened. "This is *history*," she would insist, as though introducing me to someone I should already know.

One night she tried a recipe for chicken croquettes that turned out to have too much salt. A week later the Chiltons, from next door, told us they were moving to Rhode Island and had sold their house to someone named Green. Julie failed a math test. A gutter fell off the side of the house. These incidents, too, struck my mother as historic. She noted them all with urgency. "What's next?" she often said. "Could you please tell me what's next?"

It was only after my father left and Boyd Ellison was killed that I started to wonder myself what might happen next. Boyd Ellison's family lived only two streets away, in a '50s contemporary with a Japanese maple in the front yard. I passed it whenever I rode around the neighborhood on my bike. The Halloween before, I had knocked on his door, shouting "Trick or treat" when the door opened and a dark-haired woman looked out at me. The Halloween before that, Boyd had come to our door dressed as a television set; he wore a cardboard box with real antennae tied to his head with yarn. I often saw him on the playground, although he went to a different school —a short blond boy with a square head who was always asking for things: a bite of your sandwich, a ride on your bike. He once asked to wear my glasses. He was irritating and pushy, sometimes a bully. He asked for things he knew you'd rather not give.

Steven, although two years older, had once briefly been in Boyd's Cub Scout troop. Boyd sat cross-legged in my own basement tying bowline knots and whittling soap cakes when the Scout troop met at our house one Sunday afternoon. He had asked for an extra brownie. He wanted a sip of my mother's coffee. He cut his thumb with his pocketknife and came out of the bathroom with one of my mother's fancy hand towels wrapped around his hand, wondering whether he could take the towel home.

"No," my mother had said, more gently than I thought appropriate, and gave him a Band-Aid instead.

Although it seems crazy, I find myself wondering if all that asking had something to do with what happened to him. I suppose I wondered that at the time, too. Somehow Boyd seems to have asked for it, the "it" that is always out there, ready to transform your life into something unrecognizable. Because this, too, is how life can change: you can ask for what happens to you, without realizing what you're asking for. Perhaps this is supposed to be fate.

But then again, fate could be something much more terrible: something that could have been avoided. Fate might be no more than a mischance—the look intercepted, the wrong thing said, the decision to take a shortcut on a hot July afternoon through the woods behind a shopping mall.

After five days with us, Aunt Fran and Aunt Claire departed together, both with sore throats from so much talking and smoking and both anxious to see their own families, to relax back into caring for people with manageable problems. Both of them had tried to get Ada to come back with them for a visit, but Ada refused. "I'm happy where I am," she was reported to have said. But before they left, they had each spent part of a day with Ada, "trying to get her story"; unfortunately, neither one seemed certain what to say about whatever story she gave them.

It must have been shocking, to think that all these years they had imagined she felt herself a sister to them the way they felt a sister to her.

"Well, it's not that she's any different from before," Aunt Claire told my mother on their last afternoon. They were all three crowded into the pantry, putting away our blue-rimmed dishes. "It's just that I feel I hardly knew who she was."

My mother caught sight of me sitting under the dining-room table a few feet away. "Marsha, go on out. Your aunts and I are talking."

I went into the living room and sat behind the sofa.

"I don't think Ada wanted this," said Aunt Claire hesitantly in a lower voice. "At least, I don't think she planned to want this."

"In my opinion, it's all about sex," said Aunt Fran.

"Please, Fran," said my mother irritably.

"Do you think you'll ever forgive her?" said Aunt Claire. "Really ever forgive her?" She handed my mother a wine glass to polish.

They all three held glasses to the light, looking for water spots.

"I think Ada's jealous of you," continued Aunt Claire, after a few moments when my mother didn't say anything. "She's always wanted what you have."

"Which is what?" said my mother, knitting her eyebrows.

"Children. The whole 'being settled' thing, with Larry getting successful and all, or at least comfortable. This house. You're always so busy—you know what I mean, in that way a woman with a big life is busy. School, errands, birthday parties."

"Errands," said my mother. "Birthday parties."

"Look, I'm trying to tell you something. To her I bet your life has always looked . . . so *set*."

"It's certainly set now."

"You're not listening, Lo. You don't have to let her take everything away. You still have a family. You still have your kids. I don't think Larry wants to leave."

My mother picked up another wine glass and held it upside down by the stem, dangling it over the floor. "I'm no longer interested," she said, "in what Larry wants."

"Don't do it, Lois," I heard Aunt Fran break in, and the rough pleading in her voice struck me, which is why I have always remembered this conversation. "Don't do it," she said.

It would have blown past, my father's infatuation with Ada. He was a mostly mild man with a weakness for passion, a suburban father burdened with the heart of a Russian hero without any sort of balancing grand intellect or ironic world view. The yearning itself, the recklessness, that's what lured him. Ada had it, too, the desire to do something dramatic, large, doomed. Their lives were so ordinary, and they themselves were ordinary enough to think of a commonplace way to shake it all up.

My mother, however, was not ordinary.

Very quickly her grief and anger vibrated into something less personal: my father and Ada became her punishment for ever having felt secure. She should have seen the affair coming. There had been signs, she told Aunt Fran and Aunt Claire — lingering smiles, too much help with a coat at Christmas, each one by chance mentioning the same restaurant on the same day. She had not been careful. In this way, their affair became her fault. It was her punishment for forgetting that the world is and always has been a disastrous place.

My father moved out on a Tuesday morning, the day after my aunts left, right after we had gone to school. And for a little while, our lives didn't seem to reflect the enormous changes under way. We were used to coming home and finding only my mother there; my father rarely drove into the driveway until half an hour before dinner, and often he was out of the house to meet a client before I had finished my orange juice. So for a few moments each afternoon after I stepped through the door and pulled off my jacket and dropped my bookbag on the floor, I could almost believe that nothing had happened.

First my father stayed at a Howard Johnson's near the new Watergate Hotel; after a few weeks he rented a studio apartment on MacArthur Boulevard, not far from his real estate office and near the reservoir. His front window looked across at a stocky little cement castle that had been built at one corner of the reservoir, probably to house pipes and part of the filtration system. When we visited, I often knelt on his new fold-out sofa and looked out at the castle's four crenellated towers, imagining what it would be like to live there.

My father seemed unable to furnish or decorate his apartment after installing that sofa bed. For months he ate standing up in his tiny, bare kitchen. He bought a small, black-and-white TV set, which he set up on a milk crate. He kept his underwear and his socks in one of his suitcases. Whenever we visited, we all sat on the wood floor and ate Chinese food out of the paper cartons, or ate pizza and drank Coca-Cola from plastic cups, which my father washed and kept to be used again. Otherwise he made no effort to keep his apartment clean, and after he'd been there a few weeks dust balls rolled in the corners when we opened the door while spiderwebs floated from the windowsills.

Meanwhile, every evening my mother walked around our house by herself, opening closet doors and looking into them, opening cabinets, pulling open drawers. Down in the basement she sorted through carefully labeled boxes of winter clothing, old toys, and Christmas ornaments, only to repack them all again. One afternoon I came home to discover every single one of those repacked boxes stacked on the curb to be thrown away. Over the next few weeks, she threw out boxes of books, boxes of photographs, mysterious boxes marked only "Attic" or "Keepsakes." Some boxes had no labels at all. After a while, I don't think she herself knew what she was throwing away.

At night, while we were in bed, she cleaned. Sometimes we woke to the rumbling of furniture being shifted downstairs, or the chatter of plates being run in the dishwasher for a second or third time, or the crash of the silverware drawer being emptied so that she could tear out the old shelf paper. She washed all the windows, a job that must have taken days. She scrubbed the kitchen's linoleum floor, which had yellow and green squares. One morning, all the yellow squares were white.

Around the house, she began wearing one of Steven's baseball shirts and a pair of his outgrown basketball sneakers. He was already as tall as she, and his feet were two sizes larger. She looked surprisingly young in his clothes, despite the deepening lines that ran from the wings of her nose to her mouth. One day I told her I liked her more the way she looked before. For a long moment she gazed at me, an exclamation mark of grease on her forehead. Then she said, "Too bad."

Her biggest project during this period was refinishing the dining-room table. She and Steven carried it out to the screened porch and put newspapers on the floor. For the next two weeks, my mother stood out on the screened porch at night in all kinds of weather, first sanding the tabletop by hand, then each of the legs, then staining the whole thing twice, and after that adding a coat of clear varnish. The table became a lovely cherrywood color that glowed on evenings when she decided to light the candles. She called the table her "piece de resistance."

For the first few weeks of my parents' separation, Aunt Fran and Aunt Claire called my mother every day. "Oh, hi," she'd say in a toneless voice that let me know it was an aunt, not someone for whom she had to sound cheerful. "No, I'm okay." She was usually on the telephone with one or the other of them in the afternoon when I came home from school. While I opened the refrigerator, my mother would watch me from her kitchen chair, one elbow on the table, swinging the long phone cord like a jump rope, slapping it against the floor.

If around this time she noticed the little shrine of snapshots on top of my bureau—photos of my father doing yardwork, my father eating a hamburger at Uncle Roger's restaurant, my father paddling a canoe on the C&O Canal—she never mentioned it. Perhaps she guessed my secret: that I was beginning to have trouble picturing him whenever I wasn't with him. I would close my eyes to concentrate and after a few moments I would summon his ginger-colored sideburns, then his small ears, then his aviator glasses, then at last his long face would come into focus, smiling apologetically, his blue eyes small and indistinct behind his glasses. If I made myself look hard enough I could catch their expression, which was sometimes distracted and sometimes kindly and sometimes slightly cold.

In an attempt to remain loyal, I also tried to remember the things he cared for and review them before I went to bed. Every morning in the shower he liked to belt out several bars of "Singin' in the Rain." He loved thick socks and the melancholy light of evenings in late summer. He loved to mow the grass because he said that mowing released the lawn's tender smell. "Nectar and ambrosia," he often said when he sat in his chair before dinner with his glass of Scotch and a bag of corn chips. He celebrated little necessities and comforts in a way that reminded you that nearly anything could be transporting if you put your mind to it.

He was a true voluptuary, in his own modest way, with a voluptuary's genius for softening the world around him. After he moved out on that cold Tuesday morning, our house began to seem drafty, full of hard surfaces and stale smells.

The separation was hard on him, too. One Sunday, about six weeks after he'd left our house, my father and I were sitting cross-legged on the floor in his apartment eating grapes while he watched a football game on TV. The twins lay reading old *TV Guides* on the sofa bed, whispering to each other. With the puritanism of teenagers, they had taken my mother's side almost from the beginning. Between themselves they referred to Dad as "Dud," although they stayed rudely polite while they were with him.

Outside, the sky had turned the color of an old pie tin. The wind lashed up the bare branches of the horse chestnuts across the street and drove sticks and candy wrappers across the sidewalk.

Meanwhile I was pretending that we were Polish refugees, and that my father's apartment was a boxcar. We were heading for the border, where my father had figured out a way to save us all, and even Julie was grateful. I listened to the crowd cheer on TV and ate another grape. This was the last of our rations. I pictured myself thin and pale, being carried by my father through the snow.

"How about we order a pizza?" he asked at a commercial break.

I reached out to punch his leg, just to touch him. Then I

looked up and saw his cheeks were wet. I asked why he was crying and behind me felt the twins stop reading their comic books. My father wiped his face with his sleeve and said he was allergic to the varnish his landlady had used on the woodwork.

Did my mother see Ada during that time? I like to think she must have, at least once. For all her energetic stoicism, she was only human.

They would have made arrangements to meet at the mall, somewhere public, like wary people on a blind date. My mother would have wanted no chance of hysterics, on her part or Ada's. In different ways, they were both circumspect women. Instead of weeping and scratching each other with their fingernails, they walked around and around the upper floor of the mall, two tall women in bulky parkas and leather boots, my mother carrying a purse with a broken strap, which she had mended with an old diaper pin. Their elbows pointed at each other; otherwise, they might have been shopping the Presidents' Day sales. But they kept their voices down and stared at their boots, ignoring the rack of gauzy negligees whenever they circled past the Coy Boutique.

Occasionally their elbows bumped, which made them stagger apart. Ada watched my mother's face, looking for an opening, a chance to begin excusing herself.

She had never meant for things to go so far. From what I've gathered, Ada was the most prosaic and nearsighted of the

Mayhew Girls, the one who, in the company of the sister she was betraying, the husband she was cheating on, and the man she was sleeping with, would be truly interested in the state of her nail polish.

Can't we just forget about all this? she might have said, with a trace of a whine.

But that's not quite right, the whine part. Ada was also the most fun of the sisters, the one who laughed most easily, the one most willing to forgive a slight. Every Christmas they all gave one another earrings, but my mother and my aunts always seemed to buy one another pearl studs while Ada gave them long dangling silver earrings with moonstones or turquoise or jade. They made meatloaf or pot roast for family dinners; she made lamb curry or chili rellenos. "Hey there," she cried when she saw you, as if you were someone she had been hoping to see. She was almost beautiful; she was almost generous. She was a relief to have around.

So: *Can't we just forget about all this?* she might have said, with the trace of a smile, because she actually believed forgetting was possible.

But my mother walked on. Perhaps she shook her head. Perhaps she made a chopping motion with her free hand, the one not gripping her purse strap. Perhaps she, too, wore a trace of a smile. This is what she had come for, after all, the gritty pleasure of denial.

Both of their faces stayed white. When they left the mall, they walked separately over the dirty snow to their cars, parked at opposite ends of the parking lot, and each sat for a few minutes behind the steering wheel before starting her car and driving away.

One cloudy afternoon in late March I came hope from school ahead of the twins to find a note pinned to the front door. SHOPPING, it read—in a couple of the letters the ballpoint pen my mother had used had driven all the way through the paper. It wasn't like my mother to be gone when I came home from school, but in the last few weeks she hadn't been like my mother in so many other ways that this one seemed hardly remarkable.

I had just turned around to hunt for the spare key hidden under the front steps when Aunt Ada's old red VW bug pulled into the driveway.

"Hey there," she called.

She was wearing a pair of dark sunglasses and a yellow sweater with white appliquéd sunflowers around the collar, which matched her big white plastic sunflower earrings. The frames of her sunglasses were white plastic, too, and almost square, which made her face look like a house with dark windows.

"Hey," she said again softly as I came up to the car. When she saw me looking at her earrings, she said, "Aren't these cute?" She unclipped one and handed it to me. "Keep it. When we meet again, we'll recognize each other because we'll be the ones wearing only one earring." Her square sunglasses were impenetrable and she smelled strongly of drugstore lily-of-the-valley perfume.

Then suddenly she laughed. "Oh come on, kiddo. It's just me. It's just Ada. I mean, I'm not *that* bad." She did look just like Ada, with her silver bangle bracelets and her auburn hair the same color as mine, so familiar that I had to smile.

She smiled back, then lifted up a piece of sketch paper that had been lying on the seat beside her. "I drew a picture. I came all the way over here to show it off."

In charcoal pencil, she'd drawn a woman looking through a telescope. Far in the distance, a tiny figure was walking away over a hill. That was what the woman was seeing through the telescope.

"That's me." Ada angled one finger through the window to point to the woman. Her fingernail was dirty; most of the pink polish had chipped off. "And that's your mom."

I backed away again, gripping my bookbag against my chest.

"Oh honey. I didn't mean to scare you." Ada pulled the picture back into her car, then sighed and leaned her head against her seat. Her throat looked long and pale. Now that she wasn't looking at me I could see her eyes behind her sunglasses and they looked smaller than before; the upper fold of her eyelid drooped. Her hair was shorter too, and darker. Altogether she did look different, not so much altered as sunk into some part of herself that I'd never noticed before. She closed her eyes, her chest slowly rising and falling. Her head lolled to the side. I thought she might be falling asleep.

Across the street, Mrs. Morris came outside and stood on her front steps, but after I waved to her she turned around and went back inside. Finally, Ada opened her eyes.

"Can I ask you a favor, Marsha?" She paused, looking down at her hands on the steering wheel. After a moment she said: "Don't tell your mom that I came by here this afternoon. Please? I guess I've decided that what I was going to tell her wasn't such a good idea after all."

"What were you going to tell her?" I put one foot exactly ahead of the other, toe to heel. Then I took two steps back, heel, toe, heel. I wished she would go away. My mother could come home at any moment. While I didn't understand the full extent of their estrangement, I knew enough to recognize that Ada didn't belong in our driveway.

As if she understood, Ada suddenly started the car. It took a minute to get revved up, choking into action like an old lawn mower. She made a face, leaning against the wheel, her cheeks flushed now and damp-looking. Then she said something that I couldn't hear over the noise of the engine.

Her face looked unbalanced without both earrings; although if you had walked past her, it might have taken you a minute to figure out what was wrong, like one of those trick pictures where it turns out that the girl has only four fingers or a button-up shoe on one foot and a laced shoe on the other. I thought about running after her with the other earring, but before I could make up my mind, she had driven halfway down the street and was too far gone for me to catch up with her. So I went inside and hid the earring in my underwear drawer.

A couple nights after Ada's visit, Uncle Roger came to our house and he and my mother stayed up very late talking in the living room. Uncle Roger was Greek. Doudoumopolous was his last name; for many years it was the longest word I could spell. He had a high, creased forehead and heavy-lidded brown eyes with broken capillaries netting the corners. My mother once told me that he had been handsome when he was younger—actually, her word was "slick"—but his flamboyant black mustache always reminded me of seaweed. That night he blew a kiss to where I stood blinking at the top of the stairs, but he didn't say hello.

"Go to bed," my mother told me from the landing, putting up her hand like a traffic cop. Her bare heel was the last thing to vanish into the living room; I saw it lift right out of the back of her shoe.

For a few minutes I listened to the dip and swell of their voices, although I couldn't hear what they were saying; after a while I sniffed the brown stink of Uncle Roger's cigar, something my mother had never before allowed in the house.

"Good-bye," said my mother when Uncle Roger was leaving. I woke up to hear the screen door bang. "If you don't mind, I'd rather we keep this little episode to ourselves."

The "episode," I found out much later, was that Ada and my father had slipped away together for a weekend.

That part doesn't surprise me when I think about it now. People who have gone so far always go a bit further. One careless step—then it hardly matters what carelessness follows. Or at least, that's how it can seem to the person who has been careless.

But I'm no longer sure I understand why Ada came to see my mother just before she and my father went off for their secret weekend. Maybe she wanted to be talked out of it. Or was she counting on my mother's bitterness to goad her into doing what she'd otherwise lost heart for?

I imagine her driving her little red car up our street, muttering to herself, repeating whatever phrases she had rehearsed, knuckles whitening as she gripped the steering wheel. Those small bright eyes, that defiant mouth, the rounded shoulders, all that dense, fox-colored hair. She hadn't meant to let go of her sister so easily— or to be let go of. But then, when she arrived, my mother wasn't there, only me clutching my bookbag. And she lost her nerve.

But for what kind of fight? That's the question that keeps needling me—whether in the end Ada persuaded herself that she loved my father or hated my mother. It had to have been one or the other for her to do what she did.

Or could she simply have made a terrible mistake? And once she was caught in the middle of it, she couldn't see how to get out of it. Or maybe she even fell in love with her own confusion—there was her grand passion, her way at last to be different, extraordinary, to make her sisters stop claiming that they knew who she was. For a little while at least, her mistake might even have looked like bravery.

Because the truth is, mistakes are where life really happens. Mistakes are when we get tricked into realizing something we never meant to realize, which is why stories are about mistakes. Mistakes are the moments when we don't know what will happen to us next. An appalling, exhilarating thought. And while we entertain it, the secret dreaming life comes groping out.

So my father and Ada snatched a couple of days together, went to the beach, probably Virginia Beach because it was close. They would have rented a motel room with a view of the ocean, a little cement balcony where they could sit in the evening with their drinks. They wore their coats, a cold ocean breeze chapping their faces as they glanced back and forth between each other and the sand. They watched the waves scrolling in toward shore, gazed past the surf to a flat, wide distance. That span encouraged them; perhaps it looked like an open margin between themselves and the rest of the world.

Four

In April the Chiltons moved out of the house next door, taking their sweet cross-eyed baby and leaving their broken picnic table and a square lawn full of crabgrass for the man who moved in. His name was Mr. Green. I woke up one morning and fumbled on my glasses to see an orange moving van parked on the street and chairs and tables being carried out of it.

"Somebody's moved into the Chiltons' house," I announced at breakfast.

"Have they?" said my mother, from behind the newspaper. She had begun sitting at my father's place at the table; no one sat at hers. "How do they look?" she said eventually, turning a page of the newspaper.

"Regular," I said. "It's a man."

I was pleased to be the first to notice our new neighbor; it gave me a kind of claim on him. Otherwise I noted only that he appeared to be a bachelor, which was unusual in our neighborhood but satisfied me because now I wouldn't have to worry about meeting strange children and having to invite them to play Ping-Pong in our basement. Nothing could be expected from me regarding Mr. Green, except courtesy, so I waved to him that afternoon when Julie and I walked home from the mall. He was unloading boxes from the van. I remember that he paused to balance a box on one knee in order to wave back. He was a squat man, with a pinkish face, blandly familiar, although he didn't actually resemble anyone I knew. When he bent his head, I saw that he had a bald spot, shaped like a heart.

"He looks like a creep," said Julie.

It had been wet in March and early April, then suddenly it got very hot. In just a few days, our big front yard went from a brown mat to a seething tangle of color. Lilacs and wisteria bloomed, and the azaleas and the crab apple tree. Tulips, daffodils, irises driving up like spears. Blooming saturated the air, seeping in through open windows and under doors and into the sofa's upholstery. The storm drains clogged with apple blossoms; all the car windshields gathered greenish pollen, frothing against the windshield wipers.

A kind of lawlessness infected everything. Next door, eight-year-old Luann Lauder decorated herself with toothpaste one Sunday morning and ran across the lawn in only her underpants. Boyd Ellison appeared on the playground one afternoon with a ten-speed bicycle he said was a birthday present but which looked just like our neighbor David Bridgeman's bicycle, which had recently been stolen. Blue jays screamed all day long. Even the grass looked an unearthly green, as it does right before an electrical storm, when the air starts to hum and your hair stands on end.

And yet our neighborhood was anything but lawless. With its tidy lawns, pruned dogwood trees, and sputtering lawn mowers, Spring Hill still strikes me as the most wonderfully inoffensive of places whenever I drive through it. Our house was the oldest one on the block, a bungalow throwback to when people used to summer by the river. We had a screened front porch, shade trees, and a wide front yard set up on the top of a hill, with a view of half the street.

In 1972, Washington suburbs like ours were dowdy, provincial places, like the city itself. The Whitehurst Freeway still ran past an old rendering plant, which smelled so rankly of boiled hooves in the summer that motorists rolled up their car windows even on the hottest days. The Whitehurst emptied behind the battery-shaped Watergate Complex, still known only as elegant apartment buildings. Locusts banged against the screen doors of houses all the way up Capitol Hill. The spring before, millions of locusts had crawled out of the mud after a seventeen-year sleep, buzzed like madness for a week, then died. Their fat brown bodies piled up in drifts, so that we wore rainboots when we ran outside. The whole city filled with a drowsy insect racket on summer nights, which radiated from the pavement right into the trees.

As I remember it, the Washington suburbs didn't get expensive until the Reagan years. During his presidency, money exploded into towns that had been shabby, somnolent, often little more than two gas pumps, a Baptist church, and a post office. Suddenly every backwater had a foreign car dealership, a gourmet grocery, and a colonial-style brick bank. Malls erupted. Office parks moved into Rockville; the computer industry swarmed up around the Beltway. Across the Potomac, Roslyn of the pale green willow trees disappeared beneath a wilderness of skyscrapers. Jaguars and Mercedeses backed up along Sagamore Road, twisting out past the defunct amusement park by the river. If my father had remained a real estate broker, we could have been rich. Little houses became big ones, while big houses became mansions, and the bigger the houses got, the less their inhabitants seemed to know about the people who lived near them. Until finally what you had were "residential areas," places where someone could be murdered on the next block and you wouldn't know who he was.

Nowadays our old neighborhood is settled mostly with young lawyers, a few systems analysts, maybe a lobbyist or two, maybe a retired two-star general. Twenty years ago mostly low-level government workers lived there, GS 3s and 4s, along with a few insurance adjusters, pharmacists, and small-business owners. They drove Chevrolets and dented Ford station wagons. They kept bowling trophies on the mantel in the paneled den and invited their neighbors over for iced tea and mixed nuts while their kids played skidoo in the rumpus room. Even though it was rumored that the brick Defense facility behind the mall was really the president's secret underground bunker, where he would be hidden away during a nuclear war while the rest of us melted, none of our neighbors seemed particularly nervous about the future.

Their politics were desultory and middle-of-the-road. Most of them had voted for Nixon; they had also voted for Kennedy two terms before. For them, as for the rest of the country, Kennedy had been a romantic choice. Nixon seemed more pragmatic. It was there in the flat ring of his voice, the way he said, "My fellow Americans." The times demanded pragmatism. There were the Soviets to consider, the Chinese, the student protests, the war in Vietnam. Nixon, with his shovel face, his unhappy, determined little eyes, could handle them. He was thrifty and basic. He had no illusions. He was someone you could trust.

Of course it was still early in 1972. Our neighbors called Nixon Tricky Dick, like everyone else, but joking about crooked politicians was just a way of looking savvy; they didn't believe he was any worse than any other politician. Or rather, they didn't yet believe that there was no such thing as good government—just a few bad politicians. Neither did they lock their doors at night, or dream of applying the word "dysfunctional" to families.

Vietnam was so distant for most of them, a glimpse of jungles or rice paddies on the evening news. The Cold War seemed frozen far away. About as activist as our neighbors got was to sign a petition my mother had circulated in January to save the patch of woods behind the mall from being made into a parking garage.

In those days I still loved the quiet brick view of the Morrises' and the Sperlings' split-levels from our porch, with their box-shaped lawns and square-trimmed hedges. I loved the sight of metal trash cans lined up on the street every Wednesday morning. I loved neat leaf piles. I also loved the quickening smell of lighter fluid and charcoal on summer evenings, when every house became a campsite, the street became a river, and we ran through dark backyards to the sinuous burble of television sets.

Then my father left, and a few months after that Boyd Ellison was killed behind the Spring Hill Mall, and what happened in our neighborhood began to seem less and less like what happened in neighborhoods.

My fifth-grade teacher, Miss Sullivan, had begun reading a few pages from *The Hound of the Baskervilles* every afternoon before the final bell while the class drew pictures in their notebooks or rested their heads on their desks. Those boggy, sulfurous moors haunted me like something out of a recurring dream; every afternoon I sank into them, my hair knotted by the wind, my eyes bleared with staring into the yellow night, relaxing only when I crept through the fog and the drafty gloom of the Baskerville mansion back into my seat at Clara

Barton Elementary School. Whenever Sherlock Holmes noticed a small detail, one I knew would turn out to be important later, I would grip the edge of my desk and hold my
breath. One afternoon my face must have turned red because
I heard someone laugh. Miss Sullivan looked up and fixed her
maidenly trout eyes on me.

"Marsha," she said sadly. "Is there a joke you'd like to share
with the rest of the class?"

The trick, I realized, was to notice everything.

And so it was that the day after Mr. Green, our new neighbor, moved in, I began keeping a notebook in which I docu-
mented my travels through our house. I noted the worn
patches in the hallway's Oriental runner, the scuff marks on
the stairs, the scorch at the back of the lampshade in the living room. The screen was coming away from the screen door
in one corner, curling away from the metal frame like a leaf.
The volume-control knob had fallen off the hi-fi, leaving a
forked metal bud. Steven had spilled India ink on the sofa, and
if you turned over the left cushion, you found a deep blue
stain shaped like a moose antler. I had never realized our
house contained so many damaged things. Soon it seemed I
couldn't look at anything without finding something wrong
with it.

On the cover of my notebook, I wrote "Evidence."

Mr. Green was not an especially interesting person, but
around this time I also began noticing him, at first casually
while I sat on the porch. Every morning he left his house car-

rying a bag lunch and a thermos of coffee. He climbed into his car, carefully backed out of his driveway, then drove off down the street, keeping an eye out for children on bicycles.

In the evening he returned, always at the same hour. Mothers would be calling through screen doors for their children to come in for dinner; in shirt sleeves and loosened ties, fathers dragged green garden hoses onto their lawns to water the shrubbery. I think he must have been between forty-five and fifty. His most distinctive feature, aside from the bald spot, was a long nose that seemed at odds with the pink anonymity of the rest of his face. This was the Mr. Green I began to follow every evening, and in reverse every morning as I sat on the screened porch listening to the catbirds squall in our crab apple tree.

Mostly he moved methodically from his house to his car, or from his car to his house, only varying this pattern to mow his lawn with a chattering push mower, or to pull a few weeds that sprouted, always in the same place, beside his front stoop. On weekend afternoons he sat in his shady backyard, where an enormous copper beech rose like a waterspout from its pool of dirt. But other than his initial wave the day he moved in, we hadn't exchanged any greetings.

Then one Saturday evening that spring, as I crouched near the fence in our backyard, I heard a man's voice say, "Hello there," and I looked up to see a gray shadow; and then suddenly there was Mr. Green looming bulkily from behind a lilac bush.

I'd been singing to myself as I built an ant village in the dirt in a shaded corner that I'd always considered absolutely secret. It made my heart turn to realize that someone had been watching while I constructed tiny ant ranchettes and ant apartment buildings and sang "Where Have All the Flowers Gone," a song that always brought me to tears, which is why I sang it.

"Hi," I said, blinking back at him.

We regarded each other for several moments. "What you building there?" he said finally, lilac leaves brushing his head as he cracked his knuckles.

"It's a science project."

"Aha," he said, beginning to edge away.

"For school." I felt emboldened by his lack of interest. "Last year we studied amoebas."

"Ameobas," he repeated.

"You can only see them through microscopes. Even then you have to look carefully. We also looked at a cow's eyeball under a magnifying glass."

"Yes," he said, as if he'd already known this. "Well, good-bye there," he added.

And he walked slowly across his backyard, past his copper beech tree and his aluminum chair, up his two back steps and into his house. This was perhaps the first private conversation I had ever had with a man who was not my father or one of my uncles. It left me with a peculiar feeling fluttering between excitement and disappointment, and something else that even now I'm not sure how to name. It wasn't really much of an encounter, and yet it has remained troublesome enough to make me wonder if that small violation, that quiet little intrusion, was what first set me against Mr. Green.

June arrived. School ended. Hurricane Agnes slammed into town, tore off tree branches and knocked down power lines and left lake-sized puddles in the street. A few days later the twins snuck in to see an R-rated thriller at the MacArthur Theater and were graphic for days afterward. They began interrogating each other with flashlights, one barking questions while shining the flashlight into the other's eyes. *When did you last have sex with a chicken? Have you ever eaten a pig's testicle? Was the pig still alive?*

By then my mother had taken my father's college beer stein from its place on the living-room mantel and recast it as a toilet-brush holder in the downstairs bathroom.

Because she refused to allow him to come to the house, my father often met us on Saturday afternoons in parking lots, sometimes at a bowling alley or skating rink, sometimes the mall. Steven always made a point of shaking his hand, telling him everything that had happened all week in a rush of over-confident chatter. Julie stood a little apart, smiling a cryptic smile she had practiced in the bathroom mirror. I waited until he had finished with the two of them so that I could be lifted into the air and embraced all alone, and wedge my face into his crisp white shirt, and wrap my arms tight around his neck.

One warm Saturday, not long after the hurricane, my father met us in the mall parking lot and presented each of us with a water-resistant wristwatch with a striped cloth wristband. He said he was going on a little business trip, maybe for a couple weeks. To Delaware, he said. A real estate convention. Then maybe a short vacation. Three weeks at the most. He presented my watch to me and said the time would go by "in no time."

"That's a pun, honey," he added. Then he hummed a few bars from "As Time Goes By." "Marshamallow," he said, squatting on the pavement in front of me. "Let's not cry, sweetheart."

"Oh God," muttered Julie. "Spare us, Junior Sarah Bernhardt."

She had dressed to annoy my father, squeezing herself into an old black satin sheath dress of our mother's, which had moth holes in the bodice. She had lined her eyes with black eye pencil and given herself a beauty mark the size of a thumbtack above her upper lip.

"I thought we were going bowling," she added, one hand on her hip.

My father cleared his throat and tried to pry my arms from around his neck. "Not today."

"What *are* we doing today?" said Steven.

"Today we're just going to talk."

I stepped back. The twins groaned and rolled their eyes. Julie put her other hand on her hip.

"I wanted to tell you kids." My father paused and straightened up, then leaned against his car. "I've been meaning to tell you, to let you know, that I am sorry everything has worked out this way. I wish it could be different, but it is what it is."

"What?" said Julie.

"What what?" said my father, looking surprised. He had been regarding us very earnestly.

"The way what is?"

He flushed behind his aviator glasses. "Our lives. Your mother and I—"

"Oh," said Julie. "I know all that." And she took her hands off her hips and turned away. "You know what," she told Steven. "I need to get some stuff from the drugstore."

"It can wait, can't it?" said my father.

"Dad," Julie said balefully. "I am having my *period*."

Steven snickered.

"All right," said my father helplessly.

"I'm having my period, too," said Steven, following Julie and her sheath dress across the parking lot, although he had stopped snickering by then and looked back once or twice, his silky little ponytail wagging.

After they had disappeared, my father and I leaned against the car. A seagull flew overhead, which was unusual this far inland. I pointed out to my father that it must be lost.

"Listen," he said at last. "About this little trip I'm taking. It isn't much. You'll hardly notice I'm gone. It'll be all right." Gently, he patted my head. "I'll be back soon."

Even then I knew he was lying.

Actually, that's not true. I would like to think I was prepared for what happened next; but in fact I was used to believing what my father told me, so as I trailed after the twins later that afternoon on our way back home, my thoughts were probably no more anxious than the thoughts of any child whose parents are separated and who is being ignored by her older siblings.

My father had not looked especially grave that afternoon. His aviator glasses were not askew; his hair was not standing on end. Instead, as I remember that day now, he looked only subdued squatting in the parking lot of the Spring Hill Mall, holding me at arm's length.

"I'll be back soon," he said, without a catch in his voice.

In my imagination, a seagull circles and circles overhead, the afternoon sun glinting off his outstretched wings. My father bends over me. His sideburns tickle my cheek. "It is what it is," he whispers. "What is it?" I whisper back.

On our way home the twins and I saw Boyd Ellison ride by on his bicycle. He was standing up on the pedals, leaning over the handlebars, intent as a wizard. If he waved at us, I don't remember now. "Queer bait," said Julie, as he flashed by. Steven said, "I wonder why Dad gave us these watches." "Who cares," said Julie. "Mine is hideous."

Later that same afternoon, to escape the sneering accents of the twins reading aloud from their yearbook ("Mary Alice Neider simply scintillated in the Junior Class production of *Love's Labor's Lost*"), I clawed as high as I could up the crab apple tree and hid inside the leaves.

It began to be evening. A radio was on in the Lauders' house next door and I heard snatches of words, mostly about poll results; it was an election year and even I understood the difference between Democrats and Republicans. We were Democrats. The air cooled and from the branch where I sat picking off lichen I could smell mown grass and road tar and hear kids on the next block scream *Red Rover, Red Rover*. They seemed to be calling in the evening, which drifted closer and closer as cars drove into driveways, screen doors sang and slammed, and here and there a light switched on. Until suddenly everything was blue.

My mother came to the porch door to call me in for dinner. She stood looking at our yard, twining her hand in her hair before she called me again. After a few moments, she walked slowly onto the dark grass, calling, "Marsha? Marsha Martian?"

She passed close to my tree, one hand now fingering the collar of her blouse. I could see a fork of white scalp through her brown hair and a dab of ketchup on the pale inside of her arm near the elbow. Bits of wet grass stuck to her sandals. If she had only looked up and to the left, she would have seen me watching her through the crab apple leaves. But she didn't look up. She walked to the daylily bed and for a long time she simply stood there, smoothing her cotton skirt. At last I saw her reach into the loose collar of her blouse and lightly hold her throat.

She looked over the hedge into our new neighbor's yard, where his boatlike Dodge was anchored in the driveway. A light flicked on in his kitchen. "Marsha?" called my mother again, higher this time; as she spoke my name the brassy, jungly opening bars of a jazz tune wavered out from Mr. Green's kitchen window. Across the street, the Morrises' sprinkler began to spurt. A gray cat crept into the yard with something dangling from its mouth, then slithered into the hedge like an eel. My mother swayed a little by the daylilies, pressing the balls of her feet into the grass, her skirt brushing her bare knees.

As I shifted in the tree to get a better look at her, pushing leaves from my face, a spiderweb ghosted over my hand and all in a single rush my mother slipped away and I lost my grip on the branch I was holding, and felt myself slide, hitting my head against another branch, and felt myself fall, and fell clear to the ground.

The wind was knocked out of me, and for one wild, cottony moment I thought I was dead.

By the time I sucked my breath back my mother was crouched over me, lifting me under the arms. "You're okay," she kept saying, panting hard. She pounded my back, beating between my shoulder blades.

Her lips made a perfect O as I turned my face toward her.

It took a good several minutes for either of us to realize that I had broken my ankle.

In the excitement of rushing me to the hospital, where I had X rays and then got my ankle swaddled in an important-looking white plaster cast that stiffened to my knee, my mother forgot to check the mail and it wasn't until Sunday afternoon, after we had finished eating tuna salad and rye bread and dill pickles for lunch, and she had washed the dishes, and put them away, that she found the note from my father, handwritten on a memo pad that said at the top "From the desk of Lawrence Eberhardt."

"Lois," it read. "By the time you read this I will be on The Road. Ada and I have decided to make a Go of it. I know this will be hard for you to Understand, but none of this is meant to hurt You or the kids. That is the truth. Love, Larry."

My father had not gone to Delaware for a real estate convention. He had not even driven back to his apartment on MacArthur Boulevard after meeting us in the mall parking lot. He did not appear at his office on Monday to sit behind his Scandia blond-wood desk with the green-shaded fake brass library lamp and the glass jar full of peppermint drops. That Saturday, after saying good-bye to us, my father picked up Ada in Bethesda and together they drove all the way to Connecticut, where they spent the night. The next day they drove to Maine and took a ferry to Nova Scotia.

All this I discovered later. I found out about the note that night by listening in on the upstairs extension in my mother's bedroom, with my ankle propped on a pillow, while she talked to my aunts, one after the other, on the kitchen telephone.

"Oh, for Pete's sake," said Aunt Fran, when the note was read to her. "Oh, Lois. I'm sorry, but this is ridiculous."

"It may be ridiculous to you—"

"What I don't get," continued Aunt Fran without listening, "is why he wants her so much." I could almost hear her add: Or why she wants him.

"You know how I picture myself in ten years?" my mother said. "I picture myself enormously fat and living in a trailer home with the blinds pulled down. No one visits me and I eat potato chips all day long. The only way anyone knows I'm there is that occasionally an empty potato-chip bag flies out the window."

"Lois. That will never happen."

"How do you know? Nobody knows what could happen to me."

"Nobody ever knows what could happen," scolded Aunt Fran.

Across the street the Morrises' lights went out. Four houses away David Bridgeman, still mourning his stolen bicycle, was practicing "Greensleeves" on his recorder, making quavering alto sounds as I looked out at the streetlights and at the lit-up pools of lawn.

Aunt Fran said, "Why do you think he left?"

I could hear my mother shift on her kitchen stool. After a moment she said, "I don't know. He's always thought he was missing something. Some grand destiny or something. She's the same way. You know Ada." She stopped and made a sound deep in her throat.

Then she shifted on her stool again, scraping it against the floor. "Marsha? Marsha? Are you on the upstairs phone? I want you to get off this instant."

My ankle throbbed as I eased my cast off my mother's pillow. "Do you have some medicine I could take?" I said in a small, tragic voice. "My foot hurts."

Later, after I was sent to bed with two orange-flavored Bayer aspirins, I picked up the upstairs extension again as my mother spoke to Aunt Claire.

"He once told me that he hated being able to predict how his life would turn out. He said it made him feel like he was already dead."

"Well this is certainly something unpredictable," said Aunt Claire.

"He's a real romantic," said my mother. "Romantics are usually bastards, in case you haven't noticed."

My mother almost never used bad language and it sounded mispronounced coming from her. Aunt Claire coughed. "Well," she said. Through my mother's bedroom window I could see the blue light of the Lauders' TV set through their living-room windows next door. A June bug banged against the screen.

"Do you think he'll be back?" Aunt Claire murmured at last.

"I don't know."

"Do you think he left *expecting* to come back?"

My mother didn't answer.

Aunt Claire coughed again. "I suppose he's not coming back anytime soon. He's confused," she added gently after a while. "And probably ashamed. We have to remember that. Ada's also responsible. I've said all along that she's jealous of you. She may even be the one who gave Larry the idea."

A dog barked from a few streets away. Then after what seemed like a long time, my mother said, "A week or so before Larry left, I told him that I'd filed for a divorce."

"Well, didn't he want one, too?" Over the telephone wires, Aunt Claire's voice sounded tinny and insistent. "Lois?" she said. "Lois, are you still there?"

Far away a siren wailed. An ambulance was on its way to Sibley Hospital. The Morrises' terriers began to howl from inside their house. "Help," shouted someone on a television show the Lauders were watching, but then the laugh track started so I knew it was a comedy.

My mother was in the living room the next morning before breakfast spraying Lemon Pledge on the coffee table. When I made it to the kitchen, I saw that she had already thrown away the paper shopping bags that had been wedged between the wall and the refrigerator, scrubbed the dish rack, scoured the sink, polished the toaster, and shaken out all the burnt-toast crumbs. She had even washed the wooden rack of spice bottles and alphabetized them.

"Hi Martian," she said. "Twins still asleep?" She was dressed in an orange middy blouse and a khaki skirt, clothing I had never seen her wear.

"I've been doing a little baking." She pulled a pan of snail-shaped sweet rolls out of the oven and set them on top of the stove. She patted me on the shoulder. "All right. Don't get hiccups. Want a cup of coffee?"

She had never offered me a cup of coffee before; she always said it would stunt my growth. But as I stood there staring she poured a little coffee into a mug, adding milk almost to the brim. She set the mug on the kitchen counter and put a sweet roll on a plate. Then she held my crutches while I climbed onto one of the kitchen stools, and she sat next to me while I ate.

"Listen, I know you were on the other phone last night," she said when I had finished my sweet roll.

Her thin face seemed thinner and her eyes looked red, but she was making an effort to sound composed. "Okay, it's all right, although please don't make a habit of it. But I'm going to make a suggestion. You'll feel better if you find something to do. My advice is to find some kind of hobby this summer."

"I have a mold experiment," I said. "I am growing three kinds of mold in jars."

"Well, that's a start." She got up and poured herself a cup of coffee.

That afternoon she cleaned every room in the house, including the attic, and then she washed the car. Every morning that week she baked something different for breakfast: coffee cake, blueberry buckle, pineapple-pecan muffins.

Meanwhile the twins played backgammon tournaments on the front porch, only occasionally allowing me to play and never letting me win. My mother shampooed the carpet. She did the laundry and sewed new buttons onto whatever clothing of ours had lost them. She took us along grocery shopping and bought eight bags of food, which she made us help her unpack. Every night she fixed something out of the *Better Homes & Gardens* cookbook, or she let the twins select recipes they found hilarious. One night they decided to make Creole Shrimp in a Rice Ring and Polka-Dot Melon Salad.

"Rodney, you gourmet fiend," cried Julie. She and Steven often called each other Rodney and Felicia, which they thought sounded aristocratic.

They were wearing aprons and bickering in brittle English voices, elbowing each other out of the way. My mother was upstairs lying down. I sat in the kitchen and watched them fuss around the sink, first making melon balls, then chopping the shrimp with a knife and throwing the shells down the disposal. If my father's disappearance had upset them, they certainly weren't going to tell me. Instead they spent more and more time as Rodney and Felicia, until it was beginning to seem as if the twins had also left town.

"You're not taking the mud veins out of the shrimp," I said.

"What do you know about mud veins," said Julie.

"It's shrimp poop."

"Oh please," said Julie. "Oh disgusting."

"You've heard, Swamp, haven't you"—Steven looked at me over his shoulder—"that if Mom and Dad get divorced you'll probably have to be put up for adoption."

"There's a new law." Julie tossed her hair out of her eyes. "It says all children under twelve become wards of the state if their parents split up."

"That's not true."

"Oh yes, old Swampy thing," said Julie. "Sad, really."

"Rotten luck, old girl," said Steven.

"Shut up," I said.

"Of course, no one may *want* to adopt you." He pitched a paper towel into the trash can. "Then you'll have to go to an orphanage."

"Ever read *Oliver Twist?*" said Julie, coming at me. She had fingers like pliers, which could leave a mark that lasted for hours after she pinched you.

"No," I cried. "Shut up. Shut up."

"Pathetic case, Felicia," said Steven.

"Simply awful, Rodney," sighed Julie, backing away.

I stumped out of the kitchen and worked my way upstairs

to find my mother. She was lying on her back on the bed with a washcloth draped over her eyes.

"Mommy," I began. "Julie and Steven—"

"Hush," she said fiercely, not moving her head. "I am thinking."

"What are you thinking about?" I asked.

My mother pulled the cloth off her face. "Survival," she said.

Five

A week and a half after my father and Ada disappeared, my mother decided to sell our house.

Although I have never understood it, her decision was understandable. Twice she'd been left by a man with no provision for the future; this time she had something worth money —a house and everything in it. The deed was in her name because ironically my father had believed his investments were safer that way, in case any of his clients ever sued him.

A red, white, and blue "For Sale" sign appeared on our front lawn, lonely and inimical against the soft grass and rhododendrons. To sell the house, my mother used a realtor from my father's own agency, a cadaverous man named Harold McBride, whose long fingers were double-jointed, so that he could bend his thumb back to his wrist.

"So sorry for your troubles, Lois," he said the first time he showed up, towing a young Japanese couple wearing matching blue blazers. "So sorry. Anything I can do to help."

"So sorry," echoed the couple standing behind him, looking confused.

"Oh, that's all right," said my mother, and opened the door for them.

Years of dusting and despising china goose girls wafted back to her, like the potpourri smell of the Coy Boutique: Keep your lips shut. Wear an undershirt *and* a bra. Be prepared. Like her own mother, faced with four fatherless girls after the war, she managed.

Quick as if she were gutting a fish, she emptied the joint checking and savings accounts into a new account in her name. Our allowances were cut off, something I accepted, but the twins complained about it and Julie threatened to sell her clothes. "Go ahead," said my mother. "But I get fifty percent since I bought them in the first place." When I asked her if we had any money, she said, "Enough. For now."

She began phoning numbers listed in the want ads she'd circled in the newspaper. She wrote up a work schedule for the four of us and taped it to the refrigerator: MONDAY. Marsha—set table. Julie—dishes. Steven—trash. Lois—grocery shopping/dinner. TUESDAY. Marsha—sweeping. Lois—laundry/dinner . . .

My mother's first job was selling magazine subscriptions part-time over the telephone.

From noon until five every weekday afternoon, she sat at the kitchen table with her ankles pressed together, talking to strangers across the country. As she dialed each number she frowned as if she had bitten down on a leaf of sandy lettuce. But you could tell when a customer picked up the other end of the line because her eyes widened and her eyebrows shot up. "Hel-lo. This is Lois Eberhardt with Peterman-Wolff Communications Distribution. Are you aware of our special summertime offer of two, yes that's right, two popular magazines of your choice for the low, low price of. . . . No? You *haven't* heard of our offer?" Her voice was so surprised it made her forehead wrinkle.

She had a basic script to follow, plus a fact sheet filled with alternative responses depending on a customer's questions. She said she could get "canned" if she deviated from a single line. Supervisors from Peterman-Wolff Communications Distribution could listen in on our telephone; they would report her if she even asked, "How's the weather in Sandusky?"

This rule made sense to my mother. "When you have a successful formula," she told us, "stick with it. That's the law of nature."

Her own formula for those days rarely varied. Breakfast at exactly seven-thirty on the front porch, with the radio tuned to a news station, and the card table set the night before. Orange juice, Shredded Wheat, coffee for her, milk for me, Fresca for Julie—who was dieting—and nothing for Steven, who usually slept through breakfast. We sat on collapsible director's chairs. Although I was allowed my nightgown and Julie wore a T-shirt and an ancient pair of gym shorts, my mother now wore lipstick and earrings even when she wasn't planning to go out on an interview, dressing neatly in a skirt, blouse, and sandals. Once breakfast was over and the dishes washed, she went over the want ads, or made up a grocery list, or put in the laundry. She never mentioned that by then Uncle Roger had traced my father and Aunt Ada to a tiny Nova Scotia seaport called Annapolis Royal, where they were living in a rented room. I discovered all of this by eavesdropping.

Monday and Wednesday mornings were the times she reserved for job interviews—selling magazines was what she called "a stopgap." That summer she interviewed for secretarial jobs, administrative-assistant jobs, clerk-typist jobs, saleswoman jobs, receptionist jobs. For each interview she dressed up in one of her suits—she had two, a cherry-colored linen ensemble from Woodward & Lothrop and almost the same thing in a salmon pink nubbly fabric—and then spent half an hour turning in front of her bedroom mirror, trying to see herself from every angle. "How do I look?" she would ask Julie, holding her arms away from herself. "Do I look professional?"

She always came home around eleven-thirty for lunch before she began her telephone calls. Our lunches were as unvarying as breakfast: carrot sticks and cheese sandwiches. On Sundays, my mother made twenty cheese sandwiches—two slices of bread/two slices of American cheese/a smear of butter—and stuck them in the freezer. Every weekday morning she would take four out to thaw. We had to economize, she said.

"How was it?" Julie would ask, if she had been to an interview.

"Oh, you know," she'd say, looking into her plate. "It's a lengthy process."

At five o'clock, she hung up the phone, spent twenty minutes tabulating the day's sales in a specially provided Peterman-Wolff vinyl-covered logbook, then reapplied her lipstick and went outside to sit in what was left of the sun in the side yard, joining Julie and Steven, who were oiled like sardines and splayed in two folding lawn chairs they had dragged partially behind the rhododendrons. They had begun smoking cigarettes that summer and always just before my mother came outside there would be an important flurry of tossing butts under the rhododendrons. Julie would fan the air with a magazine. Steven dug out breath mints for both of them.

"If you tell," Julie warned me from under her tennis hat, "I will put Nair on your eyebrows while you're asleep."

But I had no intention of telling on them. Their smoking seemed daring and mature, and secretly I loved hearing them drawl, "Cig, darling?" at each other, in low nasal voices.

Although breakfast and lunch were spartan, dinner became increasingly ambitious. I missed my dinnertime ritual of standing beside my father as he sat on the piano bench, turning the page of music for him whenever he gave a nod. But my mother tried to make up for this loss by whistling Cat Stevens tunes as she prepared dinner in the kitchen. Not only did she set the table with her Minton china and sterling flatware every night, she tuned the radio to a folk-rock station, lit candles, and put fresh flowers in a vase. She made cold cucumber soup and salads with artichoke hearts. She made things with olives. One night for the twins' birthday she roasted a pair of Cornish game hens and served them sprinkled with shredded coconut, which made them look like shrunken heads.

Sometimes we discussed politics at dinner, my mother's new favorite subject.

"What do you think about this," she might say. "Did you know that John Mitchell has resigned as Nixon's campaign manager?"

Julie would squint at her plate; Steven tapped his front teeth with his fork.

"He *says* it's got nothing to do with that bugging business. He says his wife asked him to quit." My mother raised one eyebrow. "You know what I think?

"Men don't quit their jobs because of their wives."

She had begun drinking white wine with dinner, something she had never done before. As dinner went on her political speculations became alarming.

"This whole country is going insane," she muttered one night with grim enthusiasm. "Nothing works right anymore. Nothing happens the way it's supposed to. We'll all probably get blown up tomorrow."

"Mom," said Julie. "We're eating."

As for Watergate, which from the beginning she followed on the news as avidly as the other mothers on the street followed *Guiding Light* and *General Hospital*, my mother's main observation was that it proved that the government was more stupid than criminal. "Those break-in guys were morons," she said, more than once. "They got caught because of a dumb mistake. A *mistake*. That's all it was. If they hadn't made a mistake, nobody would have ever known and everything would have gone on the same."

This seemed to strike her as a painful, even devastating truth.

"Just you wait, children," she announced one evening, not long after the Japanese couple toured our house. "This break-in stuff is going to turn into a big disaster. Sometimes things like this start small, but then they get out of control. That's what happens. It doesn't take long for a lousy mistake to turn into a crime."

"Dear Dad," I wrote in my Evidence notebook:

How are you? I am fine. My favorite TV show is the Partridge Family. I think it would be wonderful to be the Partridge Family and drive around in a school bus to play concerts. You could play the piano and sing. I would play the guitar. Guess what, I have the hiccups. Today it rained like crazy. Julie and Steven are being pigs as usual. I got a puzzle from the drugstore. It is hard! Well I really don't have much to say. So I will say it in some short words! Bye Dad!

Too bad I didn't have his address. Some of my letters were very affecting, I thought.

Around the middle of July—July 20th to be exact, three and a half weeks after my father and Aunt Ada disappeared—I was sitting on our porch with my notebook in my lap reading *The Adventures of Sherlock Holmes*. Every now and then I scanned the street with a pair of pink plastic binoculars I'd gotten for Christmas. From the kitchen, my mother's voice faltered through her telephone calls, stiff and cordial, speaking Peterman-Wolff as if it were Portuguese. Julie and Steven had gone to the mall to flip through magazines in the drugstore and, since their allowances had been canceled, to shoplift packs of gum from the candy racks.

Every so often I glanced up from the page I was reading and surveyed the street to make sure nothing had changed since the last time I'd looked. The Sperlings' fat tortoiseshell cat stalked across their lawn. A few moments later little Mrs. Sperling appeared carrying Baby Cameron. She walked to the middle of her lawn, swinging him, diapered bottom first, into the air. Upsy-*daisy*, she exclaimed. Then she sneezed, and her straight brown hair fell into her eyes. The cat rolled in the grass. A cloud floated overhead. From somewhere near the mall, a whistle blew.

At 4:44 that afternoon, just as I looked up with my binoculars to find where a squirrel was clucking and complaining in one of the dogwood trees, I saw Mr. Green's car drive past our house, two hours before he normally got home from work. I recognized the license-plate number.

The car did not pull into Mr. Green's driveway, but kept on going and turned left on Ridge Road.

A few minutes later, my mother took a break from her telephone calls and came onto the porch fanning herself with a Peterman-Wolff magazine. "It must be a hundred degrees," she said. "I feel like a rag."

"It's eighty-nine degrees," I said. "Guess what. I just saw Mr. Green's car drive by."

She stopped fanning and bent over the begonias, nipping off a few shriveled leaves with her fingernails. "He must be coming home from work early."

A car full of teenagers drove past, shouting something unintelligible. My mother picked up the watering can and watered the potted ficus in the corner, then checked it for spider mites.

Across the street, old Mrs. Morris passed by in her faded denim sun hat, walking her Jack Russell terriers. Mrs. Morris was English—not British the way Felicia and Rodney were British; she'd probably never read a word of Evelyn Waugh. Now and then she invited me over to have tea with her in her dining room while the Jack Russell terriers growled at each other under the table. We always ate Lorna Doones from gold-rimmed china plates and drank milky tea from china cups so thin that light glowed through them. Mrs. Morris told me the cups were all that remained from her mother's bone china. In one of those surreal misapprehensions that make childhood so interesting, I thought the cups were made from her mother's bones. I would hold my cup delicately with my fingertips, wondering which bones I was touching. A thigh? An ankle? "A spot more tea?" Mrs. Morris would ask, in her dry lilty voice, lifting the teapot. "Another biscuit?" And I would nod, feeling damp and a little tired in her shadowy dining room, with its spider plants and tiny oval portraits and the sound of Mr. Morris snoring softly in the living room.

Mrs. Morris waved. My mother waved back.

"Mr. Green always comes home from work at the same time every day," I said. "The exact same time. Six-forty. P.M."

"Why are you so interested in Mr. Green?" My mother twitched off a ficus leaf, then pointed her watering can at me. "And what have you been writing? Every time I turn around, you're writing something. Is that a diary?" She made a motion with her free hand as if she meant to pick up my notebook, where I had been taking notes, Sherlock Holmes—style, on everything that happened on the street.

"It's not a diary," I said, clasping my notebook to my chest.

"Don't be so touchy," she snapped. "Privacy is something I respect, and I hope you do, too."

The floorboards quaked as she walked across the porch. I heard her pick up the phone in the kitchen; a minute later she cleared her throat and then her voice began its loop: *Hel-lo. This is Lois Eberhardt*, and I went back to watching the street.

Mr. Green's car pulled up six inches from his drainpipe that evening ten minutes before his usual time. He looked sallow as he got out of his car, a little bruised around the mouth, and he had a Band-Aid stuck below his lower lip. As usual he walked up his front walk, pausing to hail Mrs. Lauder, who was standing on her steps watching Luann try a handstand in the grass. Mr. Green waited for Mrs. Lauder to wave back and for his pains was rewarded with a display of Luann's white underpants as her sailor dress flew over her head.

"Luann," shouted Mrs. Lauder. "Quit fooling and get in here."

Mr. Green continued up his front steps, then reached behind his azalea bush to turn on his sprinkler. It started up with a *pffft!* and pattered the leaves of one of our dogwoods.

As he stooped to fiddle with the spigot, I found myself contemplating his bald spot. He had tried to comb his front hair back to hide it. I imagined him standing in front of a smudged bathroom mirror carefully combing Brylcreem into his thin hair, turning his head from side to side as he combed. His bald spot was sunburned, which gave it a tender look.

Two weeks before I had watched Mr. Green start building a barbecue pit in his backyard. By the time I got out to the porch that Saturday morning, after helping my mother and Julie tidy up the house for another visit from Mr. McBride, a pile of bricks sat near the picnic table and Mr. Green was mixing cement in a big metal tray.

It was already hot, and he had taken off his shirt. I remember being startled at the sight of his bare chest. It was much broader than I would have imagined, more muscular. On his right arm, just below the shoulder, where his bicep bunched, was a bare-breasted mermaid. As he worked, the mermaid undulated, as if she were being rocked by invisible currents.

He knelt on the ground, using a trowel to slap concrete on the half-moon of bricks he had already laid. I watched his arm rise and lower, revealing a thatch of dark hair glistening at his armpit. And then there was my mother standing in the doorway behind me. She watched, too, as Mr. Green's arm rose and fell, scooping up cement like heavy icing and spreading it onto the bricks. His chest gleamed with sweat. After a few minutes, during which neither my mother nor I spoke, Mr. Green sat back on his heels, wiping his forehead with his wrist.

As he caught his breath, my mother suddenly sang out: "If you want something cold to drink, we've got lemonade."

Mr. Green rocked forward and blinked toward our house. Then he groped for the shirt crumpled on the ground beside him, fumbling with the buttons in his hurry to put it on, squinting at what must have seemed to him a mass of shadows beneath a mass of leaves on our vine-covered porch.

"I don't believe we've properly met," she called, stepping up to the screened door. "This is my daughter Marsha." She opened the door and gestured to me. "And I'm Lois.

"Eberhardt," she added. "Like the pencil. Eberhard Faber? Except with a 't.'"

Mr. Green stood up and brushed for a fraction too long at his bare knees. He was wearing stained blue cotton shorts and old canvas shoes; it was the first time I'd seen him untidily dressed.

"Hello," he said, neglecting to offer his own name, or perhaps imagining that we already knew it. He stepped forward a few paces and held up his hand to shield his eyes from the sun. Then he stopped, felt around in his back pocket, produced a black comb, and in two quick, stealthy motions, combed his hair backward over the crown of his head before the comb vanished and he walked around the hedge and into our yard.

"You must be dead," said my mother as he approached our porch steps. When Mr. Green looked startled, she added loudly, "Of thirst. It's *broiling* today."

"I'm all right." He still looked startled. "Thank you very much."

"So, would you like a glass of lemonade?" My mother had moved onto the top step, unconsciously mimicking him by lifting one hand to her eyes.

"Thank you very much," he said again, a tendon jumping in his neck.

"With ice?"

A pause. "Yes. Thank you very much."

"It's tropical lemonade," said my mother a little wildly. She must have just remembered that I had tinted the pink lemonade lavender with blue food coloring that morning. I thought lavender lemonade would taste cool on such a hot day.

Mr. Green waited on our lawn by the porch steps while my mother went into the kitchen. He regarded me through the screen without speaking, and I gazed back at him. A heat rash had started up his neck and sweat trickled down the side of his face.

My mother returned with a round rattan tray on which she had placed two tumblers of lavender lemonade, ice cubes clinking. A tense minute followed during which she hovered inside the porch door with the tray and Mr. Green hovered outside by the bottom of the steps. Finally my mother said, "Marsha, help me with this," and Mr. Green sprang forward to wrench at the door handle.

I stayed in the love seat while my mother offered the tray to Mr. Green. He stared a moment, but selected a glass without comment.

"A little whimsy," explained my mother.

"Thank you," said Mr. Green.

"Marsha," she called sharply; when I hobbled to the screen door, she handed me the empty tray. "Put this back inside, honey." She smiled over my head.

After broaching several conversational possibilities—the weather, the upcoming election—my mother moved quickly on to the subject of grass. Mr. Green had done wonders with his grass. Mr. Green must have a green thumb. Her own lawn looked like it had leprosy. "*Look* at those brown spots," she said, sweeping a hand at our grass.

Dutifully, Mr. Green turned to examine two or three small yellowing patches in our lawn. But just as my mother prepared to criticize our dogwood trees, the rhododendrons, and the treacherous crab apple from which I had fallen and broken my ankle, he said reluctantly, as if he regretted making such a confession: "I'm from the country myself. Sometimes I look out at your yard and something about it makes me feel like I'm in the country."

My mother seemed impressed by the frankness of this remark. Her eyelids fluttered. "Well," she said. Then she paused and examined our bushes and trees from the perspective of someone pining for a rural vista. "I think I see it," she consented at last. "I see what you mean. I should stop complaining."

Mr. Green finished his lemonade with a sharp tilt of the glass, which must have been sharper than he intended because lavender lemonade spilled down his chin and onto his white shirt. He looked down at himself. My mother pretended not to notice. The moment for offering him a paper towel came and went. Mr. Green's eyes shifted back to his little tumulus of bricks, then returned to my mother's face as she launched into a paean to country life. "No, there's nothing like it," she said, as if continuing an extended discussion. "Living in the city makes us forget that *real* life happens in the country. And the suburbs." Here she paused to glance across the street at the Morrises' cubelike boxwoods. "The suburbs are neither here nor there. In fact," she went on breathlessly, "I sometimes think the suburbs are a *distortion*."

Mr. Green cleared his throat and bobbed the empty glass in his hand. A bee buzzed between them. My mother swatted at it, already opening her mouth to introduce a new subject. A neighbor's television began to gabble.

"*Mom*." I got up, knocking over my milk crate and making the begonias shiver. "My foot itches."

"Marsha is my youngest," my mother told Mr. Green, not turning around. "As you may have noticed, she has a broken ankle."

Mr. Green glanced through the porch screen and gave me a quick little nod.

"You don't have any children?"

"No ma'am."

"They are—" I could see my mother searching for something clever. "They are a challenge," she said at last, frowning.

Mr. Green nodded again.

"You know, I didn't catch your first name."

"Alden. Alden Green. Junior," he added. He thrust his glass forward. "Thank you very much."

"Like John Alden?" My mother took the glass and held it under her chin. "Wasn't he a Pilgrim?"

His forehead was perspiring in the sun; he kept dabbing at it with the back of his wrist. My mother asked him what he thought of "this Watergate business." Across the street, the

Sperlings' Buick drove up. The Jack Russell terriers began barking from inside the Morrises' house.

"Those dogs," said my mother. "Yippy and Yappy."

Mr. Green smiled formally.

"Well," she sighed at last. "I should let you get back to work."

Mr. Green ducked his head, thanking her again for the lemonade. A few moments later he had trudged back to his yard and was kneeling once more among his bricks.

"It's always a good idea," observed my mother when she came back onto the porch, "to get to know your neighbors. You can never be too careful." The screen door banged. As she bent to take the tray, I saw that her cheeks were flushed and her eyes bright and that she was still smiling the same lavender smile she must have turned on Mr. Green.

All that week my mother made a point of waving to Mr. Green if she happened to be in the yard when he drove into his driveway or came out to his car. She always called out something to him, usually a comment about his grass or the straggle of marigolds he had planted around his front stoop.

"How do you keep slugs from biting the heads off your marigolds?" she demanded one evening.

Mr. Green had just stepped out of his car, hadn't yet even closed the door; my mother's question made him jerk around as if someone had tapped his shoulder from behind.

She pushed up the brim of Steven's baseball cap, which she had taken to wearing outside, and smiled as though she had just asked Mr. Green how he liked his coffee.

"Slugs," he repeated. His white shirt was sticking to his chest, revealing the outline of his undershirt beneath. He gripped the handle of his briefcase, edging it a little higher across his stomach.

"They're decapitating my marigolds," she announced, advancing toward the box hedge that separated our yard from Mr. Green's driveway.

Mr. Green turned to look at his marigolds, then faced my mother again, his face moist and pouchy over his white shirt collar. "Baking soda," he said in his soft, twangy voice.

"*Baking soda,*" repeated my mother. She swung her weeding fork.

"Or you can sprinkle salt on them," he added unwillingly. "So they shrivel up."

My mother stopped swinging the weeding fork. It must have occurred to her simultaneously as it occurred to me that Mr. Green had done just such a thing, waited outside with his saltshaker, watching for a silvery trail to catch the moonlight.

That Sunday she caught him sitting in his aluminum folding chair reading the newspaper. This time he seemed to be ready for her and stood up as soon as she called to him from behind the screen door.

He was in his usual weekend outfit of madras shorts and khaki shirt, which made him look like a cross between a tourist in Florida and Marlin Perkins on *Wild Kingdom*. His hair had been combed meticulously over his bald spot, and he'd used hair oil—a sign of low class, my father once said when a barber had slapped hair oil on Steven after a haircut. My father himself had thick, springy hair that curled naturally away from his forehead. He also had a lanky body and an ingratiating, loose-limbed way of moving, with none of the squat, dense heaviness of Mr. Green, who even with his pink face seemed dark as an olive.

"Isn't it *hot?*" my mother cried. She couldn't believe how hot it was; she thought if it got any hotter she'd be hard-boiled.

Rolling his newspaper into a tight cylinder, Mr. Green nodded once as he strode toward the hedge, then twice again for emphasis.

She opened the screen door. "Maybe we'll get a tornado," she said as she walked down the steps. "A quick little tornado would be so nice."

Mr. Green's face, which all this time had been lifting into an alert expression, plunged back into its customary blankness. Clearly he didn't, couldn't follow why my mother would want a tornado. Especially after we'd just had such an early hurricane.

He wasn't the first person to be confused by my mother's domestication of disaster. I recall being terrified as a child the first time I heard her announce that she was about to drop dead after vacuuming the stairs. I was terrified the first time she declared that someone was "trying to kill us" by cutting in front of our car on the Beltway. Only eventually did her near-death experiences, her brushes with mayhem, her descents into lunacy while she looked for parking spaces, lost library books, or the lid for the mustard jar leave me unconcerned. The only way to tolerate life's dangers, she had long ago decided, was to make them routine. She never seemed to understand that other people found this attitude unnerving.

"Wouldn't it be lovely to get rid of all this hot air?" she asked wistfully. "Just a short tornado, to blow it all out to sea?"

Mr. Green's smile returned, twitching the muscles in his face. Then surprisingly he laughed. He laughed the way cartoon characters laugh, enunciating the words "ha, ha."

"Ha, ha," echoed my mother, fanning herself with a hand.

I'm sure she would have been astonished if someone had told her right then that she was flirting. But what else could she have been doing? And who, besides me, could have blamed her? Even Julie and Steven probably understood, if they had bothered to notice. Of course, I still wonder if I would have done what I did if my mother had been less friendly that afternoon, or if she had kept herself and her tornado in the house altogether, and Mr. Green had remained in his folding chair, his bald spot winking at nothing but the sky.

Ada and my father had been gone three weeks by then. They hadn't called, or sent a letter, or even a postcard. They could return at any moment, or never. Aunt Fran's husband, Uncle Billy, who was a lawyer, had drawn up divorce papers by then, and my mother was waiting to send them to my father as soon as he came back. In a few months, she planned to be the only single mother she knew. Already she figured the other mothers on the street were looking at her narrowly, calculating whether or not she was likely to turn into a husband-stealer. A few years ago, Julie told me that Mrs. Guibert and Mrs. Bridgeman had invited my mother over for coffee one morning that summer, and in Mrs. Guibert's neat kitchen, with its brick-patterned linoleum and avocado-colored refrigerator, they informed her gently that this was "a family street." "Oh really?" my mother said. "Whose family?"

And so while my mother waited for what would happen to her next, she spent her days stumbling through her Peterman-Wolff pitches. At night she sat up late drinking Chablis and reading nineteenth-century English novels in which everyone ended up married in a manor house surrounded by Lombardy poplars. Or she murmured to Aunt Fran or Aunt Claire on the phone and tried to convince them not to come visit again.

But out there, out on the lawn, the air shimmered.

"It's so hot," my mother said in a trembling voice. "I think my *brain* is melting."

"Ha, ha," said Mr. Green, whacking his newspaper into his palm.

She bent her head modestly, already thinking up a new witticism. "No really," she said. "It's so hot out that—"

A jet cannonaded overhead on its way up from National Airport. My mother's witticism was lost.

Before she could repeat herself, Mr. Green interrupted her. Today, it seemed, he had a statement of his own to make. This statement wasn't going to be easy for him to deliver, however. From the porch I watched his reddening face break into a struggle between hesitance and determination, lips twitching, eyes blinking as he staggered a little behind the hedge, his forehead perspiring, even his ears turning red, until finally he managed to open his mouth just wide enough to say: "I want."

He sank back, swallowing and plucking at the front of his khaki shirt. Just as it seemed he might give up and pretend he hadn't said anything at all, he added almost vaguely: "Was wondering." Again he paused for a breath, gripping his newspaper like a man clutching the end of a rope. But he was into it now; he was going to finish or be damned. "Wondering—I wondered if you might want to come to a cookout at my house?"

My mother stared and Mr. Green flushed a heavier red, tucking his chin into his neck.

"A cookout," he repeated.

"A cookout?" she repeated right after him. Already I could tell that she was stalling.

"Yes." The front of his khaki shirt had soaked through in two long panels, but he set his jaw.

"Oh." She smiled the best of her impregnable smiles.

"Finished my barbecue pit." He gestured with his newspaper.

"Oh yes I see, it's *gorgeous*. Look at all those bricks. Really —I could never make anything like that. I even have a hard time making *toast*. What day did you say?"

"Sunday? Maybe some Sunday? Two, three weeks from now?" He seemed unwilling to name a date, as if now that he had succeeded in announcing his intention to have a cookout, he was amazed that anything else should be required of him.

"Two or three Sundays from now?" My mother smiled. She cocked her head, pretending to consult a calendar hanging just behind Mr. Green's head. Prior obligations whizzed almost visibly through the air: Visits to cousins. Pool parties. A promised trip to the zoo. We could always leave home for the day and drive around Great Falls or Silver Spring. It was convenient to have children; people always believed you when you said you had to do something for your children.

Mr. Green, who had been watching her face, nodded and looked away. "I thought," he said sullenly, "I could invite some neighbors."

"We-ell," said my mother.

She played with her metal watchband, dragging it away from her wrist and letting it snap back. Even from the porch, plastic binoculars pressed against the lens of my glasses, I could see her flesh pinch between those tiny nickel-plated sections. Spend an evening with meat-colored Mr. Green, watching him bumble over his barbecue pit? Impossible. I imagined him offering her a quaking paper plate, a sticky Dixie cup of wine, while under his sleeve his mermaid tattoo jiggled.

My mother's eyes narrowed. Her smile stretched thin, became transparent. Mr. Green swallowed and pulled a leaf off the hedge.

But then, in a gently ironic voice, a voice reserved for disappointing suitors and defenestrating unfaithful husbands, my mother said: "Why yes. Alden. Yes, I'd love to come."

Six

A grown man ran down our street at seven on the evening of July 20th, just as most families were sitting down to dinner. He ran first to the Guiberts' Tudor on the corner and shouted, banging on their door. Mr. Guibert appeared, and even from my house half a block away we could hear their excited voices. Then the man ran across the street to the Reades' house and banged on their door. Husbands, wives, children began crowding toward the windows as the man zigzagged from house to house, each time talking loudly, hardly pausing before running to the next house. We were still holding our napkins as we turned to look out our windows.

By the time he reached the Bridgemans' house, the Morrises and the Sperlings were opening their screen doors and stepping onto their front steps. You could hear the twang of door springs all up and down the street, like frogs in a pond. People were calling to one another over their fences and hedges, asking what all this was about, had something happened, what was that man saying?

A boy is missing, he was saying. *Tell your neighbors. A child is missing.*

He had run over from Buena Vista, where the Ellisons lived, and started knocking on doors to ask any grown men he found to meet up in the Ellisons' front yard. Number 26. His wife, who was sitting with Sylvia Ellison, had told him that he should get as many men together as possible. The Ellisons had called the police, but the police couldn't do anything for twenty-four hours. He's probably off with a friend, they'd said. That was the police for you.

A child is missing. A child is missing.

And so it went through the neighborhood.

Every man under seventy and every high school boy on our street volunteered to help search—Mr. Sperling; Mr. Lauder; Mr. Bridgeman and fat, goggle-eyed David Bridgeman; the Reade brothers, Mike and Wayne, both of whom I loved for their straight blond hair and slanty eyes, and for their surly grace when they played basketball in their driveway; bald Mr. Hollowell; Mr. Guibert, a French Canadian with gaping nostrils who sometimes shouted "*Merde*" at the Morrises for letting their terriers squat on his lawn. Every man, that is, but Mr. Green. As far as I can recall, no one remembered to ask him.

In less than half an hour from the time that man bypassed our house and Mr. Green's house, stopping instead at the

Lauders' door, the men on our street had gathered on the grass in front of the Ellison house, and their wives had locked all the doors and windows in spite of the heat and had herded their children onto the living-room sofas, where they all waited to watch the ten o'clock news on television.

Everyone felt tensely excited, as people do when something terrible may have happened to someone else. Of course we all hoped the boy would be found, but we also hoped that he wouldn't be found, at least not immediately and that it would be a dramatic rescue when he was, with rope ladders and dogs and EMTs.

For a few hours the neighborhood drew tight as everyone except my mother closed and locked their doors and locked their windows and checked the basement. A few small children probably cried when their father grabbed up a flashlight and hurried out the door, but most children would have been impressed by their father's sudden importance, and longed to go with him into the pinkish, loamy twilight. They sat quietly, leaning against their mother, watching figures slide across the television screen. Periodically their mothers rose to look out the windows. Fans whirred. The children sucked Popsicles. Finally they fell asleep. And then from their kitchens, mothers began calling everyone they knew.

No one had knocked on our door, probably because they realized my father no longer lived there. Everyone seemed to realize that almost before he had left. But we'd heard the shouting and along with everybody else had gone to the screen door to see what was happening.

"Rubberneckers," muttered my mother, when Mr. and Mrs. Lauder and Luann and then the Morrises appeared outside on their front steps. Then the Sperlings stepped out, too, with Mrs. Sperling joggling the baby in her arms while dark-haired Mr. Sperling waved to old Mr. Morris. It looked like a parade was about to go by. The Jack Russell terriers started barking.

"I'm going out there," said Steven.

"Me too," said Julie.

"You are not. Eat your dinner." My mother put her hands on her hips. Then she wheeled around so abruptly she bumped into my crutches.

"*Ma*," said Steven.

"Never, ever call me 'Ma,' " she said unsteadily. In the last week she'd begun drinking a glass of wine in the kitchen while she made dinner, in addition to the glass she drank with dinner, and the glass she drank afterward while she read on the sofa.

On her way back to the table she turned up the radio. "Civilized people," she added, as we sat back down, "do not gawk at the misfortunes of others."

"Yeah, right," said Julie.

It had been a hot, still day, full of wide green leaves that barely stirred and damp sidewalks. The kind of day that reminds you that Washington, D.C., is a Southern city. All afternoon locusts buzzed in the trees, while the neighborhood cats lay in the same position for hours on whatever doorstep or porch they could find that seemed a little cooler than anywhere else.

While other mothers in our neighborhood began shutting their windows and doors, and Julie and Steven stalked into the living room to watch television, my mother made me help her with the dishes, the two of us standing together at the open kitchen window, steam clouding around our elbows from the sink.

We were still standing by the sink when the phone rang. It was Mrs. Lauder from next door. I watched my mother cradle the receiver between her ear and shoulder as she dried a salad plate. Her eyebrows lifted and fell. "Oh no," she said.

She moved toward the dining room, dragging the phone cord. "Who is it? Do they know who it is?" She paused. "Yes, I'll do that. All right, Mavis. Thanks for calling."

Hardly had she hung up and placed the salad plate back in the cabinet before the phone rang again. She just had time to tell me, "A child's gotten lost," before she had to say hello into the receiver. This time it was Mrs. Sperling, who was crying because she was scared to be alone with just Baby Cameron.

"Don't worry," said my mother, now drying a bowl. "You're perfectly safe. I'm sure they'll find him. I'm sure it will all turn out just fine." Her brisk tone informed me that this was for my benefit as much as Mrs. Sperling's. "Really, I think you're getting much too worked up, Dolly. There's no reason to be afraid. They've probably found him already."

After another minute or two, she hung up, and by the dissatisfied way she stared at her dish towel, I could tell she realized that she should have invited Mrs. Sperling to come over and sit with us. A moment later she dialed the Sperlings' number, which was taped to the refrigerator on a piece of paper with the numbers of the fire department, the poison control center, and several of the other neighbors. Aunt Ada's phone number, once written at the top above Aunt Fran's and Aunt Claire's, had been neatly scissored off. The Sperlings' line was busy. A few minutes later Mrs. Morris called.

While my mother talked to Mrs. Morris, I clumped out to the porch on one crutch and sat down, my notebook ready in my lap along with my binoculars and a new Bic pen I'd stolen from Julie's room. Lately I had taken to writing in black ink, which I thought looked more serious. The Sperlings' tortoiseshell cat skulked across their lawn. A moment later, Mr. Morris's stooped silhouette passed his drawn living-room blind, like something from a Hitchcock movie. I propped my cast on the wicker table littered with Peterman-Wolff magazines and by habit looked over at Mr. Green's house. The sprinkler on his lawn arced back and forth. Otherwise the only movement I saw came from the beech leaves shifting above his roof.

· · ·

While we all slept that night, the hunt widened, spreading past the mall, I learned later, all the way down to the abandoned amusement park by the river, where search teams played their flashlights into the cracked, empty wading pools and under the old roller coaster, which creaked and moaned and looked, from down below, like the collapsing skeleton of a dinosaur. So many places to hide a child, or his body: deep within the crusted gears of the old merry-go-round, behind the splintered arcade with its fourteen plaster clown faces, in one of the termite-eaten turrets of Jack's Happy Castle. Even the air tasted secretive, mixed with the taint of river water and an ancient undercurrent of popcorn. They shouted his name, again and again. Somebody got hold of a klieg light and managed to wire it, and suddenly the park lit up, ghastly, smaller. It would be appropriate, even reassuring, to find a nightmare in that place of nightmares, Playland gone to seed. But he wasn't there.

All evening my mother sat inside on the living-room sofa, riffling the pages of a magazine. For the last several weeks, the Peterman-Wolff Company had been sending us every issue of every magazine my mother was supposed to be selling, on the off chance that she might be required to say something specific in her sales pitch. That night, while the twins defiantly watched a Japanese horror movie, she sat in a corner of the living room skimming through the magazines she had just received, looking annoyed and exhausted. "Blah blah blah," she would say periodically, tossing the magazine onto the floor.

"That's all it is. Blah blah blah." After a few minutes of gazing into the cup of her hands, she would retrieve the magazine and go back to reading.

I refused to come in from the porch even after she had announced twice that it was past my bedtime. The phone rang for Julie. It rang for Steven, then for Julie again. I kept rehearsing one sentence: *A child has gotten lost*.

A child has gotten lost. The grammatical construction of this statement baffled me. Who had lost the child? Had he lost himself? Could you lose a child the same way you could lose the car keys? Even then I was something of a determinist, as most children are; I believed that things were lost for a reason. Perhaps God collected lost things for his own benefit, keeping them until you died, when whatever you had lost would be returned to you. I imagined heaven lined with shelves, a celestial pawnshop. All it took was a moment's carelessness, I told myself, and you could lose anything. I didn't understand the implications of this observation, but I remember the thrill that ran up my spine, composed mostly of gratification at being, for the moment, predictably where my mother would look for me.

Years later, during one of our infrequent visits, I told my father about that night and how the twins and I had watched from the porch as all the other fathers gathered on the street, talking with their arms folded. "We were frightened. We needed you," I said, although I was no longer sure that this was true. "And you weren't there."

"Yes, I know." He took off his glasses to clean them with a cocktail napkin. He looked sad and thoughtful. But when he put his glasses back on, he said, "But you got through it all right, now didn't you?"

Light shone from nearly every window of every house, from attic to basement. When a dog barked from behind our house, the whole neighborhood seemed to jump. My mother, however, refused to lock the front door. "I don't believe in the bogeyman," she said. And I have always wondered whether she was being simply stubborn and foolhardy that night, or whether something darker was passing through her mind.

The light in Mr. Green's kitchen snapped off at nine-thirty, followed by the light in his bedroom at his usual ten o'clock. His house was the first on the street to go dark.

By the next morning, we didn't know anything more than we had the night before, except by then my mother had told us the lost child was Boyd Ellison. Nothing on the evening news, or in the morning paper. After that spate of phone calls the evening before, our neighbors left us to our own speculations, even after word began to seep back with the men who had gone out searching.

It was a Friday. When I woke up and looked out my window, Mr. Sperling was standing on his front steps in plaid shorts and boat shoes instead of his usual dark suit, and instead of getting into his car to drive to work, he was drinking a glass of iced tea. "Frank," I could hear Mrs. Lauder calling next door. "Frank, Frank."

Mr. Green left for work at a quarter to eight, as he did every morning. He walked down his front steps carrying his empty-looking brown leatherette briefcase with the noisy silver clasps, opened his car door, and ducked his head to climb into the driver's seat.

As he backed his car out of the driveway, I remembered what he'd told my mother the week before, about being from the country, and how our yard reminded him of where he was from. I tried to picture Mr. Green's pink face superimposed above denim overalls and a checked shirt, standing on our lawn with a hoe. But it was impossible to divorce him from his white shirt and tie, or to persuade him out of his shiny loafers and into a pair of yellow farmer's boots. It seemed clear that he belonged somewhere else, but where that was I couldn't imagine.

"Left house usual time," I wrote in my notebook.

My mother, Julie, and I heard the news together just after breakfast when Mrs. Morris hurried across the street with her terriers and rang our doorbell.

"Have you heard?" Mrs. Morris quavered under the brim of her denim cap as my mother opened the screen door. "Has anyone told you what happened?"

When none of us answered, she clutched the dogs' leashes, pulling the terriers close to the white balls on her ankle socks.

"They found him." Her head shook as it always did, a gentle wobble that reminded me of a china doll with its neck on a spring. "They found the boy."

"Oh thank God," said my mother.

"No," said Mrs. Morris, shaking. "No, no."

I watched Mrs. Morris shake her head, thinking of the time two years ago when Steven had complained that Boyd Ellison stole money from a Cub Scout paper drive. "Stinker," he had said, standing in the kitchen with his face flushed and his feet apart. I remembered exactly how he said it, standing by the refrigerator, eager and aggrieved, his brown hair sticking up from his forehead. Can you prove it? my mother had asked him. Steven looked surprised; his mouth hung open. But I know he did it, he said. I *know*. How? said my mother. Steven couldn't answer. His face folded inward, his lip jutting out. You never believe me. You never believe anything I tell you. I do not believe unsubstantiated allegations, said my mother, turning on the faucet. This is America.

I tried to stop myself from repeating *stinker*, *stinker*, shivering while Mrs. Morris's head wobbled, while her dogs lunged away from her ankles, their toenails skittering on our cement front steps, while a crow flapped into the crab apple tree, while my mother stood at the door, shaking her head in time to Mrs. Morris's shaking.

I tried to picture Boyd Ellison's face; I tried to remember how he had looked the day in the playground he asked to wear my glasses. *Let me*, he said. *I just want to see what it's like.*

Under her hat brim, Mrs. Morris's lips wrinkled and separated, revealing her neat brownish teeth. "Frank Lauder said they found him behind the mall. In those woods. Said he was unconscious. Frank thought unconscious. He didn't know for sure. Then they said he was dead. But it was him, it was the boy, and he'd—"

Here Mrs. Morris stopped, peering around the side of my mother to where I crouched on the love seat, my good leg drawn up to my chest.

"Go inside, Marsha," my mother said, glancing around. "Julie, take her inside."

"Mom," said Julie.

"Now. Please."

Julie dragged me out of my chair and stuck my crutches under my armpits, holding the door for me as I hobbled into the living room. We sat on the living-room sofa and stared at the fireplace, trying to listen to their low, rustling voices from the open window above our heads. In the distance I heard a siren.

"Boyd Ellison," said Julie, picking at her eyebrow. She shuddered. That morning she was wearing tight orange bellbottoms and a flowered halter top, with her long straight brown hair pulled tightly back by a leather clasp, which made her face look round and very bare.

Upstairs we heard Steven turn on the shower. I wondered what he would think when he discovered that a boy he'd accused of stealing from the paper drive had been killed, the boy who may or may not have also stolen David Bridgeman's bicycle. But then, he wasn't the only kid in the neighborhood who stole things. Who would have thought Boyd Ellison would be the one among us to have something so dramatic happen to him.

That's how it seemed then, that the killing itself was fated—not the person—and any of us could have been chosen. That it was Boyd Ellison suddenly invested him with new and awful importance. Almost immediately the square-headed blond boy I'd avoided on the playground acquired a kind of glamour. In spite of myself, I began to wish I had spoken to him more often, that he'd visited our house more than once. I wished I had loaned him my glasses when he'd asked for them.

Outside Mrs. Morris said something, and then she said something else that sounded like someone coughing out a fish-bone.

Finally we heard my mother ask: "Who is *they?*"

"The police," said Mrs. Morris. A delivery truck rattled by, running over whatever she said next.

"Question us?" said my mother.

Next door, the Lauders' car started up. "Luann," shouted Mrs. Lauder; a car door slammed. Mrs. Morris's voice began to spiral: "He didn't mind his mother. He took that shortcut. He went through those woods. He didn't mind. No, he didn't. He went through those woods."

"Jesus," whispered Julie beside me.

As my mother murmured, trying to quiet her, Mrs. Morris's quavering voice rose higher, losing its quaver. "Those woods some of you people were so keen on not having cut down. That was a mistake, now wasn't it? They'll cut the whole place down now, I expect. Cut it all, I expect, the whole place."

"Old bitch," Julie muttered.

I rolled over on the sofa cushion and got on my good knee to look out the window. On the other side of our yard, the Lauders' car was backing slowly down their driveway, their three white faces bunched inside; Luann's palms flattened against her closed car window as she peered out like a diver trapped in an aquarium. The Sperlings had appeared on their front steps. Mrs. Sperling gripped her baby bandolier-style across her chest, swaying back and forth, while Mr. Sperling walked slowly down the steps and onto his lawn.

Mrs. Morris stopped shouting. By leaning on the back of the sofa and pressing the side of my face against the farthest edge of the windowpane, I could see her bare elbow jutting from a white sleeve printed with daisies, and her bottom straining against her ironed khaki skirt. The wisteria and the side of the porch cut off the rest of her. My mother said something in a clear, automatic tone, as if she were reciting the Pledge of Allegiance. It was true; she had been the one who sent around the petition to protect the woods. She had even made a sign out of cardboard and poster paint that said "Save Our Trees/No Parking Garage," and stuck it on the lawn near the spot where the For Sale sign now stood. In those days she'd had quite a passion for saving things.

One of Mrs. Morris's white ankle socks in a white tennis shoe appeared. Then a calf. Then Mrs. Morris stood in the yard complete, gray hair curling under her denim cap, head gently wagging. "I know you're alone over here, Lois," she was saying, her voice back to its familiar quaver. "Don't be afraid to call us now if you feel frightened, dear. Any of us."

Invisibly, my mother said "Thank you. Edna."

Mrs. Morris gathered up the dog leashes and drove herself and the terriers back across the street to her own yard and house, where the smoky apparition of Mr. Morris in a golf cap waited inside the screen door.

I slid back down into the sofa cushions, letting my hair catch on the cretonne so that it would stand up from my head. After a few moments, my mother came into the living room.

"I don't want you outside today." She emphasized each word so that it hung balloonlike for an instant in the air between us. "You heard me," she said to Julie. Then she sighed and put her hand over her eyes. But in a moment she had taken her hand away again and gone into the kitchen to begin her telephone calls.

Seven

It seems increasingly common for people to live in places where there has been a murder. For instance, these days I live in a fairly expensive neighborhood not far from Chevy Chase, a neighborhood of center-hall colonials and flowering dogwood trees where most people do not mow their own lawns. Last Thanksgiving, five blocks away from my house, a woman stabbed her brother in the neck with a steak knife while her housemate roasted a turkey downstairs and outside the window neighbors' children in bright Gap outfits chased each other through the chilly November sunlight. No one knows why she killed him.

Here in Washington, the murder rate has risen so high that newspapers record violent deaths in six-inch columns rather than as front-page tragedies. Which probably makes sense. My least-favorite college English professor once declared: "Oedipus is a tragic figure. Richard Nixon is a tragic figure.

The guy down the street who gets shot is not." When the class murmured at this, he crossed his arms and said: "Tragedy has to be interesting. The whole world cares about Richard Nixon. Who cares about the guy down the street?"

"His wife," someone volunteered.

The professor smiled and took off his little oval spectacles to polish them by the blackboard. "Who cares," he said, blinking slyly, "about his wife?"

But you have to understand that twenty-five years ago a murder in a suburban neighborhood like Spring Hill was still an astonishing occurrence, so astonishing that for a long time the people who lived there felt somehow responsible, as if they should have foreseen something so unforeseen. Like my mother, they felt guilty for having ever felt secure.

Almost immediately after Boyd Ellison was killed our neighbors began to see strange shapes in the rhododendrons, hear human screams in every cat fight, lose their appetites. People from several blocks away sent flowers to his family, and a total stranger from Bethesda offered to paint their garage. Collections were taken up; proposals were made inside the Clara Barton Elementary School auditorium for a memorial tree. And a month later, when the Ellisons decided to sell their house for less than they'd paid for it—even with a newly renovated kitchen, an updated heating system, and central air-conditioning—a long time passed before anyone was willing to buy it.

Within the first few hours after Mrs. Morris's visit, Mrs. Lauder stopped by our house, knocking at the porch door. She sat on the edge of the living-room sofa. Apparently she only wanted to hear my mother say how awful it was, what a terrible tragedy, and to repeat the same words herself. "You've heard who it was?" she asked my mother. They exchanged stories of when and how they had heard the news, touching their throats. My mother offered her iced tea, which Mrs. Lauder declined.

"Now don't be a stranger," she added, on the way out the door.

Otherwise people seemed to avoid us, at least that's the feeling I had as I sat on the porch watching neighbor after neighbor congregate in one another's front yards. All morning a weird holiday current lit the air, with so many neighbors out on the street, the fathers all home on a weekday, and everyone talking about the same thing. Even the twins dropped their British accents and wandered around the house looking somberly approachable.

The early stories traded around that day were contradictory and convoluted. Stories swirled and eddied until each family seemed to have its own version of the events. And every version began with "I heard—"

Among the details I overheard from my post on the porch, all of which I printed in my notebook with Julie's Bic pen, are the following: Boyd Ellison was alive and had told the police everything. A man on a motorcycle had attacked him. A man with a beard attacked him. It was a bearded man with a foreign accent, maybe Dutch or Turkish. It was a hippie on drugs. Boyd was in a coma. Boyd had called out his mother's name. He didn't know who his parents were. He was dead. He was alive. He was alive but just barely. He was dead.

Later that morning, eavesdropping from my bedroom window on Mrs. Bridgeman's conversation with Mrs. Lauder on her front steps, I several times heard a word I didn't understand. Molested.

The neighborhood fathers spent the day talking together in close knots in front of their garages, eyes traveling from house to house. Mothers appeared regularly in their doorways, usually restraining a child from running outside, one hand spread against the child's chest. Or they made forays to one another's houses to deliver bulletins, twitching at their culotte skirts as they ran across the street, the wooden heels of their Dr. Scholl's sandals clunking against the heated asphalt.

Whenever my mother took a break from her Peterman-Wolff calls, the twins hurried to the phone to have hushed conversations with their friends, the ones who hadn't gone to camp for the summer. Everyone had known Boyd Ellison, although none apparently knew him well. No one had liked him very much. Besides his reputation for petty thievery, he bullied younger children then became obsequious at the arrival of their older siblings. He was chubby and bad at baseball. He laughed when other children fell off the swings or skinned their knees. But suddenly he was the closest thing to a celebrity any of us had ever known.

"Remember that time I gave him a ride on my bike?" said Steven. He leaned against the kitchen counter with his elbows, his brown hair tugged back into its usual ponytail. From behind, he and Julie looked nearly identical. "I gave him a ride to the mall."

"I sat next to him once on the bus." Broodingly, Julie plucked strings from the fringe at the bottom of her pants' legs.

"Who would kill a kid like that?" said Steven, sounding almost jealous.

In fact, in the days that followed he did become jealous, we all did, while at the same time we were appalled in a keyed-up, restless sort of way. We tried to feel afraid because we recognized that fear was the expected response and not to have it signified something uneasy about ourselves; but fear wasn't really a part of those first days. We were exhilarated. Nothing so enormous and glittering as a murder had ever happened to us before. Its darkness was the darkness of our favorite stories, the ones we whispered at slumber parties and in the school bathrooms. We were jealous of Boyd Ellison not because he had been killed—of course not that, we had never felt so alive ourselves—but because he had encountered something legendary, and was fast becoming so himself.

"If I'd been Boyd and that guy came up to me," Steven began saying at lunch or dinner. And he would outline various responses, from clever methods of distraction to exactly placed uppercuts.

"I would have kicked him in the balls," said Julie one night.

"Kneed him in the groin," corrected my mother, spooning brussels sprouts onto each of our plates.

Steven said: "If I'd been Boyd, I'd have taken that rock . . ." And he picked up his spoon and beat at a brussels sprout until it jumped off his plate.

"Oh sure," said Julie. "Like the guy would have handed it to you."

"No, no like this. First I would punch his nose." Steven bunched his fist. "And get him to drop the rock. Then I would whip around behind him and kick in his knees."

My mother looked up sharply. "Don't be an idiot," she said. "You have no idea what you would do." When Steven opened his mouth, she put her hand down on the table. "I don't want to hear it. Nobody is a hero ahead of time."

What I remember most about the theories that circulated through the neighborhood that first day was not their wildness or their exaggerations. What I remember most is that no one really seemed surprised by any of them. All that long, muggy afternoon, I sat on the porch picking at the rim of my plaster cast, listening to the opinions of our neighbors.

"I'll wager it's a black," cherubic old Mr. Morris told Mrs. Lauder, as he stood stiffly in her driveway gripping a pair of hedge clippers. Mr. Morris had been in the British army and had never quite lost the habit of standing at attention, even though he was past eighty and had arthritis.

"Well, it could be anybody," Mrs. Lauder began, then stopped and put a puffy hand to her forehead.

"I'll wager it's one of those Panther people," said Mr. Morris, not listening. "When they find him I'll wager his record is two miles long."

While my mother was taking a phone break with me on the porch, little Mrs. Sperling came over in a flowered house-dress, carrying enormous Baby Cameron, who had the hiccups. Mrs. Sperling had lived on our street only since November and in the beginning she was so lonely at home by herself with her gigantic child that she had braved my mother's reserve, trotting over uninvited every afternoon to ask questions about baby fevers and diaper rash and germs, which my mother answered as best she could, and the two of them had become almost friends. Lately Mrs. Sperling seemed to be getting her advice from Mrs. Lauder.

"Hi there, Marsha," she said cheerfully. Then she recollected herself and turned to my mother to confide in a whispery voice: "Oh Lois. That boy died in his mother's arms. I *think* that's what I heard."

She shivered and Baby Cameron hiccuped milky drool over her bare arm. "Oh honey. *Look* at you. *What* a mess." She handed the baby to my mother and pulled a diaper out of her dress pocket to swab at herself. When she had slung the diaper over her shoulder and held her arms out for the baby again, she added, "His mother works, you know. I know this is wrong, but I can't help it—I can't help thinking this is what happens when women don't stay *home*. All that women's lib stuff—doesn't it make you kind of, I don't know, *sick* sometimes? Leaving kids home alone, going off to find yourself." An uncertain expression of disgust wavered across her round face. She brushed a strand of hair away from her forehead. "I mean, there's a *limit*, isn't there?"

"Maybe his mother was home."

"I heard she wasn't," said Mrs. Sperling stubbornly. "I heard she was a receptionist."

"Well, Dolly, then maybe she had to work," said my mother, opening and closing her mouth very precisely. "Maybe his mother did everything she could for him and it still wasn't enough."

"Oh," said Mrs. Sperling.

"It's just that it may be more complicated than you think."

Mrs. Sperling frowned down at Baby Cameron's crumpled face, awaiting another hiccup. When it came, she said, "I see what you mean, Lois. It's *awful*. Poor woman." And her brown eyes welled up. She blinked at the baby for a long moment, then she apologized and told my mother she had never felt so afraid in her life.

By the time Mr. Green returned home that night and parked his usual six inches from the drainpipe, we'd heard that officers from the Montgomery County Police Department had used bright yellow tape to rope off the place where Boyd's body was found, and that crowds of people were being ordered away from the back section of the mall's parking lot.

Two police detectives had already visited every house on our street, asking whether anyone had noticed anything unusual the day before. No one had, although Mrs. Morris said she felt all day "that something was wrong."

"I had the most awful feeling," she told Mrs. Lauder. "I thought perhaps it was a gas leak in my house. It gave me such a headache."

My mother was so ingratiating to the big-chinned detective who came to our door that she must have seemed unusual enough all by herself. "Come right on in, Officer. Can I get you a glass of water or a Coke? It's so hot out there."

When he asked if we had seen any strangers on the street in the last twenty-four hours, she made an unconvincing show of turning to consult me, waiting for me to shake my head, then turning back to the detective to announce that neither of us had seen anyone. She worked up the same high-pitched chattiness she often used with the neighbors, trying to force the detective to sit down in one of the director's chairs, asking questions about his job until his long dark face seemed to flatten into a silent page on which all sorts of terrifying observations were being recorded. He had a Baltimore accent and said "youse" instead of "you." His name was Detective Robert Small, which I remember thinking was funny because he was so tall that he had to stoop as he came through the door.

Once or twice he jotted something down on a palm-sized pad of paper. "Hear anything like a scream?" he asked. "Who lives next door?" Finally, as he was pushing open the screen door, he told us politely to "keep a careful lookout," and said we should call him right away if we remembered something that might be helpful.

"Watch yourself," he said to me, just before he walked down our front steps. And I felt that he was speaking to me as a suspect, someone who might make a wrong move and betray herself, and not as a child who was at risk.

Watch yourself: it's advice I have taken to heart. My husband often accuses me of being too fearful, of thinking too much about the calamities that could befall us. I used to defend myself by arguing that I have a good imagination, which allows me to envision calamity in great detail. But the truth is, I watch myself because I can never be sure I won't do something calamitous myself. "I am *careful*," I correct him.

By the time Mr. Green turned on his sprinkler that evening, the men in our neighborhood had already met on the Morrises' lawn and partnered up to patrol the block in pairs. Like me, they had discovered the virtue of being careful. They called themselves the Neighborhood Night Watch, and they intended to patrol our neighborhood until a suspect had been caught.

Looking back, I believe no one asked Mr. Green to join the Night Watch because they forgot about him, the same way they had forgotten to knock on his door the night before to ask for his help with the search. He hadn't lived in the neighborhood long; he was a quiet, self-effacing man, almost laughably forgettable. But it's also possible that he wasn't asked because of some echo of tribalism that agreed that only married men should stand guard over the neighborhood. Whatever the reason, Mr. Green stayed inside his house that night, listening to a jazz station on his kitchen radio, while Mr. Lauder and Mr. Sperling and every other man on our street took turns walking for two hours around and around the block. The same was true of the next night, and the next, and every night for weeks.

To imagine what happened to Boyd Ellison the afternoon of July 20th is something I've tried to do again and again, and I always fail. Memory is supposed to supply facts you didn't know you remembered until you sat down and remembered hard enough, but in this case the facts disappear whenever I try to cup them long enough to examine. Actually, it's not even facts that disappear, but impressions, constructions— leaving only that rough bit of grit, the event itself.

For me, all mental pictures of that day end at middle distance, with the image of a boy in shorts and a T-shirt on a street corner. Bare stocky legs, ending in white athletic socks and black basketball sneakers, half-unlaced. Blond hair stirring in the breeze, square face turned at a three-quarter profile as he, a good Cub Scout no matter what happened with that paper drive, squints up the street to see if a car is coming.

Ahead of him lies a last wilderness: oak trees, white pine, and creeper, a litter of broken beer bottles and cigarette butts, the wooded shortcut to the mall. Soon to be a parking garage. But for now it is a green wood, a tempting darkness. He has, remember, spent the morning reading *The Call of the Wild.* Gazing at the white pines and scrubby oaks from across the street, he hears that call himself, ululating all the way from the frozen Northwest Territories to an East Coast subdivision in mid-July. The sun is shining on Spring Hill that day. It is eighty-nine degrees.

An elderly woman wearing a pink housedress walks past with her pug on a red leather leash studded with rhinestones. She smiles at the boy, who stoops to pat the dog and touch its curled tail. To the right bulks the brick Defense facility, mysterious and nondescript behind its black chain-link fence, fortified by shield-shaped "No Trespassing" signs in red, white, and blue and a sign that says "U.S. Government Property." The woman and the dog walk on.

But now, just as the boy prepares to cross the street, a car does appear, a brown car, sunspot blazing on the windshield. The car slows, comes to a stop beside the boy. Then the car door opens with a metallic grunt; someone leans over the front seat. A man's hand beckons from inside. Come closer. The boy steps closer. He bends to listen.

What kind of summons could have persuaded Boyd Ellison

to approach that car and temporarily abandon his errand to buy straight pins and sherbet? What was requested of him that day, the boy who was himself so fond of asking?

Maybe only directions. Anything worse and he would have run straight home. It is 1972, after all, which if more innocent than our own time is still an era where children know not to talk to strangers. So he backs away from the car, back to the safety of the cement curb. All this the lady with the dog confirmed. The car door slams shut and the car drives on, disappearing around a corner. Half a block away, the pug whines, is told to hush. His leash winks in the sun. And off goes Boyd Ellison, still with his head full of blizzards and gray wolves— off he trots across the street and into the raggedy, fairy-tale woods behind the Spring Hill Mall.

Perhaps the man driving the brown car meant to go right on home that day. Perhaps he wasn't the worst man in the world. Perhaps he was a man who lived in a neighborhood full of children, a man with a neat lawn and orange marigolds around his front steps, a man who bought raffle tickets and lent out his jumper cables, a man who could—if you didn't look closely—resemble any other neighbor. Perhaps he had his own romantic dreams, ones that were not perverse, ones that would not hurt anybody.

Perhaps, perhaps—that careful word. Who can tell what went awry in those next minutes as Boyd Ellison stepped into the woods and the man in the brown car drove around the block to the mall's parking lot, parked in a far corner, and walked up the hill? One step, two, three. Twigs crack; a beer can rattles, kicked aside. Overhead tree branches sway against a blue sky. A pause. There is still time. Time to turn back, time to stop. Time to recollect. But then another step, and another. Tree branches sway; another twig cracks. One step more. And there he is, a boy lost in the woods of someone else's imaginings.

After that I can see Boyd Ellison only after he has been killed, his hair blood-matted, blank eyes half open, blue lips parted. Or I picture him walking down the street, forever into that middle distance. I'd like to think that my inability to picture anything further involves something moral, but I'm as much a voyeur as the next person, probably more so. Every time I swung past the Ellisons' house on my crutches that summer, I thought about Boyd's body on the hillside behind the mall. I imagined his head twisted to the side, his arm bent under him, his T-shirt hiked up to expose his pale belly.

So strange and vulnerable a belly looks, especially a child's—like something left unfinished.

"According to Sergeant James McKenna, Montgomery County Police Department spokesman, the slaying does not appear to be ritualistic. 'We have some items recovered from the site that we are checking on,' McKenna said. He would release no further details pending the investigation."

My mother paused for a moment, then continued. "A

source, however, revealed that bloodstains found on the youth's clothing do not match his own blood type. Police believe he struggled with his assailant, perhaps scratching or biting him."

Over the next few days she read aloud newspaper reports about Boyd Ellison during breakfast, very much as months before she had read aloud news about Nixon's trip to China so that we could apprehend history while it was happening to us. Perhaps she thought it was time we recognized that history was full of crime as well as mistakes, and the very occasional triumph.

She also read aloud articles about what people were beginning to refer to as "the Watergate bugging." Convinced it was important by my mother's interest, I pasted into my notebook an article headlined WATERGATE BURGLAR RECEIVED MONEY FROM CAMPAIGN FUND.

In a confused manner, I think I'd begun to connect my father's leaving us with Boyd Ellison's murder and even with whatever it was that had happened at Watergate. Although I couldn't have explained it then, I believed that my father's departure had deeply jarred the domestic order not just in our house, but in the neighborhood, and by extension the country, since in those days my neighborhood was my country. My father left to find himself, and a child got lost. That's how it struck me.

Up until then we had lived a reasonably calm life on a reasonably calm street, where nothing extraordinary ever occurred, at least visibly. People had babies and went to work and played catch in the evening or watched television. Mr. Reade's youngest brother had been killed in Vietnam; I remember overhearing him tell my father about it one evening as they stood by the curb watching Steven and the Reade brothers play basketball. But otherwise no one else spoke of the tragedies that befell them. It was, in a way that has ceased to be possible, a quiet neighborhood. And so in a peculiar way I began very early to blame my father for Boyd Ellison's death.

Especially as the days went on and the police didn't find a suspect, and my father didn't write to us. He waited too long. The longer he waited—out of shame or confusion, or out of a mistaken conviction that we wouldn't want to hear from him—the harder it must have become to pick up a pen or the phone. Slowly he crossed the line from someone I had always known to someone I could hardly imagine. Which is how, I suppose, we became for him.

The photograph that appeared in the paper the day after the murder showed a fair, solid boy with close-set eyes. His smile looked commanded, but not unnatural. It was one of those photographs found on the living-room mantelpiece of any middle-class family's home in America, taken in the elementary school auditorium by a middle-aged sweating photographer who motioned for one child after another to step forward and sit on a stool in front of a blue screen. *Smile*, he ordered, and every child did, impressed by the flashbulb in its aluminum shell and the depthless black lens glaring at them, and by the fleeting importance of being recorded, as a person, as a human body.

But I remember a different-looking boy than the one in the photograph. I remember that he often squinted. I remember that he smelled of sandwich crusts. I remember the intimate grasp of his hand on the arm of my mother's chair, the other hand already lifting toward her coffee cup.

But mostly I remember this:

One morning in late April the year before, when the spring mud had finally hardened and we could go outside without shoes, the twins and I were in the front yard building a clubhouse with fallen branches and an old packing crate. It was a rare thing to be allowed to assist them in any of their enterprises, and although I knew I would be expelled from the club once construction on its headquarters was concluded, I ran around the yard in my striped overalls, dragging over bits of wood, offering suggestions. Finally the twins went inside to ask my mother for duct tape, leaving me to "stand guard."

That was when I noticed that two boys had pulled their bikes together in the road in front of the Sperlings' house. They were holding something between them and staring at it so intently that I walked across the street to see what they had found.

It was a praying mantis. Although I don't believe I'd ever seen one before, I felt a kind of recognition at the sight of that long segmented insect, sap green, with enormous fractured eyes on a small triangular head. It looked like a space creature.

The first boy, the one I didn't know, had taken off his baseball cap and, with his hand inside the cap, pinched the mantis between his fingers, crushing its gauzy wings and trapping its upper legs. The insect twitched; its jointed, mechanical-looking lower legs clawed the air while its head, moving freely back and forth, appeared to turn toward each of us.

"It's a vicious bug," the boy said. "It can bite its own head off."

He pinched it tighter. Then the other boy moved closer. I saw a bright glint and, as my heart beat faster and faster, I watched as Boyd Ellison, earnest as a surgeon, tried to slit open the mantis's abdomen with a penknife.

Holding my breath, I leaned in as he pressed the knifepoint against that strange, bulky body stretched taut like a pea pod. He pressed slowly, steadily, denting the smooth green belly—until finally it punctured. A white innard pulsed out from the wound; it looked like a cigarette filter. The mantis's limbs beat thinly up and down. Then the slim upper body twitched and a milky fluid leaked from its split gut. The legs kept waving silently, six legs; the upper two, now free, had cruel spiky hooks almost like hands.

Stomach heaving, I drew closer and stared, wanting to get even closer, to peer right into those alien eyes. What I felt, as I stared at that mutilated insect, wasn't pity; it was closer to a lost word between revulsion and desire. I wanted to put the praying mantis into my mouth.

None of us flinched. We were serious as scientists or explorers, watching as the mantis continued to wave its legs.

The twins had come back outside and were walking toward us. I heard Steven shout something behind me, then felt him yank me back by my arm. He pushed me toward Julie and stood over the two younger boys huddled at their handlebars.

"That's disgusting," he said, almost shrieking. "Look what you did." His voice sounded extremely high and loud, like the school fire-alarm bell. I imagined everyone in the neighborhood rushing to their windows to see what disgusting thing we had done.

The boy who'd been holding the mantis dropped it on the street by the curb, where it lay struggling on its back, ruined abdomen lifting. A damp spot appeared on the pavement beneath it.

"You're *sick*." This time Steven swung around to include me. Then he stepped off the curb and carefully crushed the dying insect under his heel.

"Get out of here," he said when he had finished. He looked straight at Boyd Ellison, who was still holding the open penknife. "Get the hell out."

At that moment, in the face of my brother's gleaming outrage, and faced with the prospect of my mother's contempt and fury once she heard about this episode, I hated Boyd Ellison more than I had ever hated anyone in my life. I wished I had a rock to throw at him as he climbed back onto his bicycle and began to pedal away, flashing rubber Keds labels, tiny blue flags, on the heels of his sneakers. I wanted to kick him, smash his square face, and knock him down. I wanted to make him pay for showing me what I had wanted so much to see.

Miraculously, Steven did not tell. Instead, as the boys rode away he slapped me on the side of the head, just above my ear. "You're out of the club," he said. "Jerk."

Julie said: "She was never in it."

For weeks, I went back to that green smear on the street, until it dried, and turned brown, and one day blew away.

Now in the kitchen, staring over my mother's shoulder at Boyd Ellison's newspaper photograph, I knew I wasn't sad that he was dead. In fact, it was impossible to believe that someone so firmly weighted in his own flesh could exist one day and the next day vanish. I couldn't imagine myself vanishing. Guiltily, I tried to see past the tiny dots that formed his image and convince myself that I felt remorse.

But I felt worse than remorseful. I felt caught out. Boyd Ellison had recognized me as a kindred spirit, an asker, a beggar, someone who kept watching, hoping to see something disgusting, the world's most disgusting sight, pain that didn't have to happen. Boyd Ellison was someone I had known well after all.

"What's wrong with you?" said my mother, glancing up from the paper. "Marsha Martian?" And she put a cool hand to my forehead.

Eight

The police investigation continued. For weeks, phone calls streamed into the sheriff's office from people who had seen a balding man in a brown car. A psychic told police that they would find the man living in a trailer in Schenectady, New York. Several anonymous letters accused Vice President Spiro Agnew of being the murderer. A boy in Baltimore said a man approached him at a bus stop and offered him five dollars to get into his car. But it was a red car, this time, and the man had a beard. In New Jersey, a little girl vanished from her own front yard.

Based on a description furnished by the elderly woman with the pug, a composite drawing was posted in police stations across the country. One of the drawings also found its way to the bulletin board in the Spring Hill Mall; it was a pencil sketch, showing a round-faced, middle-aged man with unprepossessing features—unprepossessing enough that he could fit anyone's idea of any kind of criminal. He looked like the sort of man who nowadays is easy to recognize as a child molester because we've been told so often that a child molester could be anybody, the man next door, even your own father. Back then, the man in the sketch looked too ordinary.

I thought he looked just like Mr. Green.

In my notebook, I pasted the following article from the *Washington Post*:

> Police investigating the abduction and murder of 12-year-old Boyd Arthur Ellison of Spring Hill believe someone living in the vicinity may be responsible for the crime, according to a source close to the investigation.
>
> The same source revealed that the police believe the murderer is left-handed, due to the angle at which blows were delivered to the youth's head. While Montgomery County Police Spokesman Joseph McKenna refused to discuss whether police have any suspects, he did urge area residents to exercise caution and to report any suspicious activity. "We have some leads that we're currently following. I am not at liberty to disclose further details," McKenna said.
>
> Meanwhile, Spring Hill residents continue to express their shock over the killing. Several residents say they are uneasy about remaining in the area. "This is a nice neighborhood," said Carol Humphries, 44, a mother of two who lives next door to the Ellison family home. "Everyone I know around here has the same values. That's why

we live here, because you know what to expect. Things like this just aren't supposed to happen here."

During the next few weeks, the Night Watch became a regular part of our neighborhood and even attracted some press of its own. A reporter for the *Post* interviewed Mr. Lauder, and a few days later a short article appeared in the Metro section, headlined LOCAL PATROL CALMS NEIGHBORHOOD JITTERS, accompanied by a photograph of Mr. Lauder, Mr. Sperling, and several other men standing with their arms crossed on the Morrises' front steps. I saved the photo in my Evidence notebook. They look like piano movers.

Mrs. Morris had sewn orange cloth armbands for the patrol, with black felt letters, NW, stitched to each one. "What *is* this?" my mother said, the first evening the armbands appeared. But I thought the armbands looked very official.

I began sitting out on the porch after dinner until bedtime, waiting for the patrol to pass our house, timing them from when they began at seven-thirty to see how many times they would pass by on a two-hour shift. The fastest walkers were Mr. Reade, father of Mike and Wayne, and Mr. Lauder; their record was every twenty-six minutes. I held my breath whenever they went by, the same way I held my breath whenever Sherlock Holmes made a small, vital discovery. The slowest were Mr. Guibert and Mr. Bridgeman, who got into arguments about the I.R.S.——Mr. Bridgeman was a tax inspector—and sometimes stopped walking altogether to pick through fine points of the tax code. The patrol covered about ten city blocks, including the mall parking lot, where they occasionally surprised teenagers necking or drinking beer in their cars. The mall parking lot had become even more popular since the murder. Their last shift ended at half past midnight.

Most of the men talked as they patrolled, and I loved the rumbling, sedate sound of their voices, and the drift of cigarette smoke they left behind. It was something I depended upon during those long weeks in July and August, the sight of Mr. Lauder and the other fathers on my street passing by so regularly, yellow light from the street lamp gleaming off their metallic watchbands, shining along the handles of their heavy silver flashlights. It moved me to be the object of their care. As their white, short-sleeved shirts hove into view, I felt my throat close and my back straighten, swept up by the closest thing to patriotism I have ever experienced. I fell in love with all of them. I dreamed of being carried by each man, pressed to each of their chests as they carried me to safety, passing me down a long line of fathers.

Like the freak tornado my mother had so thoughtlessly wished for, something violent had blown into our little grid of streets, changing the whole topography. But in those days people believed you could prepare for catastrophes. That's what storm cellars were for. That's why people had emergency medical kits, and a few years before, fall-out shelters in their backyards. We hadn't been prepared, and that's why a child from our neighborhood had died. We hadn't been prepared, and so a pleasant stretch of trees and lawns and driveways was now shadowy terrain, pocked with hiding places, dark corners, creaking branches. Looking back, it seems to me that those gallant fathers intended, by sheer physical effort, to return our neighborhood to what it had never actually been.

Mr. Green's failure to be included in the Night Watch made me first pity, then detest him. My memory of his brawny chest and his blacksmith's arm receded, replaced by scurrying images: Mr. Green disappearing ratlike through his front door; Mr. Green dressed fussily in madras shorts, hiding behind a bush. I created scenes in which Mr. Green was asked to join the Night Watch but refused. In these scenarios, Mr. Lauder and Mr. Sperling begged him to join them, to help them keep our neighborhood safe. "Why would I waste my time," Mr. Green sneered, "on such a *hopeless* enterprise?"

He always had a supercilious German accent in these exchanges, and a lock of greasy hair dangled over his forehead. Whenever Walter Cronkite mentioned the Watergate burglars on TV, I pictured Mr. Green wearing a ski mask. Often now when I watched him walk to or from his car I imagined him in debased poses—on the toilet, or with his finger up his nose.

If I passed close to our hedge, I tossed litter into his yard: snips of string, torn movie-ticket stubs; sometimes I spat out my gum in his driveway, hoping it would stick to his tasseled loafers. One morning I constructed a note from letters cut out of the newspaper and glued onto a piece of notebook paper. I aM gREEn, it read. I haTe KIDS. I am gOiNg to gEt YOU. When no one was out on the street, I took the note and placed it on his front steps, where it sat for an hour or so before blowing away.

A few days after Boyd Ellison's body had been found behind the mall, every house in the neighborhood received its own threatening note, a flyer on acid-yellow paper, tucked under the windshield wipers of their cars: A NEIGHBORHOOD CHILD WAS BRUTALLY MURDERED BY AN UNKNOWN ASSAILANT, THURSDAY, JULY 20TH. ALL PARENTS ARE ADVISED: KNOW WHERE YOUR CHILDREN ARE AT ALL TIMES. AVOID STRANGERS. BE CAREFUL. The flyer was signed, THE NEIGHBORHOOD NIGHT WATCH. I saved ours and pasted it inside my notebook.

That evening, Mrs. Lauder told my mother that Mr. Lauder and the other men intended to question any unfamiliar men they encountered on their rounds.

"They're going to say, 'State your business.' And if the guy can't explain why he's here, they're going to drive him over to the police station."

"I think that may be unconstitutional," my mother said.

Mrs. Lauder looked surprised. "Don't you want to keep the kids safe? That's all they're trying to do."

Mrs. Lauder was a heavy woman with short curly black hair pulled down around her ears like a dark bathing cap. I never saw her wear a blouse that didn't strain at the buttons, and her frosted lipstick often missed her mouth, but she was an oddly rigorous person. Her brother was a Methodist minister in Alexandria, and this relationship seemed to have marked her as the neighborhood Good Samaritan. She knew everything that happened to everybody. Whenever anyone in the neighborhood had a baby or lost a relative, Mrs. Lauder could tell you the baby's name or how the relative had died. Nevertheless it was hard to meet her small, watchful blue eyes without feeling guilty, even when you hadn't done anything wrong. It wasn't that she seemed accusing, exactly, it was more that she seemed to *expect* you to be bad. And yet, she was a kindly woman, cheerful, insistent about helping her neighbors. Ever since my father left, she had made a habit of dropping by once or twice a week to check up on my mother and me.

"How's it going?" she would always ask. "You folks need anything?" She seemed disappointed whenever my mother answered that we were fine.

The same evening the flyer appeared, yellow as fever, on our front steps Mrs. Lauder crossed our yard towing Luann by the hand. My mother had just lugged the hose into the front yard to water the rhododendrons.

"That boy's mother hasn't spoken one word since it happened. Not one single word." Mrs. Lauder always began talking without introduction or greeting. "It's the shock, I guess. Probably a mercy."

"I suppose so," said my mother.

"I heard the grandmother lives with them now. She tells anybody who comes to the door to go away. In Swiss or French or some language. Wears all black. She was there at the memorial service they had over to the high school this afternoon. Did you go, Lois?"

My mother shook her head. Mrs. Lauder fanned herself with our copy of the flyer, which had dropped onto the steps. Luann stood off to the side by the birdbath, staring at her pink sneakers. "Why don't you hop on in and play with Marsha," said her mother. "Go on, doll."

Luann opened the screen door and inched through the doorway, allowing herself to get sandwiched between the door and the jamb. Finally she slid free and stood against the screen, squatting a little to scratch the inside of her leg.

She eyed my cast. "Nobody sign you yet?"

I shook my head.

"Well at least that part's over," said Mrs. Lauder from outside. "But what are we all supposed to do now? What if they don't find the guy?"

"It's terrible," said my mother with a faraway sound to her voice, as if what had happened was not really terrible but only disappointing.

"You watch and you watch, and you make sure your kids are safe, and you stick the Drano and the Windex on top the fridge so they can't swallow it, and you meet their bus every afternoon, and then something like this happens anyway." Mrs.

Lauder wiped her forehead with the back of a dimpled hand and leaned against the porch railing. "It may be God's will but I tell you it's not fair. It seems like these days either you've got to spend your whole life watching, or give up and stop watching at all."

"I know how you feel," said my mother, in the same faraway voice. She turned the spigot on full, then pressed the spray gun she had screwed onto the end of the hose. Rhododendron leaves bucked wildly up and down; she lowered the nozzle and sprayed the ground below each bush, creating small marshes of mud and grass.

A lawn mower started up across the street. Luann sat down on her hands and rocked back and forth. "If I had a cast"—she gave me a cool look—"I'd put on some of them flower-power stickers."

Her pale hair hung around her face like a shower curtain; between the flaps peered a sallow, dignified little face. As the result of a car accident, she had temporary dentures instead of front teeth, which she could flip out and retract with her tongue. At eight she was already famous for this feat, which she performed upon request, and also for her nerve. Not long before he was killed, I'd watched Boyd Ellison ride his possibly stolen ten-speed bicycle right at her—something he liked to do to frighten little kids—and she never flinched, just continued to sit on the sidewalk playing jacks with herself as his front tire passed within an inch of her knee. It was known that she refused to take baths. She was the only girl I knew who would pick up a worm. When a strange dog barked at her she stared at it until it quit.

I'd never had much to do with Luann. In spite of her reputation for composure, she was only eight, and the twins made fun of me if they caught us playing together. "The Infant Duo," they called us, and made horrible cooing noises.

And though I hated to admit it, I was slightly afraid of Luann. Perhaps it was her temporary dentures, and her weary air of having survived what the rest of us had yet to encounter.

On our porch, Luann was peering up at me from the floor. I pretended not to notice and instead stared at my mother's begonias, which had acquired a layer of dust on their leaves. "Know what?" she said at last, brushing back her thin hair.

"What," I said ungraciously.

"When I was six, I got a Cheerio stuck up my nose and I had to go to the hospital. The doctor stuck a big pair of tweezers up my nose. He got it out, but there was blood.

"Yep," Luann went on, after waiting politely for a response. She rocked back and forth. "I got a Sno-Kone after."

"Good for you," I said.

Luann eyed me for a moment from the floor. "My mom says your daddy runned off," she said. "She says he's committed adult."

"That's not true," I hissed, my face hot.

"My mom says it is."

"Your mom's a fat pig," I said.

Outside, Mrs. Lauder was saying, "You know his funeral was yesterday." She paused for a moment. "I heard the parents didn't go to that either."

My mother nodded, turning to spray the azaleas and then the lily bed.

"I just about can't sleep," Mrs. Lauder said. "To think of that poor kid." For a moment or two she closed her eyes and rubbed between them with her finger and thumb. Finally she looked up. "Who could do a thing like that?"

Just then Mr. Green pulled into his driveway. Mrs. Lauder stopped talking while he inched up to his drainpipe, then cut the motor. His car door groaned as he pushed it open. When he caught sight of my mother and Mrs. Lauder, he waved his punctual wave, waited for them to wave back, and then started up his walk. He paused when he reached his front door, then drew out the flyer that had been rolled up and stuck through his door handle.

After he had finished reading it, he folded the paper into a square and tucked it in his shirt pocket. Then he unlocked the door and disappeared inside.

Mrs. Lauder looked into his yard as if waiting for something else to happen. "Now what do you think his story is?" she said after a while.

"Who knows," my mother sighed, coiling the garden hose, muddy flecks of grass spattering her hands and legs. "But I'm sure he has one, just like everybody else."

"Luann," called her mother. "Time to go home, doll."

On the porch Luann, who had been gazing out the screen, turned suddenly to me. "Want to know a secret?"

When I didn't answer, she came over to my chair, bending so close that her breath dampened my cheek.

"Luann," called Mrs. Lauder.

"Want to know a secret?" Luann demanded, looking at me the way she looked at barking dogs.

"All right," I said at last.

Outside our mothers turned toward us, their soft, tired faces like peonies in the fading light.

"Looks like a big thumb," she whispered, almost kissing my ear. "A boy's thing does."

It now strikes me as strange that in the days and nights following Boyd Ellison's murder, I never really felt afraid. But I suppose nothing changed very much in my life that hadn't changed already. The worst sort of crime had happened in my own neighborhood, the murder of a child, someone my age, whom I even knew, and still we went to the grocery store and to doctor's appointments; Julie and Steven still pretended to be members of British café society and they still ignored me and they still swiped gum from the drugstore and smoked behind the rhododendrons; my mother still sat in the kitchen selling magazines over the phone; at night we still washed the dishes, dried them, and stacked them in the cupboard.

I find myself trying to imagine Boyd Ellison's mother washing dishes after dinner, filling her sink with soapy water, staring at her reflection in a black windowpane as she scrubbed a bowl, rinsed plate after plate. The repetition would have calmed her. When she had finished the dishes, she might do them all again. I remember her as thin and tall from the single time I saw her at Halloween, thin and tall alone in a doorway, holding a dishrag in her hand, wearing a blue dress. She had dark hair and dark eyes. She looked, as I recall, something like my own mother.

My father once told me, "That whole summer I thought of you children. But for a while you didn't seem to be my children anymore. You seemed to belong to another life that I didn't belong to, and the life I was living seemed to be my only life. We went fishing and took long walks every day. Sometimes we ate at a diner down the street. We drove out into the country. That's mostly what we did."

Even during the worst times of your life, there are moments when life seems normal, and then you catch yourself wondering which kind of moments—the terrible or the normal—are the real ones. "I tried to write to you," my father said. "But I didn't have anything to say that I thought would make sense."

That's how we all seemed to feel about the murder. We didn't have anything to say that would make much sense, so after the early shock of it, while we waited to find out who had done it, and why, we didn't really discuss it much. Although my mother continued to read aloud news articles, and I continued to paste them in my notebook.

In the first days after Boyd's body was found, a blanketing quiet draped the neighborhood. Black-and-white police cars drove by, or sat parked in front of houses like enormous saddle shoes. Only adults walked alone on the sidewalks, and most people stayed inside. Air conditioners droned and dripped. Once in a while a dog loped down the middle of the road. At night only the pairs of neighborhood men came out, circling the block.

The police had no leads. They would say only that they believed the murderer was someone from the area. Possibly even someone who had known Boyd. Possibly anyone we all might have met.

By Sunday, parents had begun letting their children play outside again. The morning stayed quiet; from our porch I could hear the perky, anodyne drone of cartoon voices, like a bee hum. By that afternoon bicycles began flashing past our house. Steven went down the block to shoot baskets with Mike and Wayne Reade. Julie locked herself in the bathroom to tweeze her eyebrows and came out looking red and furious. Across the street in the Sperlings' yard, two visiting little girls in pink bathing suits ran squealing through the sprinkler while Mrs. Sperling and their mother sat on the front steps, leaning their elbows on their bare knees.

It was right around this time, day number three, when the tower of complimentary Peterman-Wolff magazines stacked on top of the television reached over my head, that my mother told Aunt Fran and Aunt Claire to stop calling.

Ever since their last visit, my aunts had telephoned two or three times a week. They thought my mother should take up golf; they had read that exercise was a "mood enhancer," a phrase that made Julie choke on her chicken leg when my mother repeated it at dinner. They thought she might want to join a women's encounter group. They recommended the benefits of knitting, yoga, consciousness-raising sessions, long bubble baths.

"Have you heard anything?" they would ask.

After the murder, both of my aunts had called every day.

"You've got to stop this," my mother told Aunt Claire one night. "You've got to believe that I'm fine."

From where I was sitting in the living room, I could see her as she paced back and forth in the kitchen, pulling the phone cord taut.

"Listen," she said. "I appreciate your concern, but you're making me feel like something's wrong with me."

Finally she paused by the refrigerator, the phone cord trailing behind her. "What does this do for you, Claire?" she said, in a flat tone I'd never heard her use before.

One rainy night that same week, we all came home from a movie to find Mr. McBride leading a well-dressed young Iranian couple into our basement to look at the boiler. My mother closed the door softly behind us, flushing as she stood in the hallway with her back against the jamb. Julie and Steven instantly evaporated, running up the stairs to their rooms on the balls of their feet.

"Please. Go right on ahead," my mother told Mr. McBride, who, with his black suit and steepled eyebrows, looked like a mortician surprised by a reanimated client. "Don't mind us. Go anywhere you like. Bathrooms, closets, anywhere. We're just . . . we're just—"

But she couldn't seem to decide what it was that we were just doing in our own house, so she looked at the neat little Iranian couple, rustling in their pale linen clothes behind Mr. McBride.

"We're selling our house," she said. "Of course, you know that already." She paused to laugh helplessly. "My daughter Marsha—this is Marsha."

The Iranian couple looked at each other, then at Mr. McBride. My mother, intercepting this glance, added hurriedly, "If you have any questions, any . . . anything, we'll be right here."

She smiled one of her broadest smiles. The belt from her raincoat trailed on the floor by her feet, her heavy black purse dangled from one shoulder, and mud had splashed on her sneakers. The couple stared curiously for a long moment, as if we were some sort of rare, drab creatures they didn't expect to encounter again; then silently they turned together toward the basement and filed down the basement steps. From the hallway, I could see the basement's bare lightbulb glint off their sleek, bluish hair as they murmured near the Ping-Pong table.

"Hi, Lois," said Mr. McBride, shifting in his crow-colored suit. "Didn't hear you drive up."

My mother smiled harder.

"Heard anything from Larry?" he asked after a moment, looking hesitantly down his long nose. "He's quit the firm, you know. Officially, I mean. Resigned. We had a letter."

My mother held her smile a moment longer, then she turned away. "I hadn't heard."

"Well, anything I can— Money. If you need any—?"

"No," said my mother, turning quickly back around. "We're all right for the moment, thank you, Harold. Shouldn't you get back to your—?" She tilted her head toward the basement.

"Oh," said Mr. McBride. "Oh, right."

My mother kept her raincoat on, as if she were the uninvited visitor, pretending to sort through some old mail on the dining-room table. After a few minutes, the Iranian couple filed back up the steps ahead of Mr. McBride, their patent-leather shoes gleaming as they crossed the hall's parquet floor. Looming again by the closet, my mother apologized twice for disturbing them.

"I hope you got to see everything you need to see," she said. "Don't let us rush you."

They gazed liquidly at her. Then the man reached for the

door to open it for his wife, and with a little start, my mother stood aside.

"Sorry to surprise you like that, Lois," mumbled Mr. McBride, hunching his shoulders as he followed them out.

"No, no. *My* fault. Mea culpa," said my mother gaily. She waved from the doorway as the Iranian couple tucked themselves like a pair of gloves into Mr. McBride's hearselike black Oldsmobile.

But the front door had not quite shut before she hurled her purse across the living room. It hit the stack of magazines on top of the television and the whole column collapsed, washing magazines across the floor. A checkerboard of faces suddenly grinned up at us—young women's faces with red lips and long eyelashes, men's faces with their mouths open in speech, President Nixon's face, Chairman Mao's face, George McGovern's face, George Wallace's face, faces of movie actresses, athletes, businessmen, a whole population of faces, as if the days and weeks of the last few months had literally acquired faces. Faces of people we didn't know. Faces not looking at us. Faces that wouldn't care if we lived or died.

Upstairs, Julie and Steven came onto the landing. I could see them peering down the steps as, still wearing her raincoat, my mother began rushing around the room snatching up magazines and tossing them into corners. Damp hair stuck to her forehead. She grunted and stooped, her face and neck turning red, looking somehow animal in her wrinkled tan coat and spattered sneakers. I suddenly pictured her the way I'd seen her that night with my aunts, naked with a towel on her head, pink scar snaking into that dark shrub of hair.

When she had hurled most of the magazines across the room, she thundered over to where I was hanging on my crutches in the front hall, rushing up so close that I could see the fine mesh of perspiration clinging to the hair above her lip.

For a moment or two we stared at each other. I don't know what she saw in my face—fear, repulsion, maybe simply surprise, which can be bad enough in certain circumstances. Maybe she saw the color of Ada's hair on top of my head. Whatever it was, it made her do something she had never done before, and never did again. Panting, almost wheezing, she jerked back her arm and slapped me hard across the face.

I fell over, and my crutches fell on top of me before clattering against the floor. Almost immediately I felt a peculiar satisfaction. Then something dark and cold swept through me, a close and desperate feeling, like drowning.

"*Mom*," Julie screamed from the top of the stairs.

The next moment my mother was on the floor pulling me onto her lap. Julie and Steven had gathered around us, but I could only see their bare legs and ankles from where I was lying. My mother said: "All right, it's all right."

She rocked me under the front-hall coat rack, her neck smelling moistly of rain and talcum powder. A vein throbbed against my cheek. I held myself very still, counting the beats until I couldn't tell if I was counting my pulse or hers, or both of ours together.

"What's going on?" Julie said, her hands hovering around her face. "Are you guys all right?" said Steven, at exactly the same moment. They sounded frightened and confused and uncertain about whether they wanted to understand what had happened.

A rumble in my mother's stomach seemed to come from mine. She stroked my hair and patted my back as the buttons on her raincoat dug into my collarbone.

"Are you okay?" Julie kept asking in a high-pitched voice. "Mom?" She had started to cry, shivering a little. "Mom? Mom?" She and Steven leaned toward each other, their faces identically smooth and worried.

"I'm fine," said my mother at last, getting up. "I'm sorry—"

And that was when the phone rang. We listened to it ring again and again.

And we all knew: it could be my father calling. It could be him, at last, calling us from Nova Scotia.

I can picture him now just as I pictured him that night. He's standing in an old-fashioned red wooden phone booth on a dark street, cars hissing past him, the collar of his jacket pulled up around his chin. The reflection of rain sliding down the glass of the booth slides down the side of his face. He bends toward the black phone box, bracing one hand against the side of the booth. His sideburns have grown longer. Someone has mended the earpiece on his aviator glasses with a safety pin. His voice says: *Hello? Hello?* He says, *I miss you. I'm coming back. This has all been a big mistake.*

Ringing filled the whole house, ringing louder and louder, closer and closer, until finally the ringing pushed us apart and my mother ran to answer it. A moment clicked by while she pressed the phone to her ear, staring down at the kitchen linoleum, her other hand touching her forehead.

"Hello, Fran," she said at last, turning away from us. "Yes, of course I'm fine." She turned around again, and then again, the phone cord wrapping gently around her neck.

Nine

It was Wednesday, July 26th, six days after Boyd Ellison had been murdered, and if you hadn't known what had happened in our neighborhood, the street would have looked like any other suburban street in America.

The fathers all left for work in their white shirts and dark ties at their usual time, maybe even a fraction earlier than usual. Mothers went back to hanging out laundry in the backyard and tying scarves over their hair rollers before driving to the Safeway at the mall, although they looked over their shoulders more often, and peered into the back seats of their cars before getting in. The children went back to day camp and summer school, or if they were children like Luann Lauder, they went back to performing minor acts of vandalism.

Down the sidewalk, past our house, Mrs. Lauder was dragging Luann, who was dressed as a majorette in a red skirt and tunic with pom-poms on her short white boots. "What's *wrong* with you?" Mrs. Lauder said, twice. She gave Luann a yank that made her pale yellow hair flap up and down. "I've told you and told you."

Luann hung her head, but I could see her peering out of the corners of her eyes.

Just that morning at breakfast, my mother had told me: "You're spending too much time alone. I want you to see if Luann can play with you today." When I protested, my mother said: "If you don't go over there this morning, I will sign you up for day camp.

"And leave that notebook here," she added. "I'm tired of seeing you drag that thing around."

"You just want to read it."

"That's not true." My mother looked up from her toast. "But to be honest, I find it unnerving that a healthy child your age spends most of her time scribbling."

"I'm not healthy," I shouted. "I have a broken ankle."

But even I was getting sick of collecting "evidence" about how Mr. Sperling across the street had had to change a flat tire before leaving for work one morning, or how long it took old Mr. Morris to water his rosebushes, or how Mrs. Morris had dropped a bottle of cranberry juice on the front walk while carrying in the groceries, which broke and splashed on the cement and onto her tennis shoes. Or even how Mr. Green next door had spent Sunday morning clipping the grass that edged his brick patio with a pair of poultry scissors. So as I watched Mrs. Lauder propel Luann down the sidewalk, I looked forward to asking her what she had done wrong.

What she had done, it turned out, was write "pissant" one hundred times behind the headboard of her bed in red crayon. Her mother discovered Luann's handiwork while vacuuming after breakfast and when she yelled, Luann had run off down the street. Apparently, this wasn't the first time that she had exercised artistic license on her wallpaper. "One time," she confided that afternoon when we were alone together. "One time I drew a picture of my mom and dad naked."

Mrs. Lauder had set us up in the backyard with Luann's old dollhouse and two glasses of orange Kool-Aid. "You girls enjoy yourselves," she said, managing to smile at me and frown at Luann at the same time. "I'll be right inside."

In silence we drank our Kool-Aid, regarding each other with interest and disdain over the rims of our glasses.

We finished at the same instant and set the glasses down on the little tin tray Mrs. Lauder had left. Then Luann sighed and took a pair of Barbies out of the dollhouse and laid them, both unclothed, on the grass. One had lost a hand but otherwise appeared haggardly intact. The other doll, however, was a magnificent sight. Luann had cut off all its hair, exposing the roots in its plastic skull, and completely tattooed its body with different colors of Magic Marker. She had drawn snakes around its arms, made its breasts into red-and-black targets, given it a verdant bush of green pubic hair surrounding a brown phallic blob. The face was colored half black and half purple. Pushpins stuck out of both eyes.

"This one's named Roy," she said, holding up the doll. "The other one's Tiffany. Which one you want?"

When I said I wouldn't touch either one, Luann shrugged and made both dolls sit in the grass facing each other. "Watch here," she said. "Roy likes Tiffany but she don't like him."

For a few minutes Roy and Tiffany exchanged spirited repartee, with Luann as their medium, mostly concerning what Roy would like to do to Tiffany and how repellent Tiffany found Roy. "I'm going to bite your boobies," Luann intoned for Roy. "I wouldn't go on a date with you for a million bucks," said Tiffany.

After exhausting the possibilities in this vein, Luann made Roy leap on top of Tiffany, where he smacked himself against her while she cried: "Help! Help!" And he growled, "This is what you get for being so hoity-toity."

"Now I put them back in their house," said Luann. "So they can nap."

"How come Roy has breasts?" I asked sarcastically. I had found this display extremely exciting, but would have suffocated myself before letting Luann know it. I was also nervous that Mrs. Lauder might have seen us from the kitchen window and would report Roy and Tiffany's adventures to my mother.

"Roy's all mixed up," explained Luann, calmly laying her Barbies in their pink-and-white living room with a piece of real shag carpeting, where she had also housed a collection of

Diet-Rite bottle caps, a tampon, two empty pill bottles, and a rubber mouse. "He don't know which way he's going."

"You should see what I've got under the sink at home," I said after a moment, feeling that somehow I had lost standing. "I've got three kinds of mold growing in jars."

"One time Roy made Tiffany strip in front of the entire navy," Luann continued. "But an admiral saved her and kicked Roy's butt."

"Some of my mold has grown blue fur."

"Roy always comes back, though." Luann folded her arms. "He's always ready for more."

For a moment we both contemplated the quiet dollhouse, where Roy and Tiffany now dozed peacefully amid the wreckage. Across the street, Baby Cameron Sperling began to wail.

I imagined little Mrs. Sperling standing by his crib in her nightgown, bursting into tears herself, which she had told my mother she sometimes did when he wouldn't go to sleep. "It's a lot to manage," she once said in a shaky voice. "A family isn't an easy thing at *all*."

For a few minutes neither of us said anything. Luann picked at a mosquito bite on her calf. I began to feel I was boring her.

"You know who is weird," I said, leaning forward. "I think Mr. Green next door is really weird."

"Yeah?" Luann looked up.

"He sits outside at night and when slugs come out, he pours salt on them and they dry up while he watches."

"Huh," said Luann. Her eyes flickered back to the interesting chaos inside the dollhouse.

"I think he puts out poison for dogs," I said. "He wants the Morrises' dogs to eat the poison if they pee on his lawn."

"I got bit by a dog once." Luann reached into a bedroom to extract a torn gold lamé ball gown. "He bit me right on the face under my eye."

It irritated me to have to wangle for Luann's attention. She was a stupid eight-year-old, hardly worth noticing, a human housefly. All she deserved was a good swat. But as I was formulating this opinion, it occurred to me that if you can't get such a person to pay attention to you, then you were even less worth noticing.

"Mr. Green built a barbecue pit in his backyard," I said loudly. "He hides in the bushes with a net and waits for peoples' dogs to walk by. He likes to barbecue their bodies and drink their blood. First he skins them, to make a coat." The image of quiet, dumpy Mr. Green dressed in a coat of dogskins pleased me; it seemed to suit his essential foreignness, the way wooden shoes suited Dutch people. I pictured him standing on wintry tundra wearing earmuffs made out of the Sperlings' cat.

"My uncle's a minister. He says you got to eat the blood and body of Christ." Luann delivered this information as neutrally as if her uncle had recommended wearing suntan lotion.

"That's totally different," I said. "That's not the same thing I'm talking about."

"Look at Roy!" Luann yelled. "He's after her again!"

Sure enough, Roy had awakened from his refreshing nap to seize Tiffany by her strawlike hair. The ensuing struggle rocked the foundations of the dollhouse. Bottle caps rolled. Tiny plastic purses and shoes flew out of the windows. It seemed only a few minutes later that my mother appeared on the back steps to call me in for dinner.

"That must have been fun," she said, as I lurched into the kitchen on my crutches. "You two looked like a regular pair of co-conspirators."

"I don't look anything like Luann," I snapped.

That evening I locked myself in the upstairs bathroom and stood on the pink bathmat scrubbing myself with a washcloth and soapy water, thinking about Roy and Tiffany. I stuck my head in the sink and ran water over my hair and worked in some shampoo and then rinsed and dried my hair with a towel. I shook a little baby powder into my palm to rub between my legs.

"Well aren't you Miss Clean," said my mother, as she bent to kiss me goodnight.

Right around this time I began going through the twins' rooms whenever they left the house. I'm not sure what I thought I was looking for as I checked under their beds and opened their dresser drawers, trolling among loose socks, underwear, gum wrappers, wadded tissues, but the act of searching excited me. It seemed that if I only looked hard enough I *would* find something, something I needed to find. What I would do with whatever I found remained unclear, but by that point I was too sunk in the habit of looking to care. Both of the twins had hidden candy in various places around their rooms, behind books, under the rug: toffees, caramel creams, red Swedish fish, licorice bull's eyes, candy you could filch from open bins in the Safeway. Whenever I found a piece of this stale, ill-gotten candy, I ate it meditatively, letting it stick to my teeth.

I did find a few odd, revealing things, all of which I carefully recorded. In Julie's room I discovered a cardboard ring box full of tiny polished stones, a nickel-plated P.O.W. bracelet, and a baby-food jar containing the intricate corpse of a wolf spider. I also found a poem she had written, slipped between the night table and the baseboard: "Who am I / I am Nobody / I have no Face / I have no Body / I can Only Cry," which I thought was a very good poem, although I couldn't understand how someone with no face could cry.

Then one morning, when the twins had gone to Amy Westendorf's house up the hill because she had a swimming pool and her father had a basement mini-bar stocked with airline liquor bottles, I was poking through Steven's room when I uncovered a shrine to bathing suits in his closet. The entire back wall had been plastered with magazine pictures of bosomy women in bikinis. In the center, set a little apart from the others, he had pinned a picture of a tall gleaming black woman in a leopardskin. She gazed challengingly out of the photograph, her lips drawn back, one leg thrust forward as if she meant to leap right out of the closet.

Followed by the eyes of this intimidating woman, I bumped gingerly through the room, trying not to move anything without putting it back in the same place. But something about her savage expression filled me with a new kind of daring. For the first time I lifted Steven's mattress, which made me tremble, although nothing was there. But under his bed I found a broken compass and an unopened pack of Juicy Fruit gum, both of which I pocketed, and also a small, square foil package that held, when I opened it, a mysterious pale balloon.

His room, I noted, had acquired a seamy smell, like the clothes hamper when it hadn't been emptied in a while. Julie's room, on the other hand, reeked of the same drugstore lilies of the valley that Ada had smelled of the last time I saw her, a disturbing connection that suggested some sort of clandestine understanding between them. It also suggested that Julie had swiped this perfume, since my mother never wore it and would never have permitted Julie to buy perfume herself. I toyed with the idea of spraying it here and there throughout the house, just to see what sort of reaction it caused, but rejected the idea without examining why.

As usual, I emerged from this small orgy of intrusion feeling exhilarated and guilty. To redeem myself, I decided to help my mother by doing housework, maybe even offer to weed a flower bed. But when I wobbled into the kitchen on my crutches, my mother frowned and turned her back on me, concentrating on whomever she was wheedling into buying magazines over the phone. When I tried to get her attention by skipping the phone cord, she clamped her hand over the receiver. "I can't talk to you right now," she rasped. "I'm working."

So I took that pale balloon lifted from Steven's room, carried it outside, and dropped it on the sidewalk in front of Mr. Green's house.

Then, although I had been forbidden to leave our street, I swung myself all the way down to the mall so I could listen to the squeak of my rubber tips against the mall's terrazzo floor. The floor had just been waxed, so I used my crutches as poles and slid around on my good foot like a one-legged skier, leaving long gray streaks in my wake. In spite of what had happened right behind it, the mall seemed a restful place in the middle of the day, almost churchlike with its high ceilings and cool fragrance of floor wax.

The mall was nearly empty that day. I bought a bag of M&Ms and ate them with my forehead against the pet-shop window, cracking the candy coating gently between my teeth before biting into the chocolate innards, pretending I was scuba diving as tropical fish floated by. When only the green M&Ms were left, I dropped them surreptitiously onto the floor and crushed them under my heel.

I was still standing by the pet shop when I saw Steven run out of the drugstore.

He was followed a moment later by a skinny black man in red pants and a white shirt. The man was shouting, "Come back here, you little shit. I saw what you took, you little shit. I'm calling the police."

Steven was running as fast as I'd ever seen him run; he ran right past without seeing me, smiling a tight, stunned smile. His sneakers slapped against the polished floor and his ponytail flipped back and forth. He had a rectangular box in his hand, which he flung away as he ran; it skittered across the mall floor and came to a stop behind a large potted fern near the bank.

"Come back here, you little shit," cried the man, pounding after him. His long dark face was sweating and he was kneading one side of his chest with his hand. But Steven was far ahead of him and in a moment had reached the mall's double glass doors. The doorway was filled with sunlight that afternoon and for an instant Steven hung there, a sharp silhouette, arms spread-eagled, legs flung wide, as inexplicable to me as a Chinese character. Then he was through the doors and gone.

Wheezing, the man stopped and swatted the air with his fist. His shiny shoes must have pinched, because he lifted one, then the other tentatively, hunching his shoulders as he stared out the glass doors at my vanishing brother. Finally he turned around.

"Hey," he said. "Do you know that boy?"

I shook my head.

"Little shit," he muttered, squaring his shoulders. He wiped his forehead and stalked over to the potted fern. "Look at that. Tried to steal a whole carton of cigarettes."

He glared at me again. "You know that boy, you tell him to stay out of my store. He's in here all the time, taking stuff. Next time I see him in my store I'm calling the cops." He brandished the box of cigarettes.

I shrank against the pet-shop window. As if noticing for the first time that he was shouting at a little white girl on crutches, the man looked slightly stricken. He looked over his shoulder, fingering the plastic nameplate stuck to his breast pocket. *Hi, I'm BYRON. Have a Nice Day.* "Go on," he said finally, shooing at me with his other hand, the one holding the carton. "It's no loitering in this place."

By the time I got home, Steven was alone in the kitchen with the radio on. I could hear the Jackson Five piping, "ABC, it's easy as one, two, three," as I came in from the porch. He was bobbing up and down to the music, fixing himself a sandwich.

For a moment I contemplated rushing into the kitchen and telling Steven that I'd witnessed everything. You thief, I would shout, with a beautiful self-righteous expression on my face. You criminal. But an odd kind of exhaustion came over me as I stood by the door. "One, two, three," sang Steven in the kitchen. "Baby, you and *me*." In the end I stumped upstairs to my room and lay on my bed.

The fact of it was, there had been something dreadful in the vision of my brother running past me through the mall, his legs pumping, his mouth stretched into a sneer of fright. He had looked so unfamiliar. And at the same time, as he darted down that long echoing hallway and through those blazing glass doors, I felt I had never understood him so well.

I guess what I understood was that Steven had enjoyed himself, that he had been waiting for a moment like this to happen, and even that he had been careful in choosing which store to steal from. There was a kind of power in acting so bad so deliberately, a wild heady power, and it made him run like the wind. No one could have caught him. Or maybe I've only realized the last part since, thinking back on that furious black store manager with his pinching shoes.

The next afternoon the twins got themselves invited to go to Cape May for two and a half weeks with the Westendorfs. Amy Westendorf was in the same tenth-grade class as Julie and Steven. She had a crush on Steven, and had therefore cultivated a close friendship with Julie. She was short and gnome-like, with a long mat of red hair and oatmeal-colored skin; she picked at her red eyebrows and giggled compulsively, but neither of the twins seemed to mind.

"She's a bit of a doofus, Rod," sighed Julie. "But what a nice stereo system. Lovely speakers." All Steven said was, "I wish she'd brush her teeth."

The Westendorfs were the wealthiest family we knew, and

besides their swimming pool they had their own beach house. Julie and Steven were ecstatic at the thought of going away.

"Oh Mom, *please* say yes," cried Julie that night at dinner, dramatically clutching my mother's sleeve. "You don't know what an opportunity this is."

"Yes, I do," said my mother, smiling.

"Then can we go?" said Steven, grabbing her other sleeve. "Please, Mom?"

My mother thought for a few moments, or pretended to think. It was pretty to see her surrounded like that by the twins. Their eyes were bright and excited, and she was laughing to have so much of their attention. It must have been easier, I couldn't help thinking, in the days when she had just them.

"Of course," she said. "Of course you can go."

For the next couple days, Rodney and Felicia took over completely and skimmed around the house looking for their bathing suits, ironing their best tie-dyed T-shirts, demanding money to buy flip-flops and beach towels at the mall, strewing so many clothes on the floor in their rooms that my mother could hardly wedge their doors open.

In their excitement to leave us behind, they even warmed to several degrees within friendly. Julie allowed me to accompany her to the drugstore when my mother drove us to the mall, where she stole a bottle of baby oil and a pair of cheap sunglasses. She slipped them into her African straw bag.

"You," she said coolly, "saw nothing."

Steven must have told her all about his close escape a few days before because she took pains to pass by the store manager twice, and even asked him where she could find sanitary napkins.

The twins left in the Westendorfs' Volvo station wagon on a Friday evening, right before dinner. I had been looking forward to their going, and to having the house to myself so that I could investigate their rooms in a more leisurely manner, but soon as the porch door banged behind them, I couldn't imagine what I'd do with myself while they were gone. Suddenly the house, which had been full of their singing and arguing, their astringent British accents, and their gabby, interesting telephone calls, became almost silent. I could hear the sunburst wall clock tick in the kitchen.

Outside someone was mowing his lawn. Several cars drove by. The light slowly slipped out of our yard as my mother made us spaghetti for dinner, which neither of us felt like eating. Afterward she turned on the news and settled down with her glass of Chablis.

"Come sit with me," she said. But I pretended not to hear. I took my notebook and sat on the porch and watched the neighborhood patrol go by on their rounds. It was Mr. Reade and Mr. Guibert that night. I waved when they passed our house, but they didn't see me. Or at least, they didn't wave back.

Ten

"For Your Marigolds," read the note, written in blue ink on a white index card. The message was signed "A.G."

My mother found it early the next morning propped against a yellow box of baking soda on the front steps. She carried them both inside and set them on the porch table, where she had already laid everything for breakfast.

"Look at this," she said, holding up the card as she sat down to sip her coffee. "Who do you think A.G. is?"

Locusts rattled in the poplar trees outside. Julie and Steven had been gone less than twenty-four hours. Outside hot morning sunlight spilled through the leaves, dappling the crabgrass on our lawn.

"It's Mr. Green," I said finally from behind the Cheerios cereal box. "Alden Green. The slugs. Remember?"

I wondered if Mr. Green could have somehow heard me talking about him to Luann. It's always been my experience that coincidence does not so much happen as get summoned. And I have never entirely relinquished my vision of heaven as a celestial holding pen, where lost things wait for eternity, if necessary, but also where negligent comments and gestures hang briefly before descending to revisit you in unexpected ways.

"Oh Lord," my mother murmured, picking up both the baking soda and the card and squinting at them.

"You asked him about getting slugs out of your marigolds." Deliberately I talked with my mouth full, in the manner my mother found most objectionable.

But she wasn't paying attention; she kept staring at the note, which was written in a careful, looping script. "By the way, Mavis Lauder called last night," she said after a moment, still staring at the little white card, "after you'd gone to bed."

My heart began walloping in my chest. Behind the Cheerios box, I searched for a way to deny any involvement in Roy and Tiffany's sordid exploits. My mother, although no prude, disapproved of children's sex games. "Get a book if you want to learn anatomy," she had told Steven when she discovered his pictures of "tooties" under his bed. "What are you doing?" she always called up the stairs if she heard suspiciously creaking bedsprings. Luann is very mixed up, I decided to say. She doesn't know which way she's going.

My mother laid the card next to her plate with a sigh. "Mavis said Luann found a condom on the street a couple of days ago. Do you know what a condom is?"

I shook my head, although before she had even finished saying the word "condom" I knew what it was and where Luann had discovered it, and my heart pounded even harder.

My mother gazed at her plate. "It's something men wear on their private parts. Do me a favor and never pick up anything that looks like— like a—"

"Balloon?"

"I knew it," she said, trying to sound angry but looking up half-relieved. "I knew you knew what I was talking about."

"No I don't," I said. "But I guessed."

My mother frowned. "It's very sad," she said, "when children try to act smart. At any rate, Luann found this thing near our house and her mother says she's going to call the police if any of you kids come across another one. So just be careful, all right? Don't you go anywhere without telling me, even next door."

She buttered a piece of toast and took a bite of it. "Mavis also wants to know if we want to make something for that bake sale she's organizing this afternoon for the neighborhood patrol."

"Great," I said, with too much enthusiasm. "Are they going to buy guns or something?"

My mother narrowed her eyes. "In my opinion, this neighborhood is getting a little too excited about being vigilantes. This is not the Wild West, you know. This is not the O.K. Corral. This is Washington, D.C."

"A kid died, Mom."

"I know that."

But instead of getting irritated, she watched me over the rim of her china teacup.

A bee fumbled outside, bumping against the screen. Across the street, Mr. Morris shuffled down his front steps to get the paper, his terrycloth slippers scraping against the cement, while in the distance gathered the rumble of a departing jet.

Unless what you're expecting is benign, no one likes waiting for something to happen. Not knowing what will happen to them makes people edgy and superstitious. Coincidence vanishes; everything is significant. I've had some experience in waiting for things to happen and not knowing what the outcome may be, and in almost every case I've been driven to reading the world around me as a lexicon of signs and symbols. The reddish stain in the snow means a bad lab report. A missed bus means a bad day ahead. Finding a penny on the sidewalk means good news. Cross your fingers as you pass a cemetery. Knock on wood.

Not knowing brings out the primitive in people. My mother, for instance, has always claimed to be slightly clairvoyant, a reputation I tend to dismiss or exaggerate depending on the degree of my desperation when I request her advice. I remember the summer after law school when I took the bar and asked her over and over whether she thought I'd passed.

She always said, "Yes," without pausing to consider. When I finally asked her why she was so definite, she said, "Because someone has to be definite."

While not entirely reassuring, this answer did remind me that my mother doesn't believe in playing games with fate. She would never resort to my craven tactics of pretending that I don't believe something will happen so that the gods will recognize my humility and allow whatever it is I'm praying for to take place. The gods are fond of surprises. To succeed in life, if you follow my reasoning, the odds have to be poor. As a child, I invoked this rule frequently. "I know I failed that exam," I would eagerly tell other children, fingers crossed in my pockets. "I'm positive."

And if I did fail, well, no one was surprised.

"Ask for what you want," my mother has always prodded me. "Make your case. If you don't get what you want, then at least it won't be because nobody knew what you wanted."

As the days after the murder stretched on, what I wanted, what everyone wanted, was for the police to find the man who had killed Boyd Ellison so that we could all stop waiting for him to be found. Uncertainty had thinned from horrified excitement to a fearful impatience that buzzed through the whole neighborhood. You could almost hear it, a persistent, electrical noise, something like the steady hum of our refrigerator. It got louder as the days went by and the police had nothing to report. The bag boy who'd seen a brown car drive out of the parking lot quit his job and went to visit cousins in

Pennsylvania. The florist who'd heard a cry on the hillside closed up her shop for a week and left for the Jersey shore. And although it was the coolest place in the neighborhood, no one ventured into the woods behind the mall, where ribbons of yellow police tape still fluttered from the trunks of a few white pines.

Mrs. Lauder had put herself in charge of the Night Watch bake sale, the proceeds from which would go to buy a pair of walkie-talkies for the patrollers—what they would do with these walkie-talkies seemed undecided, but everyone agreed they should have them. The bake sale was held in the mall parking lot. Announcements on yellow construction paper had been posted throughout the neighborhood for the past few days; even my mother had acquiesced to tacking one to our crab apple tree.

Mrs. Lauder presided over two card tables set up near the mall's main entrance under a lamppost, to which she had taped a large, hand-lettered sign: NIGHT WATCH BAKE SALE. But she hadn't left enough room for all the words, an oversight that she tried to correct by squashing some letters together and shrinking others. From a distance the sign appeared to read "Night Witch Bakes."

Most of the neighbors had made something. Mrs. Sperling supplied a plate of chocolate-chip cookies, the charred ones craftily arranged on the bottom. Mrs. Morris produced pecan sandies. Mrs. Guibert donated a Bundt cake. Mrs. Reade made brownies; Mrs. Bridgeman made lemon squares. Mrs. Lauder herself had baked two dozen blueberry muffins and an angel-food cake, and had thrown in a tray of mocha fudge, which had begun to liquefy in the sun. Everything was comfortably overpriced. By the time we arrived with my mother's poppyseed lemon pound cake, Mrs. Lauder had already collected fifteen dollars.

"Have a seat." Garbed in an orange floral muumuu, she nudged a plastic webbed lawn chair toward my mother almost as soon as we climbed out of the car. Behind her mother's chair, Luann hovered, clutching Tiffany by one bare leg.

"Sit down, Lois," Mrs. Lauder said. "Don't stand there getting sunstroke." Next to her voluminous muumuu, which I thought looked splendid—like something worn by a Hawaiian queen—my mother's navy skirt and pink blouse seemed clerical.

"Oh no. Really, I'd love to but I can't," she said. "I've got to work— You know I've been selling—"

Mrs. Lauder smiled. "But it's Saturday, Lois."

My mother flushed and set the pound cake on the table. "Well," she said. "Maybe for a few minutes."

"That's right." Mrs. Lauder's dark hair seemed more askew than ever under her straw helmet of a sun hat but she was perfectly in her element there in the parking lot, orange muumuu luffing regally in the breeze, engaged in charitable work that required bossing people around.

"It's six dollars for the whole shebang," she told a young pregnant woman with spiky eyelashes who had stopped to gaze at Mrs. Guibert's Bundt cake. "Better buy it now or you'll wish you had later. Don't listen to what they say about keeping your weight down. Fat lady makes fat baby."

Mrs. Lauder laughed. The young woman moved off toward the brownies. Mrs. Lauder watched her, adjusting her straw helmet. "Here, you can be cashier." She handed my mother a cigar box rattling with coins.

"I really can't stay long," my mother insisted.

"Can I have a soda?" said Luann, kicking a chair leg.

"As I always say," Mrs. Lauder continued. "Two heads in business are better than one."

"I'm thirsty," said Luann.

"I heard you," said her mother. "Why don't you and Marsha go play under that tree."

"Just ten minutes," said my mother, lowering herself into the lawn chair next to Mrs. Lauder's. "Then I do have to go."

"Sit," Mrs. Lauder hissed at Luann.

So Luann and I sat in the meager shade of a maple sapling. Luann occasionally spat on the sidewalk to see if it was hot enough out to make her spit sizzle. I had brought along my notebook and showed Luann a few pages about Mr. Green.

"He is Satanic," I said, trying out a new word from my Sherlock Holmes book. Luann nodded listlessly. The sun shimmered above the asphalt. If any day would be hot enough to bake a Night Witch, this was it.

By five o'clock, two-thirds of the cookies, muffins, and brownies had disappeared. Grocery shoppers, mainly women, had been the best customers. A few people from the neighborhood dropped by; a policeman bought several of Mrs. Sperling's chocolate-chip cookies, then frowned when he bit into a charred one.

Nobody bought a slice of my mother's poppyseed lemon pound cake, although she appeared not to notice. Several people from outside the neighborhood stopped at the little table to ask Mrs. Lauder if there had been any news about who committed the murder. Then everyone compared the hushed stories they had heard: it was a serial killer; it was a drug fiend.

From where I sat, I could hear my mother talking with Mrs. Lauder in between customers, even laughing. Several times she counted up the money in the cigar box; she seemed to enjoy making change out there in the hot sun, bumping elbows with Mrs. Lauder as they traded observations about a chubby girl who passed by in a yellow halter top.

Finally, she pulled a pack of Kools out of her purse, very hesitantly; but before she could ask whether Mrs. Lauder minded, Mrs. Lauder said, "*Cigarettes.* I quit two years ago but I've been dying for one all day."

While our mothers smoked, Luann and I sat on our curb and stared at the backs of their heads. "I wish I had a orange soda," Luann said moodily.

A seagull wheeled over the parking lot, which reminded

me of the afternoon my father had told us he was going away. It seemed such a long time ago, but actually he and Ada had been gone barely five weeks by then. "It is what it is," he had said that day, looking down at me with his aviator glasses winking. What had he meant? Had he even known what he meant? Of course he must have known. Hadn't he said it? But what had he said?

My head began to ache. Luann spat again on the sidewalk. Overhead, the seagull cried and I remembered Rehoboth Beach, where we had gone the summer before with my father and Uncle Roger and Aunt Ada. Julie and Steven and I swam all day, and because none of their friends were around, they let me follow them up and down the boardwalk. We bought Cokes and drank them while we walked, something my mother never allowed because she considered eating on the street bad manners. The twins would make funny comments about the people we passed, and sometimes I would laugh while I was drinking my Coke and the carbonation would backfire up my nose. I felt that same piercing ache now when I thought of what they would say if they could see me sitting next to Luann Lauder. "Lagoon Lauder," Steven called her. Julie said Luann had the personality of wet toilet paper. Of course, she said the same thing about me.

"I've got some money," I told Luann. "I'll get us both sodas."

Dizzy from the heat, I staggered to the mall and pushed through the double glass doors, pausing gratefully inside the sudden coolness to look at the bulletin board, fluttering with advertisements for used sofa beds and almost-new electric guitars. One of the yellow flyers about the murder had been posted beside an announcement for a modern-dance workshop. Next to the bulletin board were two blue metal signs: "Positively NO BICYCLES" and "No Dogs Allowed."

"Sorry, Swamp," Steven always said when we passed that sign. "Guess you'll have to stay outside."

I hurried past the drugstore, looking out for the black store manager in the red pants; but he wasn't anywhere visible. I still hadn't told my mother about Steven's stealing, but I had overhead him inform Julie that he'd "almost been nabbed." He sounded proud of himself. "Oh damn," Julie said in her best Noël Coward accent, yawning languidly. "We'll have to start snitching ciggies from the *madre*. Think, Rodney. Menthol. *Quelle* horror."

Two women in the Safeway stared at my crutches while I slipped quarters into the Coke machine, which sat near the conveyor belt. It had always been one of my passionate desires to ride the conveyor belt with the gray grocery tubs, to pass through the black fringed curtains and be unloaded into my mother's waiting car. I sometimes thought it would be worth working in the Safeway, just to get that chance.

By the time I swung back outside, clouds had blown in over the parking lot and the breeze had quickened, rustling plastic wrap on the bake-sale table, and bringing with it the pewter smell of river water. Luann was waiting for me and looked almost grateful when I handed her a bottle. Together we drank our orange sodas, burping quietly deep in our throats, watching the parking lot darken around us.

My mother hadn't noticed I was gone. Mrs. Lauder was describing a church scandal involving a youth director and the choirmaster, and forgot to lower her voice when she reached the moment they were discovered partially clothed in the recreation room behind the bongo drums. "Right under a banner that says 'Love is Eternal,'" she said. "Oh no," said my mother. "Oh *yes*," said Mrs. Lauder, accepting another Kool.

A baby screamed from across the parking lot, which was darkening by the minute. With her cigarette burning, Mrs. Lauder ate a pecan sandy and a brownie. A letter, she said, had later been presented to the congregation. Far off toward Bethesda, bells began to chime.

"I say forgive and forget. People will do their sinning. There's no way around that." Mrs. Lauder sighed and stared across the parking lot. "I mean, look at what happened right here. Look at what's happening everyplace. What's really interesting about people," she continued in a low voice, "is how bad they can be."

My mother nodded. Then she blew a smoke ring that floated above her own head like a halo.

"So what did happen, anyway?" Mrs. Lauder said. "With you and your husband?"

My mother sat very still. At last she shifted in her chair. "Larry?"

"Of course," said Mrs. Lauder patiently. "Of course Larry."

The bells continued to toll from Bethesda. The sky bulged. A sudden swoop of wind sent a can rattling across the parking lot. Mrs. Lauder peered at her from under the brim of her straw helmet.

"Larry," said my mother, dropping her voice. "Larry left me because he was having an affair with my sister."

Mrs. Lauder settled back in her chair, making the plastic webbing creak. She reached for another of Mrs. Morris's pecan sandies while my mother told her about my father's flight with Ada to Nova Scotia.

"Well, that's terrible," Mrs. Lauder said after a considerable pause. "But you know these things do happen. It's not much help, but as I said, people make mistakes. They do awful things."

My mother continued to stare straight ahead.

"It's hard on the kids, I bet. Hard on you." Mrs. Lauder brushed crumbs off her bosom. "But the important thing now is for you to get on with *your* life, Lois. Don't let their mistake be *your* mistake. That would really be a crime. Do you hear from him at all?" she asked after a moment.

"One letter. A note, really, to say they were going."

"Did you write back?"

"No address," said my mother.

The parking lot began to empty as the sky turned a dusty purple. Beside me, Luann was hugging her knees and singing a song to herself. There was something comforting about her restrained, scratchy little voice in that wide parking lot, even inspiring, no matter what the twins thought. I hoped she wasn't listening to what my mother was telling her mother.

A dragonfly glinted by. "So anyway, where did you find that condom thing?" I said at last, looking at my knees.

Luann stopped singing and turned to regard me gravely. She didn't seem either startled by this question or particularly interested in it. "I got it on the street. My mom threwed it down the toilet. It's for gathering the seed," she added mysteriously. "That's what my mom says."

While I digested this piece of information, Luann said, "I'm going to my uncle's church this Sunday. We're having a prayer sing." She stuck the tip of her tongue out of the corner of her mouth.

Our mothers were standing up, gathering paper napkins and paper plates together. I wondered if Luann would see the youth director and the choirmaster, if she would speak to them. I pictured two skinny, squint-eyed adults huddled under a "Love is Eternal" banner, furtively pinching each other's bottoms. It was clear to me that my mold experiment could never interest someone like Luann. Nothing I knew surprised her. Even Steven's tootie pictures seemed mundane in comparison to the marvelous depravity of Roy and Tiffany, the youth director and the choirmaster.

Just then a brown Dodge drove up and parked close to where my mother was sliding leftover brownies in with the leftover lemon squares. The door opened; a moment later, one of Mr. Green's tasseled loafers appeared on the ground, followed by the second one, followed by Mr. Green himself. Against the darkening sky, his face looked pinker than usual.

"Now isn't this a surprise." Mrs. Lauder patted down the front of her muumuu, which had filled beautifully like a sail in the breeze. She gave my mother a sidelong glance as Mr. Green approached the table. "Hi there, neighbor."

Mr. Green chuckled nervously and rubbed his hands together. "Did you bake something?" he asked my mother, his Adam's apple dunking over his collar.

"Well, as a matter of fact." She pointed to her poppyseed lemon pound cake, which had sagged after two hours in the heat and had acquired a greasy sheen. Luann, who had gone back to humming, fell silent.

"Very nice," said Mr. Green. He glanced over at Luann and me, then back at the cake. "Looks very nice."

"It's lemon poppyseed," said my mother. "More or less."

"Aha," said Mr. Green.

Mrs. Lauder, who had been glancing back and forth between my mother and Mr. Green, quickly broke in. "It's fifteen dollars." When my mother turned to her in astonishment, Mrs. Lauder added, "That's a very special cake."

Mr. Green coughed, holding his fist to his mouth. Then he reached into his back pocket and pulled out a black leather wallet.

"Here." He handed Mrs. Lauder a ten and a five, not looking at either her or my mother.

His face had gone from pink to a kind of cardiac maroon.

My mother stared at him, her mouth slightly open; then she looked down at the open cigar box lying on the table and began restacking the one-dollar bills she had just finished stacking.

"Well thank you, Alden. It's Alden, isn't it?" Mrs. Lauder was saying chattily. "Nice to see you outside your yard, by the way. You work so hard on that lawn of yours you hardly have time to get to know anybody. You know, we really should have some kind of block party one of these days. Get all the neighbors together. The Chiltons, the people who used to own your place? They were always having these little get-togethers. Iced tea on Sunday, lemonade for the kids. As I always say, in a neighborhood everybody should know everybody."

She smiled at Mr. Green from under her straw helmet. "Now don't be a stranger," she added as she handed him my mother's pound cake.

Mr. Green glanced up, mumbled something, and began backing away toward his car. But before he opened the door, he gave us an uncertain little salute with two fingers grazing his forehead. It reminded me of movies I'd seen when a soldier salutes after he's been given a difficult command. Then he pulled the car door open, climbed inside, and drove off too fast, staring straight ahead.

Mrs. Lauder watched the taillights of Mr. Green's car disappear around the corner of the mall. "I wonder if he's ever been married," she said.

"I don't think so," said my mother, still restacking bills in the cigar box.

"Why not, I wonder?" Mrs. Lauder had a speculative look.

"Who knows," said my mother discouragingly.

"Well, he certainly seemed set on buying your cake. Fifteen dollars." Mrs. Lauder raised her eyebrows. "I wonder if I could have sold him the rest of these brownies."

"I have a ant bite," announced Luann. The wind was picking up. A few raindrops had already started to fall, pattering onto the sidewalk.

Mrs. Lauder gathered up the rest of the plates and shoveled them into a paper bag. "Really, though. You've got to wonder about someone like him."

My mother said: "What should we do with these plastic forks?"

The dogwood leaves began to shudder, flipping up their pale undersides as a bright streak of lightning lit the sky, followed a moment later by a shock of thunder. It was going to be a proper summer storm. Another jag of lightning cracked across the clouds, then another thud of thunder.

"Well. Thanks for your help," shouted Mrs. Lauder, grabbing Luann's arm and herding her toward their car.

"Thank *you*," my mother shouted back, her hair blowing around her ears as the wind tugged at her skirt.

But before we reached our car the rain came down on us, coming all at once, beating so hard against the pavement that the droplets sprang back upward. In a moment my mother's hair was streaming and her pink blouse was soaked, exposing the lacework on her bra underneath.

"Get in," she panted, wrenching at the car door, rain running down her face, beading off the end of her nose. "For God's sake, get *in*." But as she pushed me into the back seat, shoving my crutches in after me, and slammed the door, I saw her smile.

Eleven

It was either that night or the next that I woke up screaming.

I had dreamed that Mr. Green had been transformed into a naked blue monkey. He squatted by the bureau in my bedroom pulling at his penis. "Just like a thumb," he cackled. "Nothing to be afraid of." He grinned and waved, gesturing with a little wrinkled hand for me to come closer. When I drew near, his penis bobbled and grew suddenly enormous, the size of a watermelon. Then it burst and Mr. Green flew squealing around the room, a pale balloon losing its air, while grass seed dribbled out of him. "Come back here, you little shit," he cried.

"Are you all right?" called my mother from the hall. A moment later she appeared in the doorway tying the sash on her flowered bathrobe. When I didn't answer, she came in and sat on the end of my bed and held my good foot. "Was it a bad dream?

"Can you tell me what it was about?" she said after a little while, laying a hand on my neck.

Eventually, as she stroked my hair and tucked the sheet around my shoulders, I told her that I had been dreaming about Mr. Green.

"He's disgusting," I said, trying to muffle myself in my pillow.

"What?" She leaned closer. "What did you say?"

"He's weird," I whispered, more desperately than I'd intended. But I was remembering Mr. Green, tattooed and bare-chested, squatting in his backyard laying bricks for his barbecue pit. Then I remembered how he'd glanced at me that day through the porch screen. Some sort of a claim had been implicit in that glance, some sort of recognition.

"He *looks* at me," I shrieked into my pillow, then burst into tears.

My mother's hand withdrew. With my face in the pillow, I couldn't see her expression, but I could feel the temperature of the room change.

When she spoke again, her voice was chill. "Tell me exactly what you mean, Marsha, when you say that Mr. Green looks at you."

I have never been one of those people who can retract a lie, who can explain that I spoke carelessly, that I hadn't meant what I said. Once I have lied, I've propelled myself into a story that has its own momentum. It's not that I convince myself that I'm telling the truth, it's that the truth becomes flexible.

Or rather, the truth appears to me as utterly relative, which is a frightening thought but also inevitable if you examine any truth long enough, even reassuring in a cold way.

So I babbled about Mr. Green staring at me when he got out of his car, staring at me from behind the lilac bush, staring at me when he came out to mow his lawn, becoming more hotly committed to my story when I rolled over and saw the tilt of my mother's eyebrows. I said he stared at Cameron Sperling's bottom when Mrs. Sperling once carried him naked into the front yard. I said he'd stared at Luann's underpants once when she was doing handstands in her yard and her dress kept flying over her head. I said he hung around the playground and stared at kids going down the slide. Nothing very serious, of course, but serious enough when a child has been raped and murdered a few blocks away and the man who did it still hasn't been caught.

"Has he ever touched you?" my mother said, in that same chilly voice.

I thought of Mr. Green's blunt fingers patting his bald spot, his other hand trembling as he reached for the glass of lavender lemonade my mother offered him.

"No," I said. "But he's weird."

"Listen to me." She grabbed my shoulder, her fingernails digging through my nightgown. "Listen to me. If Mr. Green scares you, then stay away from him. But I don't want you talking about this to anyone else. Is that clear? You tell me if he does anything to make you nervous, but otherwise you don't talk about this. Is that clear?" Her voice held a high, uncertain note. I stared back at her. A moment later she let go of my shoulder.

"What you've told me could make a lot of people around here very upset," she continued more quietly. She picked up my right hand and held it between both of hers, squeezing each of my fingers, one at a time. "Everyone is frightened right now, and when people are frightened they can do things they feel sorry for later."

She looked out my window at the telephone wires strung across the street. From my window it was possible to see the lights from the Defense facility near the mall; perhaps she was looking at those lights, wondering who could be working there so late. I pulled my hand away and lifted my glasses from the night table, holding one lens up to one eye as though I were peering through a telescope. I studied her face, examining the small V of her chin, the calm planes of her cheekbones, the soft flaw of her broad upper lip. Her hair hung lank and dry around her ears; the top of her head looked flat.

I said: "I don't care. He makes me sick."

My mother gazed down at me. "Do you want me to go talk to Mr. Green? Do you want me to tell him what you've told me?"

"No," I shouted.

"Does this have anything to do with your father?"

For a moment I pictured the two of them standing side by side, Mr. Green and my father. Mr. Green in his fussy shoes and madras shorts and khaki shirt and my father—so relaxed and normal in his aviator glasses, suit, and tie—standing together in the front yard. Anyone could see that my father had nothing in common with Mr. Green. Even my mother should be able to see it.

For another moment I pictured my father's slightly triangular blue eyes and his slender, gingery eyebrows, which he could raise one at a time. His teeth were small and white and square, except for one gold crown that glittered far back in his mouth. "My secret treasure," he once called it, smiling like a pirate.

"Marsha," murmured my mother. She put her hand on my back, rubbing up and down my spine. "Watch yourself." Which is the same thing that detective had told me weeks before, advice that, to my great regret, I was soon to ignore.

By then I had curled myself into a corner of the bed, my face shoved into a space where the bed met the corner of two walls. While my mother sat beside me breathing in the dark, I kept my back rigid and counted my breaths. Until at last my mother got up and left the room.

The plaster walls felt cool against my cheeks. I pushed harder into the corner, glad when my head began to ache from the pressure. When I woke up the next morning, I was still in the same position, pressed against the wall.

It was on Wednesday, a little less than two weeks after Boyd's murder, that we received our invitation to Mr. Green's cookout. Sometime very early that morning, he left a small white envelope propped on the front steps, much like the morning when he left my mother a box of baking soda. From our porch, I spied white envelopes resting on the Morrises' and the Sperlings' doorsteps, too, like small flat doves.

My mother got to the envelope before I did. She picked it up and tore the back flap open, letting the screen door bang shut behind her. Inside was a card, which she read standing on the front steps in the morning sunlight, pale wisteria leaves drifting around her head. Then she came back inside and handed the card to me. She sat down and drank her orange juice and after a moment buttered her toast, scanning the front page of the paper.

The card was cut in the shape of a teddy bear holding a balloon. Printed in red block letters were the words A PARTY! followed by AT THE HOME OF, then a blank line, then the word WHEN, and another blank line. On the first blank line, in blue ink, was the same painstaking, looping script that had been on the file card accompanying the baking soda: "Mr. Alden Green Jr., 23 Prospect Terrace." After WHEN he had answered: "Sunday. 5:00 P.M. Children Welcome!"

If Julie and Steven had been home, they would have had something appropriately cutting to say about this invitation. "Oh Christ," Julie would groan. "He can't be serious. I mean, who's he having a party for, the Bobbsey twins?" But I couldn't summon up more than a bleak grimace at the teddy bear and his jolly little balloon.

I propped Mr. Green's card against the napkin holder and watched my mother eat her toast. She finished reading the front page, turned it, and kept reading, neatly wiping her buttery fingertips on her napkin. She stirred cream into her coffee, still reading, and lifted the cup to take a sip. She turned another page. Finally she looked up at me.

"Yes?" she said. "You rang?"

"I'm not going."

She took another sip of coffee, setting the cup back into its saucer with a hard little chink.

"Are you going?"

"Maybe."

"Why do you like him?" I said.

"I like a lot of people." She gave me a narrow look.

"Well, I don't have to go."

"No," she agreed, displaying the half-smile she reserved for neighbors and grocery-store cashiers. "No, you certainly do not."

That evening I watched Mr. Green investigate his barbecue pit. He had been making a tour of his backyard, pacing back and forth between the house and the copper beech tree, circling the picnic table and his two folding aluminum patio chairs placed at conversational angles, when he found himself in front of the barbecue pit. For a few moments he stood there, admiring his tidy chimney and two built-in shelves. He even squatted down to lift the new grate, and peered into the pit itself.

I couldn't look at him without remembering the blue monkey in my nightmare. Neither could I look at him and find anything wrong with him. He was so careful. Never in the months that we lived next to Mr. Green had he made a loud noise, not even when he was laying bricks or hammering a loose shutter back into place. No potato chip bags blew across his lawn; no weeds sprang from the sidewalk cracks in front of his house. He was the perfect neighbor.

Sitting on the porch love seat, notebook across my knees, I could picture his cookout as if it had already occurred: the cocktail napkins he would have bought weeks ahead of time, printed coyly with a martini glass or a smiling drunk wearing a lampshade on his head; the red-checked paper tablecloth; the bubbled-glass candle holders. I envisioned him pushing his cart up to the Safeway check-out counter, unloading paper plates, plastic forks and knives, plastic-wrapped packages of hot dogs and hamburgers, buns, bottles of Coke, cartons of ice cream.

Mr. Green stood up from poking around his barbecue pit, dusting bits of grass off his knees. Then he walked over to the Chiltons' abandoned picnic table, which he had repaired so that it stood up straight again. For a few minutes he considered the table, resting his hands on his hips. Eventually he turned to go back inside his house, but not before he had glanced in the direction of our porch. In the evening light he couldn't have made out who was sitting there, but he lifted his hand anyway and gave a little wave.

The phone rang while my mother was folding sheets and towels in the basement. Even before I picked up the receiver, I knew it was my father.

By now he would have heard, he would know what had happened while he was away. The newspapers here had been full of Boyd Ellison's murder; surely a newspaper in Nova Scotia would have mentioned it. One day he must have stepped into a pharmacy for a pack of gum and there it was, right on the front page: CHILD MURDERED IN QUIET MARYLAND NEIGHBORHOOD.

"Hello?" I said, almost shaking.

"Marsha?"

It took me a moment to recognize Mrs. Lauder's voice. "Is your mama there?"

My mother had appeared beside me; I'd heard her run up the basement stairs as soon as the phone began to ring. Now she pried the receiver out of my hand.

"Yes?" she said, too casually. "Oh. Oh hello, Mavis."

Then she said: "I'm sorry. Am I going where?" She exhaled slowly, turning away from me toward the sink, where she could look at her reflection in the black window. "Yes, we got one."

After another pause she said, "I haven't decided yet."

She picked up a dish towel and pressed it against her chest. Even with her back turned toward me, I could hear Mrs. Lauder's voice at the other end of the line. I heard the words "foolish" and "whole neighborhood" quite clearly.

"I guess he thought it was something he could do," my mother said finally, cheeks flushing. She had turned around to face me again so that she could snap her fingers and point at the door. When I refused to move away from the refrigerator, she glared and shook her head. "You told him about the Chiltons inviting neighbors over. Oh really, Mavis. He probably didn't think about it being too soon——"

Here Mrs. Lauder must have cut her off because my mother stopped speaking and ducked her head. After a while she said stiffly, "I'm sure he didn't mean any harm."

Downstairs, the washing machine chugged into a new phase of its cycle; water swished and the pipes rattled. Outside, a car rushed past our house, honking its horn.

"All right," she said, staring down at the dish towel she was still clutching. "I will. Thanks for calling." Across the street the Morrises' dogs began barking, adding to the chorus of banging pipes and the chuntering washer and the humming refrigerator and the slow ticking of the sunburst wall clock by the door.

My mother hung up the phone. "Don't speak to me right now."

"I wasn't going to," I said sulkily.

"Thank you." She draped the dish towel back over the rod

by the sink. Then she pulled an open bottle of wine from the refrigerator and poured herself a full glass.

She carried the glass into the living room and switched on the news. Walter Cronkite's mustached face filled the screen; my mother once told me she wished she could have had Walter Cronkite as her father. Every evening she watched Walter Cronkite as he delivered the CBS evening news, his eyes filled with unobtrusive compassion for the world's disasters. "What a nice man," she sometimes remarked. "You can tell he really cares about what's happening to this country."

Tonight Walter Cronkite informed us that the inquiry surrounding the "Watergate break-in" was "widening." He seemed sorry to announce this, gazing straight into the camera, straight into our living room, his deep voice deepening seriously as though he knew more than he thought wise to reveal.

"Of course it's widening," said my mother to the TV set.

After the national news, my mother switched to a local news station. The bald anchorman—whose voice was much higher than Walter Cronkite's, and therefore seemed less compassionate—described a shooting in Baltimore, but had nothing to tell us about our own murder. That's how I'd come to think of it, as "our" murder, the way you might think of a local football team as "our" team or a neighborhood celebrity as "our" So-and-so. In fact, the anchorman didn't mention our murder once, which surprised me, as I had difficulty believing that anything else could be news.

Twelve

Right after breakfast the next morning a detective in a blue sports coat and brown pants from the Montgomery County Police Department knocked on our screen door. He lifted up his badge and said he had a few more questions to ask us, if my mother wouldn't mind.

A blue jay screamed from the crab apple tree. It was another hot, windless morning, one of those mornings when the air is thick with the soap-sweet smell of laundry, and leaves hang off the trees like damp towels.

My mother opened the door and offered the detective one of the director's chairs, then she pulled out one for herself. It took me less than a moment to recognize Detective Small, the same rawboned, boot-faced detective who'd questioned us before.

"I'd like you to go inside, Marsha," my mother said, smoothing her skirt tight over her knees as the detective sat down. "Right this minute, please."

"Actually ma'am, if you don't mind, I'd prefer it if the little girl stayed." Detective Small didn't smile, but he gave me an attentive squint.

"Oh?" said my mother, pretending not very persuasively to laugh.

"Well, you know children sometimes hear things that adults don't."

Just like dogs, I told myself, although at the same instant I gripped my notebook fiercely at the thought of being questioned by a detective ("an officer of the law," I began to call him).

And who would have been a better source than I? Hadn't I saved every newspaper clipping about the murder? Didn't I have an entire notebook filled with what the neighbors had said, and who had thought what, and why they thought it? Wasn't I someone who had known the boy himself?

By this time Boyd Ellison's house had become part of my regular beat, by which I mean that I passed it three or four times a week as I swung around the neighborhood on my crutches, always forcing myself to wait a decent interval before circling back to swing past it again. As much as I wanted to—as much as I was drawn to—I could never bring myself to stare directly at the house as I went by. It was too ordinary looking. So instead I flung myself forward on my crutches, relying on glimpses I caught out of the corner of my eye. Snatches of brick, a pane of glass reflecting the sun, a rolled newspaper on the front steps.

But the day before, I'd invited Luann to come along with

me while she was sitting outside in her yard with Roy and Tiffany. She stood up wordlessly and followed, not even glancing over her shoulder. I pumped my crutches along the pavement, puffing in the heat, humming a TV jingle with exaggerated nonchalance. Luann wandered behind me, yellow hair wisping against her neck, eyes fixed on her crayoned Mary Janes. But when we reached the Ellisons' house, she lifted her head and peered at the house's front windows. While I pushed furiously ahead on the sidewalk, she kept up a measured pace behind me and stared.

It was only when we got back to my porch steps and collapsed under the wisteria vine that I could ask: "What did you see?"

She shrugged and said that a thin, dark-haired woman had opened the door and stood looking into the street.

"Did she look sad?" I demanded.

Luann shrugged again.

"What was she wearing?"

"A dress."

"Was it black?" I said after a moment.

"I am trying to help solve this crime," I told her. Luann admitted that she had noticed a man's furled black umbrella on the Ellisons' front stoop, and that all the upstairs window blinds were pulled down.

"Look at this." I settled one elbow on the step behind me and riffled the pages of my notebook. "Somewhere in here," I said, tapping a page, "somewhere in all this, is probably a clue.

That's what we're doing when we go by their house. We're looking for clues. You have to notice everything if you're going to see anything important."

She nodded, rubbing absently at a streak of dirt on her knee. Across the street, the Jack Russell terriers began howling and scratching inside the Morrises' front door as the mailman turned up their front walk. They must have woken Baby Cameron next door because he started to scream from an upstairs window.

At last Luann glanced up from her knee. "My dad says it's a pervert who killed him."

"I know *that*," I told her. "Everyone knows *that*. You probably don't even know what it means."

"I know." She looked offended.

"Him." I jerked my thumb in the direction of Mr. Green's empty driveway. "*He's* a pervert."

Luann glanced over at Mr. Green's house, at his trim azaleas and the marigolds blooming by his front steps.

"He is," I said, my voice rising. "I've got pages here. He hides in the bushes. I've seen him. He hides in the bushes, sometimes right by the Ellisons' house. I've seen him."

By this time I didn't care what I was saying anymore, only that Luann was looking at me with a rapt expression. "Didn't you see something rustling there today, something in the bushes right by their house?"

"A cat?" breathed Luann.

"No," I said, exultant now. "It was him."

Luann stared. After a moment she went back to rubbing her knee, making little sighing sounds out of the corner of her mouth. "My dad says it don't help to catch anybody anymore," she said finally. "He says they's just somebody else there waiting to do the same thing."

A shaft of sunlight through the poplar leaves had pooled onto the tops of our heads. I reached up and felt my hair and the heat seeping into my scalp. It seemed to take hours for the mailman over at the Sperlings' to cross the street and stride up our front walk with a sheaf of magazines for my mother. He said hello to us as he stuffed them into our mailbox, dark moons of sweat under each of his arms.

"Go home," I told Luann when the mailman had reached the sidewalk again. "Why don't you just go home."

She stood up and began a kind of shuffle-hop across our lawn back toward her house. It was only as she reached her driveway that I realized she was mimicking the way I moved on my crutches. Her shoulders were humped up close to her ears and she walked with a peculiar draggy limp, like a person trying to walk with someone else hanging onto her leg.

When she climbed up her own front steps she turned around and grinned, then she fisted both hands into binoculars and trained them on me.

"You won't mind if I need to ask you a few questions?" said the detective. I shook my head.

He clicked his ballpoint pen several times over his notepad. In spite of the heat he looked cool, even though his forehead was moist. My mother smiled nervously. He gazed at her for a moment or two, perhaps waiting to see how nervous she became, before he started his questions. How long had she lived here? Was she friendly with her neighbors? Had she known the dead boy?

Yes, she answered to everything, but I could tell by the way her chin jutted that she was feeling untruthful. She acted the same way in department stores whenever an alarm bell went off, as if she was afraid that she was the one who had stolen something. It wasn't long before she began answering questions that hadn't been asked.

"Boyd—the child who—he once came here to a Cub Scout meeting. My son—"

Detective Small nodded, neither encouraging her to go on nor discouraging her from continuing until my mother had told him everything she could remember about Boyd Ellison, including Steven's unproven accusation that Boyd had stolen money from the Cub Scouts' paper drive.

But soon it was clear that he was mostly interested in what she knew about Mr. Green. "He's new around here, isn't he? Lives alone? Not many visitors? Would you say he was the social type or kind of secretive?"

"I'd say," said my mother, after a pause, "I'd say that he tries to be a good neighbor."

"I understand he's having some sort of party?"

"A cookout. He's been planning it for some time. Three weeks maybe? Before any of this happened."

Detective Small's ears protruded like doorknobs from his narrow head. The morning light behind him glowed red through his earlobes, which had the effect of making him look electrified. To intensify this impression, his short black hair stuck straight up from his forehead, and his heavy eyebrows had a way of shooting upward as he listened, as if even insignificant replies to his questions administered a mild jolt.

"So how long ago did Mr. Alden Green move in? Any family you know of? Where did he live before?"

"Look, I want to help," my mother said. "But I don't have anything to tell you." She sat back in her chair, dropping the hand that had been hovering around her lip. The blue jay screamed again. "Mr. Green seems like a very nice man," she added, "but I hardly know him."

Detective Small raised his eyebrows in either disbelief or resignation.

"I'm telling the truth," she said, and I wondered if she realized how untrustworthy this statement made her sound. "Haven't you talked to him yourself?"

"Not yet." The detective's eyes went officially blank.

"And nothing—?" My mother was pulling at the hem of her skirt.

"Anyone else around here move in recently?"

My mother shook her head. "Do you really think the man

who did—do you think whoever—lives in this neighborhood?"

Detective Small's eyes were the same deep brown as his knit pants. Broken capillaries threaded toward each iris. The skin beneath each eye looked smudged. "Why do you think so?" she asked respectfully.

"It's not that we think so. It's that we don't have any reason to discount the possibility." Detective Small clicked his ballpoint pen rapidly several times. Then he gave a shrug and straightened his tie, and we understood that the interview was over. "Could you spell your last name for me, please," he said, writing on his notepad. "And give me your telephone number."

"What will happen now?"

"We keep looking. We'll find him."

Now that he was prepared to leave, I found myself reluctant to see Detective Small go. I liked his sports coat on our porch, crisply blue against the faded wicker furniture and wilting begonias, which my mother kept forgetting to water. We were as safe as we would ever be with a policeman on our porch. Perhaps safer than we'd ever be again. Detective Small already seemed to know all about us. I liked his capable air of having done everything he was doing before; he was someone who wouldn't be amazed by anything, no matter how awful or unexpected.

Also, he hadn't asked me any questions. I had been waiting to be asked a question.

"Would you like a cup of coffee?" my mother offered suddenly, perhaps struck by the same wish to hold onto him.

Detective Small shook his head, but smiled this time. "Here's my card," he said. "I have your number. In case I need anything else."

My mother took the card, then put her hand up to her lips and nodded.

"When will your husband be home?" He stabbed his pen into his breast pocket. "I'd like to ask him the same stuff I just asked you."

"My husband left me in March," she said. "I haven't seen him since the end of June. He went to Canada."

For a moment Detective Small continued to gaze at her as if deciding whether or not she was telling him the truth. "Okey-doke," he said finally and stood up, flipping his notebook closed. "Sorry," he added, reddening a little and cupping his hand around the back of his neck.

"It's all right."

As he opened the screen door, he paused and glanced back at us, his face realigned into a judicial expression. "Thanks," he called, halfway over his shoulder. "Appreciate your help."

But before he was quite through the door, and before my mother could interrupt me or wave me inside, I decided to say what I'd been waiting to say, had been hoping, even pining for the chance to say. I said: "We don't like him. Nobody does."

"What?" Detective Small's black eyebrows darted up and down. "Don't like who?"

"Excuse me, Detective," my mother broke in firmly. "Pardon me, but please realize that my daughter is upset about everything that's happened." She stared first at him, then at me. "She doesn't particularly like men at the moment."

"Is that true, Marsha?" asked the detective, not looking quite as confused. "How about me. Do you like me?"

"I don't know you," I said, ignoring my mother.

By then Detective Small had let the door snap shut and was leaning against the jamb with his big arms crossed. It was impossible to gauge how interested he was in what I had to tell him. In fact, he tipped his head so that a shadow slanted across his face, obscuring his eyebrows.

"So Marsha," he said, "who is it you don't like."

My lips had gone dry. "Mr. Green," I said finally, my throat dry, too. "He watches me. He watches kids in the neighborhood."

"Watches how?"

"I don't know."

"You don't know?"

"No. He just watches," I said. My mother kept staring at me as if she intended to stare right through my skull and examine what was happening inside my brain.

Detective Small continued to lean against the door, perhaps counting to ten as he must have been taught to do at the police academy. ("Give the witness time. Allow him to feel the pressure of a silence.") Above his head, just to the left of the lintel, a little brown spider dangled in a web, its fine legs busy.

From down the street came the faint *pock-pock* of someone hammering stone. I would have liked to have said something more, but right then I couldn't think of what else to say.

Finally Detective Small sighed and pushed himself away from the doorjamb. "All right, Marsha. Probably not important. But if you have anything else to report about this Mr. Green," he added, "anything at all, you let me know."

The screen door twanged. A moment later we watched the rumpled back of his blue sports coat diminish down the front walk, past the shaggy grass, the overgrown forsythia, the dandelions and drooping rhododendrons, and out into the bright sun of the sidewalk. He turned right to study Mr. Green's neat house for a long moment, hands on his hips, which pushed open his jacket just enough to reveal his black holster, before he headed across the street to ring the Sperlings' doorbell.

The Sperlings' door opened, revealing Mrs. Sperling wearing her pink bathrobe. After a moment she stepped back. The detective stepped inside. The Sperlings' door closed.

"Well," said my mother at last in a quiet voice. "I hope you're proud of yourself. I hope you realize what you've done this morning."

"Yes," I said.

"Good," she continued, in that same quiet voice. "Because a person should realize when she's made a mistake and done something that she'll regret later."

Outside a strange golden retriever trotted across our lawn,

tags clinking, his nose to the ground. He didn't stop, but kept nosing this way and that in the grass, not finding what he was looking for, but absorbed in searching, until he passed out of sight.

"I didn't make a mistake."

My mother stuck the detective's card under one of the begonias, then stood up and turned her back on me. "Let's hope not."

That's when I threw my notebook at her. I threw it as hard as I could, every tendon and ligament aching as I drew my arm back and then flung it forward. The notebook flew across the porch. It hit her between the shoulder blades, where the clasp of her brassiere pressed against the thin white fabric of her blouse.

She stumbled a little, reaching out toward the screen. The notebook fell open at her feet, just behind the heel of her left sandal. One of the pages had got bent in the throwing, and for some reason, this bent page shocked me; it seemed as grievous an offense as what I had just done to my mother.

"Pick that up." She didn't turn around.

When I didn't move, she said again: "Pick it up."

It seemed too difficult right then to pull myself up on my crutches and maneuver across the floor, so I left them leaning against the table and got down on my knees instead.

I crawled to where she still stood by the screen door and put out my hand to pull away the notebook. I was close enough that I could see her skin through the weave of her nylon stockings, and to see where a stray hair had caught inside the nylon just above her ankle. Her leg quivered.

But she didn't move. She waited until I had dragged myself back across the porch. Then she turned around, not at all fast, but naturally, as if she had forgotten something she meant to tell me.

In a slow, dull way, I realized that I'd been waiting all summer to hear what she was going to say next. Ever since my mother had found herself alone in the house with me and the twins; ever since the night she slapped me and knocked me down; ever since the moment I'd told her that I hated Mr. Green, she had been waiting to tell me something.

And perhaps if she had spoken to me then, even told me to go to my room or to wash the dishes, everything might have turned out very differently. But all she said was, "I've got to get to work." Stepping over my legs, she left me alone on the porch with my notebook.

Thirteen

"All right, Marsha, could you wear this?" Holding up a mildewed Baltimore Orioles jersey my father had given Steven two summers before, my mother demanded, "Would you wear it?"

"Yes." I had answered the same thing about a pair of denim pants that were too short, a tan corduroy skirt with a ripped hem, and a two-piece bathing suit that had lost most of its elastic.

The twins had been gone a week. It was Sunday afternoon—a sultry, breathless afternoon—and, exasperated by the heat and each other and the hiss of sprinklers from the neighbors' lawns, we had agreed to spend a few hours doing something "useful." So we stood in her bedroom gathering together a pile of clothing to be given to Goodwill.

For the last several days we had been operating along a polite timetable of meals and small tasks, going to sleep a little earlier every evening. Neither of us had apologized. It seemed, it still seems, that any apology would have been superfluous.

The breakfast dishes never got cleared that morning after the detective visited us. They sat on the table all through lunch and into the evening, a fly circling lazily over the cups and plates, congealing butter and toast crusts, the spill of orange juice on the tablecloth. My mother finally cleared the table late that night, after I had gone to bed. When I bumped my way downstairs the next morning, the table was set neatly, the butter in its butter dish, orange juice in its pitcher, a fresh tablecloth laid down. Only the plates were not quite clean. She had not washed our plates.

Neither of us spoke of this. We ate our breakfast silently on dirty plates. By the next morning the plates had been washed.

Now, while my mother sorted barefoot through a cache of the twins' outgrown blue jeans and musty T-shirts, I lay back on her bed by the window and listened to the creak of a cricket from somewhere below. Mr. Green's cookout was only two hours away and my mother had not yet said whether she was going. Based on the fact that she had tossed his invitation into the kitchen trash can, I had decided my mother wasn't going, but that she hadn't figured out how to tell him. Which was why she'd decided to clean out the upstairs closets.

Once she finished with the twins' clothes, she started on her own. A beige housedress sailed onto the Goodwill pile, followed by a pair of cracked white patent-leather boots that zipped up the side and a paisley blouse. She added a white straw handbag decorated with ladybugs and then a shimmery thing that might have been a nightgown.

Abruptly she paused in front of the full-length mirror beside her bureau, holding up a strawberry pink cotton dress with plastic sunflower buttons the size of poker chips. The buttons looked almost exactly like the earrings Aunt Ada was wearing the day she came to our house and asked me not to tell my mother that she'd been there. In fact, it could have been a dress Ada had bought to go with her earrings and then loaned to my mother. At the recollection of Ada's visit and the sunflower earring still at the bottom of my underwear drawer, I lay flat and quiet.

But my mother was not paying attention to me. She was looking at herself in the mirror, examining her reflection as she held up the pink dress, turning her head from side to side. It was a mini-dress I hadn't seen her wear for years, bought for a trip to Miami Beach that she and my father took for their tenth wedding anniversary. He had called it her "hotsy totsy dress."

"What do you think," she said finally. "Stay or go?"

She went into the bathroom to try on the pink mini-dress, then came back out. "Now what do you think?" The short bright dress made her look skinny and tired, but determined. She held her arms away from her side with her back to the mirror.

"You look like a lipstick."

"What color of lipstick?" She smiled for the first time that day. "Magic Magenta? Violet Embrace?" Laughing, she did a little shimmy in front of the mirror. "Ruby Glow Decadent Mist?"

Watching her pose in front of the mirror reminded me of the stories she used to tell about herself and her sisters. I hadn't known until that moment how much I missed them, the Mayhew Girls, those resilient sisters in scarlet lipstick, hiding pillowcase underwear under black shantung skirts, declining Latin verbs (*amaveram, amaveras*) with the clipped, dedicated arrogance of queens. All sitting together on one bed, painting one another's toenails. Smoking cigarettes under the pink insulation in the eaves of their mother's house, coughing and laughing in the camphorous, nicotine fug. A tangle of long arms, long legs—one daughter, four heads. You know Fran-Claire-Lois-Ada. They had been so wonderful, so unassailable. It had always been the four of them. There had never been room for anybody else.

"Pink Passion," said my mother, swinging her hips.

At that moment a red balloon floated past the bedroom window. It hung in the air, neatly framed by the window sash, then a breeze caught it and wafted it away.

I sat up on the bed and leaned out the window to see Mr. Green below in his madras and khaki, arranging four folding chairs in a semicircle near his barbecue pit. His bald spot appeared and disappeared as he stooped to pull out the retractable legs of a card table, then straightened up to set the table near the chairs. He stood back for a moment to examine this arrangement, finally picking up the table and moving it to the left of the barbecue pit. Heaped beneath the copper beech were several bags of paper napkins, packages of paper plates and plastic forks, and a transistor radio. Here and there a balloon bounced against the bricks.

He vanished through his back door, rematerializing a minute later carrying a plastic pitcher and a package of hotdog buns, which he set on the card table. Busily, he stacked everything onto the table, then with a final flourish turned on the radio, adjusting its dial until he found a folk-music station.

Where have you gone? bleated a nasal male voice, accompanied by a train whistle. *Will I see you again?* Mr. Green stepped back to assess the card table. Then he shifted the paper napkins beside the paper plates and lined up the package of plastic forks beside the pitcher. He stepped back again. A moment later he moved the hotdog buns beside the paper plates. He fiddled with the radio dial.

An orange balloon rolled against his heel. Just then a lawn mower started up in the next yard with a hard stutter that leapt to a snarl. Mr. Green raised his head at the noise and frowned.

"Marsha," breathed my mother into my ear. "Get back from the window."

By four-thirty that afternoon, Mr. Green was sitting in one of his four folding chairs. He got up once to open the bag of charcoal that leaned against his barbecue pit. He shook out some coals, then closed the bag, carefully folding the top over twice. Then he picked up a can of lighter fluid and squirted fluid onto the coals, lit a match, and dropped it into the barbecue pit. The match went out.

He lit another, then another. At last flames flickered up from within the barbecue pit, licking almost to his outstretched hand before settling into the coals.

After a minute or two, he leaned over the barbecue pit to inspect the fire with a dissatisfied expression. He was just picking up the can of lighter fluid again when my mother, who had gone from cleaning out her closet to cleaning the upstairs bathroom, still in the pink mini-dress, came up behind me and pressed her palms against the windowsill.

"It's lit," she called down. "You just have to give the coals a chance to get hot."

Mr. Green stared up at us, squinting into the sun. His face immediately lost its dissatisfied expression.

He waved, then he put down the can of lighter fluid, and before my mother could call out to him that she wouldn't be able to come to his cookout—due now to begin in a quarter of an hour—before she could say that she was so sorry, but she had a last-minute emergency, one she couldn't avoid, such a shame; before she could even clear her throat, he had disappeared once again inside his house.

Plucking at a sunflower button, she stepped past me on her way to the doorway, pausing for a moment before going downstairs. "I've seen people burn themselves very badly with lighter fluid," she told me. "People who think the fire has gone out. They squirt on more lighter fluid and the fire catches the stream and comes right back at them and blows up the can." Fretfully, she touched her forehead with her wrist.

"By the way," she said. "I've been meaning to tell you. I got an offer on the house." Her bedroom smelled of stale perfume and the banana skin I had left on the nightstand. The air glinted with dust motes. She turned away, and I watched the slim slope of her bare shoulder as she walked toward the door. "It's a good offer," I heard her say. "At least it's reasonable."

She stepped out into the hall, where she hesitated for a moment. "Well, I don't know about you, but I'm going to start fixing something for dinner." A cloud blew across the sun, darkening the room. I closed my eyes, then opened them again.

Mr. Green reemerged into his yard. Once more he sat in a folding chair, crossing his legs this time. Faint music twangled from the transistor radio perched on the card table. From where I sat, his reddening bald spot looked as red as a target in the late afternoon sun. As if he sensed that his bald spot was under scrutiny, he reached up and combed a few strands of hair over it with his fingers.

A moth fluttered palely behind him like a scrap of torn paper. He lifted his arm and angled his wrist to glance at his watch, then took hold of the folding chair's metal armrests.

He was still sitting in his folding chair at a quarter to six.

Downstairs my mother had begun to fry up hamburger meat; the sound of it sputtering in the pan floated upstairs. The refrigerator door opened and shut.

Outside, Mr. Green had not moved from his position in his chair for close to half an hour. He stared straight ahead, both hands gripping the metal armrests as if the chair were moving at high speed and he feared it might crash right into the barbecue pit and catapult him into the next yard. Gnats swarmed in a little gray wreath around his head. Up in the trees, locusts rattled and buzzed like a shaken tin can full of beads.

A song ended on his radio and another began. From the Sperlings' house came the faraway tinkle of "Pop Goes the Weasel." Overhead a jet boomed on its way from National Airport, momentarily stilling everything else. "Lu-ann," Mrs. Lauder was calling when the jet had passed. "Lu-ann." A screen door slammed. Someone was bouncing a basketball a few houses away, maybe one of the Reade brothers. *Kadoom*, *kadoom*, then the jangle of the ball hitting the hoop. From across the street, the Morrises' terriers barked twice in unison. Mr. Green gazed straight ahead in his aluminum folding chair, as distantly preoccupied as an astronaut. I watched him grow smaller and smaller, as if the longer he sat waiting in his chair, the more that happened in the rest of the world to exclude him.

As soon as he caught sight of my mother walking toward him across the grass, Mr. Green let go of the chair's metal armrests and clasped his hands in his lap. Then he limped up from his chair—one of his legs must have gone to sleep—and took a stagger or two toward her.

When she drew close, he raised a hand. She was barefoot, and still wearing the pink mini-dress.

"This is for you," she said, and lifted a pineapple toward him.

He dropped his hand and stared at the pineapple with grave surprise. Then he took it from her and placed it on the card table.

"Thank you," he said. "Please sit down."

He pointed to a chair, and with an awkward half-curtsy, my mother sat down and then looked at the jumbled card table, on which her pineapple now rested, like a small startled head, amid packages of potato chips and hotdog buns.

Mr. Green sat down in the folding chair beside hers, which looked unstable beneath him, as though he had neglected to pull the legs out completely. He rubbed one hand over the other. "Would you like a glass of wine?"

"Oh thank you," she said, as if a glass of wine were what she most wanted in the world.

After pouring her a plastic cup of white wine, Mr. Green hurried over to his barbecue pit to wave a newspaper at the coals. Then he hurried back to the card table to pick up a bowl of potato chips, which he offered to my mother. He seemed relieved to see her take a small handful. He offered her more wine.

"I'm fine," she said, and lifted her cup to show him that it was still full. "I can only stay a little while."

He nodded abstractedly. "I think," he said, "that I should put on the hamburg. Or would you like a hotdog?"

I could tell that my mother was about to say that she didn't want either, but she slapped at a mosquito instead. He had returned to the card table to fiddle once again with the radio dial and must have accidently readjusted the volume, because a voice suddenly blared, "Get the *lead* out! Drive the *clean* gasoline." He glanced back at my mother over his shoulder, his smile frozen.

"I'll have whatever you're having," she said.

"You could have hamburg or a hotdog," he offered, turning off the radio altogether. "I have everything."

He stared at the heaped card table with his hands hanging at his sides. But when she made a movement as if to get up from her chair, he straightened and gave her an almost haughty glance down his nose. "I guess I must have wrote the date down wrong on the invitations."

"Oh. I'm sure—these kinds of mistakes happen all the time. I heard about a party once—no one came, you know, and it was because the hostess put down the wrong *month* on the invitation. April instead of May. Can you imagine? It was—" She stopped abruptly, perhaps hearing the hitch of hysteria in her own voice.

"I think I would like a little more wine, thank you," she added after a moment, and held out her cup.

As he bent to refill her cup, their eyes met and she smiled up at him. "It's still early," she told him. "They might still come."

"Yes," he said.

Two stories above them, I propped my chin on the back of a hand, leaning on the windowsill. Had she remembered to turn off the burner from under the pan of hamburger meat? Had she noticed, on her way out, if the freezer door was ajar?

When I look back I don't have trouble understanding how my mother got herself into Mr. Green's yard that night. All the time she had been preparing dinner she must have been glancing out the kitchen window, watching him as he sat alone in his unsteady chair, stiff khaki shirt fading into the early evening. I suppose it was the cumulative effect of that vision that finally made her fumble toward the door as if the hamburger meat had already burned, as if the whole house were filled with smoke. Because as I recall it now there *was* something dire in the sight of Mr. Green that evening. Something powerful enough to send my mother rushing from the house, barefoot, half-dressed, pausing only to snatch up that pineapple from where it sat beside the toaster. Turning from the complicated astronomy of her own kitchen, she must have gazed out and seen Mr. Green clutching the armrests of his folding chair, a lonely planet in a dark green yard surrounded by a constellation of colored balloons and paper plates. Pity wouldn't have much to do with her decision to leave the house. It was a kind of rage, I imagine, and a kind of fear.

What must have made my mother's eyes sting that summer evening, what must have made her almost run to the kitchen door, had to be the fury of mortal fear—the fear that comes from understanding all at once that you are by yourself in a vast world, and that one day something worse than anything that has ever happened before will happen, you will get sick and die, or be killed, even your children may die, and no one will be able to stop it, if anyone even tries to stop it, and you will be left alone.

As my mother stared out the kitchen window, she must have seen that such a thing could happen to her. It would happen to her. Meanwhile, it was happening to someone else.

Of course I could be making too much of my mother's defection that night, when she left my dinner unmade to present herself like a fruit basket to Mr. Green. It's possible that she simply empathized with his freakishness. It's even possible that she liked the idea of being a better Samaritan than Mrs. Lauder. Or maybe she only wanted me to know how tentatively we were bound together those days, she and I. That she could choose, just like my father, just like that. It's also possible that it was a confusion of all of these feelings that sent her running bare-legged across the lawn, in full view of the entire neighborhood, wearing a mini-dress, carrying a pineapple.

Now Mr. Green stood before her with a glass jug of wine, bending at the waist like a waiter.

"You know," she said brightly, "after all—I'm sorry—I don't think I should have any more." She withdrew her cup.

"I have a lot of wine." He lifted the jug and gazed at her until she held out her cup again.

After a bit he sat down again beside her, drinking nothing himself. In fact, his hands seemed peculiarly empty; he held them in front of him as if he were wearing rubber gloves.

Across the street the Morrises' terriers began barking again. I wondered how many of the neighbors were watching.

"My husband—" my mother said suddenly; then she gave a shrill laugh that echoed the barking dogs. "My husband. Larry. Larry is my husband's name. I'm sorry you haven't had a chance to meet him—Larry. You know he hasn't been home for a while. In fact, he's traveling. Otherwise you would—you will—" She lifted her paper cup to her lips.

Mr. Green remained quietly attentive in his chair, his face and khaki chest presented toward my mother like a blackboard. Under his shirtsleeve paused the mermaid, waiting for him to flex his arm and send her dancing.

My mother reached down to set her cup on the grass. As she leaned over she must have smelled his musky onion scent and, looking up, seen the shaving rash burning on his throat, maybe even glimpsed the sly tip of the mermaid's tail. She cleared her own throat and sat up. "I am separated—as you may have guessed. My husband—"

She paused for so long it seemed that she had forgotten what she meant to say.

At last Mr. Green said, "Your husband—?"

"Left me."

"Left you—?" Mr. Green stirred in his chair.

"It's all right," she said, which was the same thing she had said a few days before to the detective.

Perhaps it was the memory of Detective Small standing on our front porch, emblazoned blue against wicker and a blear of plants, that made her lean too far over in her chair at just that moment, reaching for the paper cup she had just set on the grass, and tip sideways. In another moment she would have gone over. But Mr. Green suddenly reached out and grabbed the side of her chair, righting her again.

His hand touched her arm. A vivid ache sang through me, like cold water against a sensitive tooth. When my mother looked up, I saw that she had felt it, too.

For a minute they sat completely still.

"I really should be getting back."

"Don't go yet."

Light slowly drained out of the backyard as the shadow from the copper beech edged across the patio and over the chairs. Lit rectangles shone in houses down the street; here and there someone's television set shimmered blue. From the card table, one of Mr. Green's bubbled-glass candle holders glowed red. The streetlights had come on, each with its yellow funnel and spiral of moths.

Night sounds started up: another cricket, a dishwasher running, the draw of a window shade. Footsteps passed—it was the Night Watch going by, silent tonight. Like everyone else, they were listening.

I imagined Mr. Lauder, Mr. Sperling, then Mr. Guibert, Mr. Bridgeman, all the fathers on the block gathering just outside the nearest streetlight arc, watching from the street as my mother crossed and recrossed her long legs, her voice whickering softly. Now and again a watchband gleamed as they raised and lowered their arms, gesturing to one another. A faint crackle from their new walkie-talkies. A stifled cough.

By the time my mother had eaten her hamburger and refused a second, she and Mr. Green were neatly surrounded by the dark.

"Don't go yet," he repeated.

In response she bent her head, only the side of her face turned toward him. A siren wailed in the distance.

Mr. Green dragged his chair nearer to hers and asked her what she thought of the news lately.

She drew in her breath, then laughed, bringing up her head. "No news is good news."

"Don't you think," he said deliberately, "don't you think the news has been very bad."

She drank a sip of wine. "Well, if you mean this Watergate business, I agree."

"Watergate?" He sounded bewildered. "I am talking," he continued, with a resolute air of trying again, "about the news in the newspaper."

"Oh. The news—? You mean about that little boy?"

"What it is, it's never what you think it will be," Mr. Green went on as if she hadn't spoken. Now that he had begun to talk, he seemed resolved to continue. "All that comes up. It's never what you think." In the dimming light, he looked like a bulldog. Then he looked like a lion. "Every day," he said, "it's something different."

"It does seem that way," my mother answered vaguely.

"You always have to worry," said Mr. Green, expansive now. He unfolded his arms from over his stomach and leaned toward her. "Worry all the time. That's what they tell you. Even about things you shouldn't have to worry about."

My mother nodded.

"Like food," he brought out, after a short consideration. He tilted his head closer to hers until she must have felt his breath against her cheek, warm with the smell of the meat he had eaten. Together they stared at the ground like two people studying a jigsaw puzzle.

"Your food," he said. "And what you drink. And—air."

"I guess you're right."

"One minute you worry about this, then you worry about that. Then by the time you get back to worrying about the first thing, it's gotten worse. You can't worry about everything at the same time." His voice grew husky. Perhaps he had never said so much all at once; the effort seemed to excite him. "But then again you have to," he said. "You have to try to worry about everything."

"I know about that," she murmured.

"Yes," he said, almost into her hair. "That's how it is."

His voice was as deep now as Walter Cronkite's, as deep as the shadows all around them. And in the darkness it seemed my mother swayed closer, then closer to rest against him as a balloon drifted against her ankles.

Fourteen

Mom?" I cried out.

Down below, my mother and Mr. Green lurched apart. "*Mother*," I called again.

"I'm sorry," she said, standing up in Mr. Green's backyard and overturning her cup of wine in the grass. "I didn't realize—"

"No—" said Mr. Green, rising also.

"I have to be getting back." When he made a move toward her, my mother put a hand on the back of the chair she had just left, stepping behind it so the chair was between them. "You know, I just meant to drop by to say hello—have a glass of wine. I didn't mean—and now here we are sitting out here—"

"Please," he said, standing also.

"Really, I have to go," she said too loudly, as if just noticing that the rest of the neighborhood had hushed. "I do really have to get home."

Mr. Green stared at her until she looked away.

She gestured upward. "I hadn't meant to come over at all," she said in the same loud voice. "You see, I was making dinner—hamburgers, too, isn't that funny—but I hadn't meant—but when I saw you sitting out here all alone—well, I—" She tried to laugh, but the laugh caught somewhere in her throat and thinned to a gasp.

After a moment she tried to speak again but stopped. I saw her glance over at the pineapple, bristling on the card table. "Do you need help," she managed finally. "Maybe you need help with carrying these things back inside?"

He didn't answer. Instead he walked over to the still-glowing barbecue pit and threw an unopened package of hotdog buns onto the orange coals. A moment later he tossed in the unused plastic forks and spoons and the paper napkins. The stink of scorched plastic curled into the air.

"Oh don't." My mother held out one arm, her hand raised with fingers spread. From where I sat watching, she looked small and toylike with her foolish arm outstretched, as if someone could reach down and pluck her up by that little arm and carry her away.

"Please don't," she said. "I know you'll wish you'd saved those things for another time."

When he didn't turn around, she dropped her arm, letting it swing free as if she had only been waving. Then she walked very quickly across his neat side lawn and through our own overgrown grass. Mr. Green stayed where he was, standing in front of his barbecue pit with his back to the neighborhood.

The screen door opened, then banged shut. My mother's footsteps crossed the porch, and for the first time that summer I heard her close the front door and turn the lock.

By the time I clumped downstairs that evening, my mother was sitting in the dark on the living-room sofa, one magazine spread open in her lap, several more beside her, the room lit only by the street lamp outside and the light from the kitchen. She had poured herself a glass of wine. After a moment, during which she did not glance at me, my mother patted the cushion beside her.

For a while we sat quietly, looking across at the bare fireplace and at the piano, which no one had played since Julie had picked out "Heart and Soul" a few days before she and Steven left with the Westendorfs. My notebook lay across my knees and once or twice I flipped the pages. My mother drank her wine. It seemed a very long time since the nights when my aunts had filled this room with their swooping voices and long legs, or since the twins had lain on the floor with their chins in their hands watching television, or since the night my father had sat here staring at Aunt Ada.

This marks a new era, my mother had said that night, staring at Nixon shaking hands with Chairman Mao on the television screen.

The windows were open, and as the warm night breeze

brushed against our faces we heard guitar music from some-one's radio down the street. The moon was up. Through the windows it looked blurred as an old coin rising over Mr. Green's rooftop.

As I watched the moon, I saw a strange thing, if seeing is the right word for it. I looked out the window and saw myself walking down the street toward our house. But then, I wasn't myself; I was a stranger in the neighborhood walking alone at night, looking in at the yellow lamplight of other people's living rooms. Most of our neighbors didn't bother to draw their curtains and it was easy to glance right in and see the green fronds of a plant, the corner of a corduroy armchair, framed photographs of babies and brides smiling on the mantel. On warm nights like this one most people's windows would be open, and up and down the street I could hear the sounds of running bathwater, the clatter of pots, children's voices, all mingling and interrupting one another until the whole street sounded as if it belonged to a single enormous family. As I passed each neighbor's house, each window lit up so that I could see bright flowers in vases and books on bookshelves and rooms full of people moving back and forth. But when I reached my own house I didn't hear anything; the lights were out and my house was as quiet as if no one lived there.

Beside me, my mother sighed and pushed back a strand of hair that had fallen across her forehead.

Sometimes I wonder if it was only to break the silence

between us that I reminded her of what I had seen two and a half weeks before, on Thursday, July 20th, at 4:44 in the afternoon. Sometimes I wonder if it was as simple as that. But not very often anymore.

My mother sighed again. "What do you have to say?" she said at last, reaching up to switch on the small lamp beside her. "Because I have the feeling you want to say something. So if you do, say it now. Otherwise I'm going to bed."

Perhaps, perhaps—that careful word again—perhaps I might never have said anything at all if she hadn't challenged me that evening. But then again, I know this isn't true. I had never been so prepared to do anything in my life.

"What?" she said, looking finally at me. "What is it?"

Though my fingers were trembling, I opened my notebook and showed her the page dated July 20th where, at 4:44 in the afternoon, not a minute sooner or later thanks to my water-resistant wristwatch, parting gift from my father, I had seen Mr. Green's brown Dodge drive by two hours before he usually got home. It was right there in my notebook. It's there still.

"What day did you say?" she whispered harshly.

I pointed to the book. Then turning each page slowly, almost reverently as I went along, I showed my mother every detail I had recorded about Mr. Green and all the newspaper clippings I had saved.

There was the black comb found at the murder site, a black comb that could be exactly like the one Mr. Green used so frequently. And the police's theory that the assailant was left-handed, just like Mr. Green. There was the elderly woman on Ridge Road who had witnessed a boy talking to a balding man in a car just before five o'clock; the bag boy at the mall, who had possibly seen a brown Dodge drive out of the parking lot approximately at the same time as the murder would have occurred; the Band-Aid on Mr. Green's chin that day. There was the scratching and biting the boy was said to have done.

And there was this clipping, which I had pasted all by itself on a page and framed with a heavy red crayon border. It began: "Police investigating the abduction and murder of 12-year-old Boyd Arthur Ellison of Spring Hill believe someone living in the vicinity may be responsible for . . ."

We sat together in the living room, within that brief circle of lamplight, and I turned the pages of my notebook while my mother drank one and then another glass of wine.

"Stop it," she said finally, not looking at me. "This is crazy. It's crazy and mean. And I don't want to hear any more."

"Wait," I said.

But she got up and went into the kitchen.

For a few moments I sat staring into the empty fireplace. It had never occurred to me that my mother wouldn't believe my story. It was all there; I had saved everything. Anyone could see what a good job I had done. Outside the Sperlings' cat began to yowl. It was a low, ugly noise, and after a few moments of listening to it my face grew hot and I felt like throwing something out of the window at the cat, a mug or a paperweight, something that would hurt. I flipped through my notebook again, riffling the pages so they fanned my face. I turned to the page where I had taped Detective Small's card, rescued from underneath a begonia pot. After that there was nothing else on any of the pages, just thin blue lines running across them, and one thin red line running down each left-hand side.

From the kitchen I heard a glass break. "You know what," my mother said in a narrow voice, coming quickly back into the living room, her hands fisted by her sides. "I'm tired. I'm tired of you. I'm tired of myself. I'm tired of everything."

"No you're not," I tried to say.

"Oh yes, I am. Sick and tired." And as furious as she suddenly seemed to be, she did look tired, even sick, standing there with the kitchen light behind her, outlined like one of those terrible sidewalk drawings that show where the crime victim lay. Her shoulders slumped and although I couldn't see her face well with the light in back of her, it seemed to me that it was shut and blank, as if she had already left me and gone to bed.

"But I haven't told you it all." I was beginning to whine.

"I don't want to hear anything more."

"But I know he did it," I said, kicking the coffee table with my good foot.

"You don't know," my mother said, folding her arms as she turned away and headed toward the staircase. "You only think you do."

"I do know."

"You only want to know. That's all it is, Marsha," she said bitterly, turning back to me for a moment, her mouth a sharp line. And suddenly it seemed the most important thing in the world to make her stay, to keep her from vanishing up those stairs and leaving me alone.

"Mommy," I cried, holding out a hand. "Wait. I have something else to tell you."

"My God. Stop it. Just stop it," she almost shrieked from the bottom of the stairs, her hands flying to her ears. "Why can't you ever just stop it?"

I heard her run up to her bedroom, her footsteps falling like stones on the staircase. The Sperlings' cat started yowling again, this time closer to the window near where I was sitting. It was moaning and snarling at the same time, sometimes dropping to a guttural murmur, then pitching upward to something like a scream, making such a nasty, sad, desperate noise that I banged the window shut, then limped into the kitchen.

I laid my notebook on the table, next to the telephone and my mother's Peterman-Wolff vinyl logbook, and sat down. Upstairs my mother walked back and forth in her room, and as I sat there staring at her logbook I wondered what she was doing. Maybe she was packing a suitcase. Once or twice something fell on the floor above me, a book, a shoe. A door opened and closed.

"Mommy?" I called softly. "Mom?" I said, louder this time. But she didn't hear.

Finally I picked up the kitchen telephone and, after another moment or two, dialed his number. He answered at the beginning of the second ring, as if he had been waiting to hear from me, which of course he had not.

"I have something to tell you," I said, in a voice loud enough that even all the way upstairs, my mother had to listen.

Fifteen

Fifteen minutes passed, or perhaps it wasn't even that long, and then there were two quick knocks on the screen door.

For a moment nothing happened. I sat where I was, back on the living-room sofa, not daring to look up from the floor. Then, from the top of the stairs, my mother called, "All right.

"All right," she repeated as she came down the stairs and crossed the room to let him in.

We sat on the sofa, my mother and I, and Detective Small sat down on the piano bench across from us. He was wearing his light blue sports coat. I imagine he said hello, although I don't remember it. In fact, I don't remember him entering the room at all, just suddenly being in it.

But by the time he sat down, everything about him had acquired a penetrating clarity, the way trees and leaves outside come into sharp focus after a rainstorm. I saw the creases in his black leather loafers and the ribs of his black socks. I saw where his brown knit trousers had begun to fray at the cuffs. As he hunched over, elbows on his knees, big hands clasped before him, I saw that he was older than I had first thought, that in fact he was middle-aged, probably my father's age, and that there was a dab of mustard near his mouth. Not long ago, he had been eating dinner.

For a full minute no one said anything. My mother stared at her knees. Detective Small stared at me. I thought of the twins sitting cross-legged on a beach in Cape May with Amy Westendorf, listening to her gnomelike giggle under the stars, themselves laughing as the tide washed in darkly across the sand. Something sour rose in my throat.

Detective Small shifted on the piano bench, unclasping his hands. "So what do you have to tell me, Marsha?" he said, kindly enough, and, perhaps hoping to encourage me by sinking to my level, he got up from the bench to squat down in front of me. "It sounded on the phone like you had a pretty important thing to say."

He tried to smile, yet as much as I wanted to get it over with, I still couldn't speak, and only the sight of my mother's tense white face so close to mine kept me from simply bursting into tears.

But as I've already mentioned, for better or worse I'm not someone who can stop what I've set going, especially not with my mother looking at me with such stark dread and confusion that I couldn't bear to be alone with her, even as I could scarcely bear to let her out of my sight. And to be honest, I also felt a sickening excitement, a kind of imploding fascination at what I was about to do that was stronger than any impulse to stop it from happening.

I lifted my head and said: "He tried to talk to me in the backyard. By the lilac bushes."

Immediately an image sprang forward of the first time Mr. Green spoke to me, that spring afternoon as I dug in the dirt and sang to myself. A plain, reliable image. I pictured his red face framed by green lilac leaves, his short neck rising up from the lapels of his khaki shirt. His fleshy nose threw a triangular shadow across his cheek in the late afternoon sun. "Hello there," he said, and cracked his knuckles. We had talked about ameobas.

"He came up behind me when I wasn't looking," I said.

Now that I'd finally begun, a deep calm settled over me and I felt myself lean back against the sofa cushions. This had happened. This was true.

"Who is he?" said Detective Small.

"Mr. Green."

He kept his gaze on my face. "When was this?"

"In the spring," I said distantly.

"Did he say something to you?"

"He asked me if I wanted to know a secret. He said a boy's thing looked like a thumb."

My mother blinked and gave me a piercing look, then she shuddered and took my hand in her hot, dry one. I snatched my hand back and sat up.

"He said he wanted to bite my boobies. He said that's what you got for being hoity-toity. He told me if I ever let anybody know what he said he would cut off my head and stick it in his barbecue pit."

Detective Small rocked back on his heels. After a pause he said, "Did he try to touch you?"

"Yes," I said.

For a moment no one spoke. Then, very gently, in a careful voice that made me despise him, Detective Small said, "How?"

I envisioned Mr. Green behind his hedge the morning my mother had asked him if he wouldn't like a little tornado. Just a little tornado, she said, to blow everything away. And he had stared back at her, slapping the *Post* against his palm, face reddening, lips twitching, forehead perspiring.

"He hit me with a newspaper."

Detective Small briefly lost his balance. He put a hand down on the floor to steady himself, then straightened up and went back to the piano bench. My mother glanced intently at him and back at me; her eyes were large and dark, but she said nothing.

"He hurt me," I heard myself whimper.

"What happened next?"

"I ran away. I ran into the house. I never wanted to see him again, but he was always around. She liked him," I said, looking sideways at my mother. "Everyone else on the street thinks he is weird."

It all began to make sense as I heard myself talk. It was all quite convincing.

"That's why I've been keeping all those notes," I said. "Because I was afraid." Then I closed my eyes and concentrated on breathing in and out. Breathing had begun to require an effort. I remember having the impression that I could forget to breathe at any moment.

"What notes?" said Detective Small.

"She has a notebook," said my mother eventually, when I didn't answer. "Full of lots of little details about—mostly about Mr. Green. She showed it to me tonight, only I really Detective, I don't—"

"Can I see the notebook?"

It was lying on the floor near my feet. I felt my mother hesitate; then she leaned over, her warm body resting heavily across my knees, and picked it up.

For a few minutes the only sound in the room was the sound of turning pages. I kept my eyes closed and pretended I was in a cool, dim room all alone. My mother sat quietly beside me. Once she reached up and brushed my hair away from my forehead, and there was something so terrible about this gesture, the old intimacy of it, that I flinched.

"Is there anything else you want to tell me?" Detective Small said at last. When I opened my eyes, his own shrewd brown eyes were fixed on my face. It amazed me that he looked skeptical.

My mother said, "Hasn't she said enough?"

I'll always remember the sound of her voice that night, how anguished it was, and that this made me glad, because in a way I figured everything about to happen was really her fault, not mine. Looking back on it now, I would guess she thought so, too.

Detective Small stood up, still staring straight at me. "I understand that all this has been very hard for you, Marsha. And you're a good girl to talk to me. But I want you to go back over everything you've just said. I want you to tell me if there's anything that isn't true."

"Please," my mother begged. It wasn't clear whom or what she was begging. Detective Small ignored her and continued to look at me. After a moment, my mother looked at me, too.

Another child might have seized this moment gratefully, broken down, confessed that she was lying—wailed that she was scared, that she'd had a nightmare, any number of plausible, forgivable things—and even then it would have been all right. The whole episode would have been smoothed over somehow and after a few years maybe even forgotten. Unfortunately, I had ceased to be another child some time ago.

"I saw him hiding in the bushes near the Ellisons' house," I said coldly. "He was standing right in their bushes. Right in their yard. You can ask Luann next door. You can ask her about when we saw him in the bushes by Boyd's house.

"He *hurt* me," I said.

And then I began to cry. There was nothing calculated or forced about it. This wasn't planned. I had been wanting to cry for days, for weeks, months, for so long I had forgotten how long. All I wanted at that moment was to throw myself into my mother's lap and feel her hand on the back of my neck and cry and cry, and know that I could. I *could* do it. Like Steven running through the mall that day, so stunned and headlong, looking almost as afraid to be caught as he was afraid to get away. I knew I was telling the truth, although how I was telling it was not true, and what I was saying would be misunderstood, which was inevitable, and I knew that, too. But such a fierce, raw release it was, to cry like that.

The police showed up early the next morning, just as Mr. Green, dressed for work with his briefcase beside him, was starting his car. They blocked his driveway with their black-and-white cruiser, gliding up as noiselessly as if their car had been on the Safeway conveyor belt. From behind the curtain in my bedroom window, I watched two policemen climb out of the cruiser with that absurdly casual, brutal grace policemen have, as though all the time they are opening their car doors, climbing out, shutting the doors, walking toward you, they are also performing these movements for a much wider audience. Bare fleshy forearms held a little away from their sides, elbows bent slightly, they walked toward Mr. Green sitting in his car. I can still hear the stiff leather of their shoes squeak.

In the early-morning light, their bodies looked heavy,

dense, and their uniforms seemed bluer than usual. Their sunglasses lent them a deeply expressionless expression, as if anything in the world, any devastation, could happen in front of them and they would keep right on walking forward.

Finally they stopped on the edge of the lawn.

"Sir, would you get out of your car, please," said the taller one in a neutral voice. "We have a few questions we'd like to ask you."

Not quickly but quietly, Mr. Green got out of his car. As he stood up, both policemen drew closer and he pressed his back against his car door as if a sudden hard gust of wind had flattened him.

Then he took a step forward and, at a gesture from one of the policemen, walked across his decorous lawn, past his orange marigolds, up his three front steps and took out his keys. He fumbled with them for a minute or so; perhaps his hands were shaking. Across the street, screen doors twanged as first one, then another, then another neighbor came to stand inside open doorways and stare, their gaze moving from the cruiser to the policemen to Mr. Green fumbling with his keys on his front step. Before another sixty seconds passed, all three had disappeared inside.

An hour went by. I clunked downstairs and stood in the hallway. My mother was sitting in the kitchen by the telephone, but she didn't make any calls. She sat with her ankles crossed and looked at the kitchen wallpaper.

She stood up, though, when Mr. Green's door opened and

the three of them, Mr. Green between the two policemen, came outside again. She took my arm and drew me against her. Together we watched from the front window as the three men walked down the front steps and strode across the short spread of grass toward the sidewalk. They managed to walk fast without actually seeming to move at all. The impression I had was that the luminous grass flowed under their feet and rushed them toward the sidewalk.

Mr. Green was carrying his briefcase with the shiny clasps; he looked straight ahead as they reached the cruiser. One of the policemen was smiling as if he remembered a tune he liked and was playing it inside his head. He opened the back door, while the other policeman cupped one hand gently around Mr. Green's elbow and guided him inside.

Sixteen

Two blocks from the Spring Hill Mall is one of those square brick professional buildings that inside always seem to smell of cleaning fluid and new carpeting, and there from 4:55 until 6:20 on the evening of July 20th, Mr. Green was either sitting in the waiting room his dentist shared with another dentist, flipping through dog-eared copies of *Reader's Digest*, or stretched out in the dentist's chair, getting a back molar filled and trying not to choke as he had an impression taken for a crown.

The dentist and his receptionist both confirmed this was true, as did a woman who was sitting in the waiting room next to the dusty Boston fern when he arrived. In fact, she had glanced at her watch just as Mr. Green pushed open the glass door to the waiting room because her own dentist was running late. When asked by the police whether her watch might have been incorrect, she replied that it was a "brand-new Timex."

That Mr. Green returned home immediately afterward could be verified by my own notebook: "G. home. 6:30 P.M." According to the police report quoted by the *Post*, Boyd Ellison must have been attacked between 4:50, when the elderly dog-walker saw him waiting to cross the street, and 5:30, when the florist went out to her car with a box full of wedding orchids and heard that small cry.

Mr. Green passed our house at 4:44 P.M. by my notebook, which would give him roughly eleven minutes within which to drive to the Spring Hill Mall parking lot, leap from his car, run up the hill, grab the boy, attack him, hide from the florist, watch her slowly walk up the hill and then back down, wait for her to drive away before running back and committing the murder with that chunk of limestone, then straighten his clothing, check for bloodstains, run back down the hill, jump into his waiting car—parked where anyone would have been able to see it—and drive to the dentist's office in time to appear, unrumpled, breathing easily, at 4:55 P.M. Timex time for his appointment.

Of course, whenever you construct a chronology like this one it looks ludicrous, like a black-and-white movie of the Keystone Kops performing every action in quick time. You have to remind yourself that seconds and minutes measure the extremes of rage, pain, terror, as surely as they measure how long a cake needs to set or when the wash will be done. No wonder it's tempting to think of time as something that watch companies manufacture.

Mr. Green spent three nights in the Montgomery County Jail, held over for questioning by the state police. In addition to my accusations, they had found several clippings about the murder taped to his refrigerator. He had saved the same clippings I'd saved, as a matter of fact. Plus the police found a photograph of a bare-chested blond boy on Mr. Green's bedroom dresser—a boy who eventually turned out to be his nephew posing after a swim meet. And they found an unloaded, unregistered pistol in his bedroom dresser, a rather antique-looking pistol. It turned out to be a World War I relic, but it was enough to hold him.

The evidence, such as it was, seemed both scanty and damning, circumstantial at best, but suspicious enough. Luann more or less corroborated my story about seeing Mr. Green in the bushes near the Ellisons' house, although she admitted that she herself didn't get a good look, that all she saw were some branches shaking, and then she volunteered that it might have been a cat. Of course there was my notebook with its pages of details, confiscated the same day, later returned with coffee stains on some of the pages, the very same notebook I have before me this minute. Someone had also turned in the poisonous little note I'd pasted together several weeks before from letters cut out of the newspaper; apparently it had blown into an open car window.

Suddenly it seemed that most of our neighbors had noticed something odd about Mr. Green. Mrs. Sperling told the police that she had twice looked out her window and seen him standing in his yard at night. "Just looking around," she said. "In the dark." Mrs. Morris claimed that Mr. Green had once made a threatening gesture with a trowel when one of her terriers got loose and ran across his lawn. David Bridgeman's father reported that Mr. Green had driven too close to David when he was riding his bike toward Mr. Green's driveway. Added to all that was Luann's unexpected declaration that one day she had bent down to pick up a dropped penny on the street only to find Mr. Green staring at her when she straightened up. "He saw my panties," she told Detective Small with an air of unwilling injury. "And they were a hole in them."

So naturally no one disbelieved my story once it began to be passed around. Just as earlier no one had disbelieved the stories about my father that circulated from house to house, or the stories about Ada, or the stories about my mother, or any of the stories that we tell about those of us whose private unhappinesses can't stay private. And in my own defense, though the evidence against Mr. Green certainly now looks flimsy, he did drive down our street, heading toward the mall in a brown Dodge matching the description of the car sighted later that afternoon right after the murder.

He kept a black comb perpetually in his back pocket, just like the comb found at the murder site. He was left-handed, like the murderer, and balding. Most damning of all, he was a single, middle-aged man who had no friends to speak of, no past he alluded to, no clear reason to be where he was at all— in a family neighborhood.

Everyone was very sympathetic to me those first few days after Mr. Green was arrested. Mrs. Lauder baked us an apple crumble. Mrs. Morris actually bought me a Nancy Drew book. There was talk of forming some kind of a neighborhood association, of vetting potential home buyers before they were allowed to move in. Neighbors stood together in the street, describing their feelings at discovering a murderer right next door; Mrs. Sperling and tall, black-haired Mrs. Reade embraced by the Sperlings' mailbox. Someone threw eggs at Mr. Green's front door.

But largely the mood in the neighborhood was, if not exactly celebratory, then at least lightened. Roses bloomed. The sky was blue. Women sat outside talking on each other's front steps. Once again children ran out when the ice-cream truck jingled onto the street. The Reades hosted an impromptu wienie roast one night and people carried over bowls of potato salad, bags of chips and popcorn, whatever they had in the house, and the Lauders brought a watermelon. Everyone went except my mother and me. She had a headache, she said.

Yet after those three days, the police let Mr. Green go, not because of his alibi at the dentist's office—Detective Small, who questioned him, knew about all kinds of eleven-minute Houdini acts—but simply because Mr. Green's blood type did not match the blood found on the boy's clothing.

He denied assaulting me with a newspaper, of course, or ever threatening to cut off my head and stuff it into his barbecue pit. Or even ever speaking to me at all. He denied hiding in the bushes by Boyd Ellison's house. In the end it was his word against mine. And in those days the police tended to believe adults more readily than they did children, especially a child who refuses to repeat her story. Although everyone was disappointed that I wouldn't testify, they told my mother they understood. It would be like living through it all over again. Once was enough.

When he returned to his house Thursday morning at eight-fifteen, Mr. Green was driven by a tall, heavy-set, sandy-haired man whom I had never seen before. From my bedroom window, I watched a blue Pontiac drive up to the curb, its engine left running as the passenger door swung open, grating against the curb, and Mr. Green climbed out, looking the same as he always looked, his hair neatly combed, only his white shirt slightly crumpled and damp enough to show the outline of his undershirt beneath.

In a strange way, I was glad to see him. He was so familiar that I felt as if I had missed him, despite my absolute terror of ever seeing him again.

He carried his briefcase as if he had just returned from a day at work. He bent down and said something to the car's driver before stepping back and shutting the door. Without watching to see the car drive off, he turned and headed up his front walk toward his house.

When he reached the top of his front steps he paused to look at the dried eggs splattered against his front door. Then, holding his keys, he turned and looked directly across his yard at our screened porch. His face held a restrained, even negated expression, as if he had been wearing a very different one the instant before. After a moment he lifted his door key to the lock, turned it, and went inside. Fifteen minutes later he reappeared in a freshly ironed shirt, got into his car, and drove away. He was back that night, parking his usual six inches from the drainpipe as if nothing had happened.

For the next week or so, in fact, nothing did happen. Mr. Green cleaned the eggs off his front door, although a few pale blotches remained where the eggs had eaten through the paint. He came and went at the usual times. It's true that no one on the street spoke to him and that he spoke to no one. Every time he came outside, everyone else seemed to evaporate back into their houses, so that he was always alone on the street, as if he were the only human being who lived there. But he managed to mow his lawn one evening and put out his trash cans on the curb; he appeared to be going about the regular business of his life. Then a "For Sale" sign appeared on his front lawn about even with the one on ours.

We'd heard about the dentist appointment the day Mr. Green returned from the police station. Mr. Lauder's brother-in-law's cousin was the desk sergeant at another station and knew all the details. Mr. Green had been a cooperative prisoner, even waiving his right to call a lawyer before he answered questions.

"He's airtight," Mrs. Lauder kept telling my mother that day as she stood in our kitchen. I was reading comic books in the living room, but through the doorway I could see her fat arms resting on the ledge of her bosom. "They finally catch someone," she said, "and the man's airtight." As if Mr. Green were a submarine, able to live submerged for days, even months, while the rest of us foundered.

"Well, there's still what happened with Marsha," she said, more comfortably, lowering her voice. "Nobody's excusing that."

"No," my mother repeated faintly. "There's no excuse for that."

"In my opinion," said Mrs. Lauder, uncrossing her arms, "it by itself was enough to hold him till kingdom come. And he sure has got no place in a neighborhood like this. Frank went over and told him that. He said, 'Look, we all know about you.' Too bad you all couldn't press charges. They made a mistake letting him go. I bet they'll find that out."

"It was a mistake," echoed my mother, staring out the window.

And yet a few evenings later she walked across our lawn and around the fence, and up the steps to Mr. Green's front door, where, in full view of the Morrises, who were sitting on lawn chairs in their yard, and Mr. Guibert, who was walking by with a rake, she paused for a minute, then rang the door-bell. She was carrying a small bunch of white carnations. But when Mr. Green opened the door and saw who was there, he closed the door again.

There was nothing left for her to do but walk down his steps again and cross his lawn and come back to our house, where I was waiting for her.

"Luann's going to Bible camp for the rest of the summer," Mrs. Lauder told me when I rang her doorbell the next afternoon. "She's not going to be able to play with you anymore, doll."

It was a quiet Sunday afternoon, hot and brilliant. Across the street the Sperlings were sitting on their front steps, watching Baby Cameron try to clap his hands. David Bridgeman rode past on his new bicycle. I could hear Luann singing, but I couldn't make out the words.

Mrs. Lauder's broad body filled the doorway; her hands were floury and there was a splotch of flour on her chin like a white goatee. "There now, honey. I think it's for the best."

She looked concerned to see me still standing on her doorstep. "Honey," she said. "You go on home now."

The twins had called that morning to ask if they could stay with the Westendorfs for another ten days. My mother had said yes. Now she was inside in the living room pretending to read a magazine. We had been avoiding each other for the last few days; or rather, she had been avoiding me, while I had been hunting her ruthlessly through the house, even coming into her room at night when she was asleep to stare at her, not because I wanted to be with her but because I couldn't bear my own company. The night before she had woken while I stood by her bed.

"What are you doing here?" she said, not turning on the light.

"I think I lost something," I said.

She stared back at me for a moment, her dark face almost indistinguishable from her pillow except for the two darker places that were her eyes. "Go back to sleep," she said finally.

Through the living-room windows, I could see her bent head as I passed that side of the house. I'd meant to go right inside through the kitchen door, but the sight of her bowed head and the determined stillness of her face made me veer toward the backyard.

For a while I stood by the rhododendrons, neatly screened from the street. It occurred to me that I might find a few of Julie and Steven's cigarette butts in the dirt, so I scratched at the ground with the tip of one of my crutches for a few minutes.

I'm not sure what I intended to do with the cigarette butts if I found any, but the old act of looking was comforting. As I scraped around I uncovered a hairy caterpillar, a metal pop-top, a muddy movie ticket stub. It always astonishes me what you can find if you keep your eyes on the ground. By the time I had dug a shallow trench in the mud and discovered the carcass of a Japanese beetle, I'd forgotten what I was looking for.

In fact I had forgotten where I was altogether when I heard something snap and then a thick cough behind me, and as the hair prickled on the back of my neck, I turned around to see Mr. Green watching me from his side of the hedge.

He was wearing his khaki shirt and his madras shorts, as he always did on Sundays, with his black socks and fussy loafers. But his face seemed thinner and he looked pale. His hands hung loose by his sides. That his hands were empty seemed obscurely wrong to me. I recall thinking that he should have been carrying something, a rake, a pair of shears. He looked unprotected.

A low ringing filled my ears. My heart was banging so hard in my chest that I must have been visibly swaying. And yet in a way I'd been waiting for this moment, which I had always known would come about. Mr. Green's face fell in and out of focus. The sun hit him from the top down and then seemed to radiate out from him so that as I watched he seemed to be standing inside a bell of sunlight.

Still he said nothing, but only looked at me, his hands hanging by the pockets of his madras shorts. One lapel of his khaki shirt was folded the wrong way, as if he had pulled the shirt on quickly. A grease spot the size of a quarter bloomed near his breast pocket. Otherwise he looked the same, although he also began to look completely different, almost unrecognizable, the way people do when you stare at them for a long time. Perhaps the same thing was occurring to him as he stared at me.

A bee brushed past, buzzing stupidly. Overhead the leaves of Mr. Green's copper beech shifted, sifting the breeze. I could smell new-mown grass and the shampoo I'd used on my hair the night before. Seconds glinted by, minutes, hours. A jet boomed overhead.

I was growing almost used to standing there, watching Mr. Green watch me. It was the worst moment of my entire life and yet I was surprised to find it tolerable. It was even, now that it was happening, one I would have prolonged. In some part of my mind I understood that this moment would end somehow, that I would go on to have the rest of my life, but as I stared at Mr. Green that afternoon in the sun it seemed impossible that anything else would ever happen to me again.

He kept his eyes on my face, squinting a little. For another instant or two he simply stood there, sunlight streaming around him.

"Why," he said at last.

Just that single word, not even followed by a question mark. I think I'd begun to hope he would shout at me, raise his fist, do something that would justify what I had said about him. But his voice was absolutely flat, almost factual, as if he were supplying me with information he felt I should know.

When it seemed that he wasn't going to say anything else, my heart stopped banging and I felt saliva flow into my mouth again. Gradually the world fell back into place, hedges, grass, trees; even the sun faded a little.

Then he was gone. I watched him walk slowly back across his grass, sunlight sliding across his back in smaller and smaller patches as he passed under his big tree and then walked up the few steps to his back door, until he had vanished inside. His screen door slapped shut. And though by then I had opened my mouth to say something, I will never know what.

Seventeen

Mr. Green moved out of his house a week later, on a humid, tar-scented Saturday in August. It was right around the Republican convention, to which my mother listened obsessively on the radio, the same way she would a year later follow the Watergate hearings on TV.

From my bedroom window, I watched Mr. Green carry cardboard boxes out to a small rented van one at a time, just as I had watched him carry them in only five months before. No one helped him. When Mr. Morris or Mr. Sperling happened to step outside, they pretended not to notice Mr. Green's steady pilgrimage back and forth between the house and the curb. Mr. Morris got busy with his garden hose and Mr. Sperling stooped to examine the hinges on the screen door. As soon as possible, they ducked back inside. In the background, our kitchen radio transmitted an incessant dull cheering, broken only by speeches that to me all sounded exactly the same.

Although it wasn't raining, as the morning went on the sky pressed down closer and closer until the tops of the trees seemed to bend beneath it and a singed smell, like burning fur, drifted up from the pavement.

No children rode their bikes up and down our street; the Reade brothers quit playing basketball; even the Morrises neglected to take their terriers for a walk. Mr. Green carried out box after box, each sealed with masking tape, its contents invisible. Around ten o'clock he carried out a TV set, followed by a small cane chair, a single-bed mattress and box spring, his card table, and those four aluminum folding chairs.

No one asked him where he was going. For some reason I have the impression that he moved south, to Tennessee or Georgia maybe, some state where he could go back to being from the country. After all these years, I still find myself wondering about why he ever decided to move into our neighborhood in the first place. Maybe he had saved his money and someone told him to invest in real estate. That's the sort of advice I could imagine my father giving out. Good neighborhood, good schools, easy commute to the city. What could go wrong with an investment like that? He could have met a nice neighbor woman with a few kids, a recent widow or divorcée, someone a little odd, a little awkward and shy, and gotten married just when he thought his life was set and nothing new would ever happen to him again. Maybe that was what he'd come for, or at least to be near the possibility.

How could he have known how unsettling a quiet, nondescript bachelor could seem to an entire neighborhood? A man who was polite and regular in his habits, who kept his yard neat and washed his car weekly. A man whose worst crimes now appear to have been clumsiness and a tragic lack of imagination, which kept him from perceiving how neatly he embodied everyone else's bad dreams.

The last item Mr. Green carried out of his house, before he shut the door and locked it with his key, was a large, ornate, gilt-framed mirror. It was the sort of mirror you would expect to find these days in a restored Victorian, one of those tall, drafty houses full of antique rocking chairs and chintz wallpaper. As he walked down his front steps he held it carefully sideways, looking down into his own reflection. Even from my bedroom window, I could see that it was an old mirror, with darkly speckled glass.

Perhaps someone had given it to him, or maybe he found it at a garage sale in the days before people realized that their grandmothers' furniture might be valuable. But somehow it struck me that he must have inherited a mirror like that, with its gilt and strange dark glass. It had the look of owning *him*, and I think of how he must have carried it with him, from place to place, wherever he tried to go.

Julie and Steven returned from Amy Westendorf's beach house the day after Mr. Green moved away. They came home suntanned and leggy and restless, addicted to private jokes that they whispered across the table and then laughed at too noisily. Both of them seemed much older. Soon after they got home, my cast was taken off. It felt odd to see my foot again; it was white and shriveled and didn't look like the foot I remembered.

Around the same time, my mother quit selling magazines for Peterman-Wolff and got a better-paying job selling cosmetics at Lord & Taylor on Nebraska Avenue. It was a job that would lead eventually to the realm of store manager, a position that required her to wear formidable-looking suits and pearl earrings as she presided over a pale green office that smelled of gardenia air freshener, a position from which she retired only last year, with a party, a pension plan, and a gold scarf pin. But all that was still in the future. For the moment, nobody asked her to lunch and she had to wear a white smock, which made her look vaguely medical. For the last week before school started, the three of us children stayed alone in the house during the day while she was at work.

"Have you been in my room?" the twins both accused me as soon as they got home.

"Little creep," said Julie, pushing her face close to mine. "I know what you did."

Most afternoons we lay on the carpet in the living room with a fan blowing, kicking one another's feet. Sometimes we watched television game shows and tried to answer the questions. The twins wanted to know all about Mr. Green's arrest, but my mother had told them not to ask me anything.

"It's been an upsetting time," she said. "Leave her alone."

At first I was glad they were home, but after a day or two it seemed they had never left. Julie painted her fingernails green and tried to make Popsicles out of grape juice in ice-cube trays. She called her friends on the phone and talked for hours, twisting her hair around her fingers.

Spying through the keyhole into Steven's bedroom, I would find him hunched on his bed with his sketchpad, no longer drawing pictures of breasts, but now naked men and women twisting around each other, their mouths full of teeth. And once I saw him lying back against the pillow with his shorts peeled back, his big knees drawn up, one hand a furious blur between them. For an instant he had looked up, straight at the door, and I thought he'd seen me. But his eyes were blank and he was smiling that same tight, appalled smile I had seen the day he'd almost succeeded in getting caught stealing cigarettes from the drugstore.

Then came one Saturday afternoon, a warm Saturday in September just before Labor Day, when my mother dropped all three of us off at a pizza parlor in Rockville, saying she would be back to pick us up after she finished shopping.

"Be good," she said, not waving to us as we stood on the curb. Then she drove away.

He was sitting all alone in a booth near a window. The light cut across the top of his head and he sat very straight, not looking toward the door. Although I recognized him immediately, he seemed more like someone you recognize in a dream: himself, but in the guise of another person.

He stood up as we came close to his table and, like Julie and Steven after their vacation, he looked both older and a slightly different color. He wore a tan suit, a white shirt, and a wide blue tie with pink squiggles on it, which reminded me of sea worms, and his ginger sideburns were bushier than before. When we reached him he held out his arms, lifting his elbows away from his waist in a gesture that might have been one of perplexity. Only Steven stepped forward.

Then Julie went up to him. She collapsed a little at the knees as he hugged her, but a moment later she stepped primly away and sat down at the booth beside Steven.

"Hi there," my father said to me.

He held out his hand and after a moment I took it. We shook hands; then he pulled me against him and for a moment I smelled his lemony aftershave again, which hadn't changed, and felt his heart beating through his shirt and his sideburns scrubbing my cheek.

"I broke my ankle," I said, pulling back.

"Is that so?" He gave me a puzzled smile, because of course my cast was gone, and to him I must have looked all in one piece.

I don't remember what else we talked about in the beginning, only that I sat next to my father and stared at the side of his face, amazed that it could seem so normal to be in a pizza parlor with him when only a few hours before he had been as far away as another person can be and still share the same planet. I felt I had been holding my breath until this moment, but at the same time now that he was here, it seemed too late, as if he had missed whatever he had come back for. He drank two Cokes, I recall. And he smiled at everything Julie and Steven said, whether or not it was funny.

"Something more to drink?" he asked, sounding like old Mrs. Morris with her teapot. "Another slice of pizza?"

After a while Julie opened a packet of sugar and poured it on the table, then made designs in the spilled sugar with her fork. Whenever my father asked her a question, she said "yes" or "no," in a voice like a sigh. Talking fast, interrupting himself, Steven described the Westendorfs' beach house, how he had learned to sail a Sunfish, how he and Amy had sat in the Westendorfs' sauna drinking jug wine stolen from Mrs. Westendorf's refrigerator. He told a story about sleeping outside one night on the beach, and how Amy Westendorf had found a garter snake in her sleeping bag. He winked and sniggered extravagantly. My father seemed not to be listening. "Is that so," he said several times. When Steven finished talking, my father smiled.

Slowly he began to look more familiar. While he talked to the twins, I watched people walk by our table. I marveled that anyone walking by would have thought we looked like such an ordinary family. My father looked like an ordinary father in his tan jacket and tie, except that it was Saturday, and most fathers would be wearing shorts and a short-sleeved shirt.

"What else did you do this summer?" he asked the twins.

"Nothing," said Julie.

"Nothing?"

"We survived," said Steven in a tone that was meant to be sarcastic.

"Well of course you did," said my father.

Outside cars drove in and out in the parking lot, sun flaring off their hoods. Slowly the pizza parlor emptied out until there was just us and an old woman in a yellow polyester pantsuit sitting alone in a corner booth, occasionally coughing into her napkin. Someone had left a vacuum cleaner in the aisle near our table, its long neck looped over itself. Julie opened another packet of sugar. Steven started to say something else about the Westendorfs' beach house, then stopped and looked out the window.

"Check, please," said my father, holding up his hand.

While he was paying the bill, Julie suddenly asked, "So where's Aunt Ada?"

My father ran his finger down the bill's short column of numbers. He didn't look angry but only puzzled as he added up the numbers again, looking to see if they really totaled up right.

"Wasn't she with you?" Julie asked.

"She was." My father looked up and his aviator glasses caught the glare from a passing car.

"Why isn't she with you anymore?"

He cleared his throat and leaned back against his seat. For a minute or so he seemed absorbed in staring at the old woman in the yellow pantsuit, as if he recognized her but was trying to figure out how. Maybe she had bought a house from him once. Or maybe she reminded him of someone he used to know. Finally he sighed and looked back at us again. He said, "You know, things don't always work out very well for people, kids. Sometimes that happens."

He paused, staring at his hands, which he had stretched out flat on the table. A few minutes went by. No one said anything. Far away in the kitchen, someone dropped a tray of dishes.

At last my father looked up again and we all saw that his eyes were red. "I'm sorry, but it's very complicated. Nobody means for life to get complicated. I never meant it to. It just does. Sometimes it gets more complicated than you know what to do with, and so you just do the first thing you can. I don't mean to give you the runaround, kids," he said. "But I'm afraid that's the best answer I've got."

"Right," agreed Steven.

"You didn't have to go," Julie insisted.

"At the time I guess I thought I did."

Julie put her hands in her lap. She had on her carefully arranged aloof expression, the one I had caught her practicing in the bathroom mirror. She said: "It's been rotten for Mom."

At the mention of our mother, my father winced. He took

off his aviator glasses and polished them with his crumpled napkin. He put them on again and squinted at my sister.

"I don't expect for you to understand."

Julie curled her lip, but she was shredding her napkin under the table. Bits of napkin fluttered onto the floor.

"I am sorry," he said, "about everything that's happened. But I couldn't have prevented any of it."

In many ways my father had always been a soft-hearted man, someone who hated to punish his children, who pretended not to notice small acts of boorishness or spite, but for the first time I began to understand that, like a true romantic, he had very little tolerance for guilt. That Saturday afternoon he embarked upon what was to become a long process of shifting responsibility away from himself, until he was able to tell me at my own wedding reception a few years ago that he'd always felt my mother *wanted* him to fall in love with Aunt Ada.

"She pushed me," he said almost plaintively, fingering his boutonniere. "She knew I was attracted to Ada. For years she said, 'Admit it, isn't Ada the sexiest of all of us? Isn't Ada the one men want?' But you know, Marsha, I never would have done anything about it. I don't think I would have. Your mother, though." He shook his head, then tried to smile because Aunt Fran was taking our picture with her Kodak. When she was done and had turned away, he said in a soft fast voice, "Your mother almost made me feel that something was wrong with me if I *didn't* have an affair."

Perhaps this is true. My father was essentially a quiet person, except at the piano. I remember how he rocked from side to side, sometimes crooning to himself. Sometimes he let his fingers drift over the keys, making up riffs and sad, discordant refrains. If you called him in to dinner while he was playing the piano, even tapped him on the shoulder, it would take him a moment or two to look up. And then when he did, you were never sure if it was really you he was seeing. He was the type who requires a push. And that afternoon at the pizza parlor, I decided to give him one.

Steven reached for the saltshaker and began to spin it on the table. Our waitress passed by carrying a tray of ketchup bottles. Behind us, the old lady in the yellow pantsuit had started to cough again.

"A boy got killed in our neighborhood," I said.

Everyone turned to look at me.

"He got killed behind the mall. People thought Mr. Green did it. Mr. Green was our neighbor," I told my father.

Once I'd opened my mouth, I couldn't close it again. I spoke faster and faster, trying to remember everything that had happened since my father had been gone. It seemed that if I could tell him everything, without leaving anything out, then he would understand what had happened. And if he understood what had happened, it was possible that he might have an excuse for it, or a reason, and perhaps it would all suddenly seem all right.

I told him about Boyd Ellison lying on the hillside behind

the mall, and the crowds of people who went to stand there; and how Mr. Green had invited the whole neighborhood to a cookout but nobody went except my mother, who brought him a pineapple and forgot to wear her shoes; and that Mr. Green had moved away because of what I said about him; and that a tall detective came to our house and asked me questions; and that my mother had hit me and that she had made Aunt Fran and Aunt Claire stop calling her; and that Roy and Tiffany were dolls who never wore clothes and Roy had pins in his eyes. I said that Mr. Green had tried to talk to me in the backyard one day when I was alone. I said the Watergate burglars were morons.

I could hear myself speaking and I knew what I was saying, but by the end I think I realized that I wasn't saying anything anyone else really wanted to understand. In fact by the end I'm not sure I was actually saying words at all.

"Hush," said my father, looking around the restaurant. "Marsha, honey, please. Stop it."

The twins stared at me. Finally Steven said, "Nuts," and drew a spiral around his ear with his finger.

"No," said my father, reaching over to pull his hand down.

We all sat for a while longer at the table, looking out the window at the cars coming and going. Julie got up to go to the bathroom. Our waitress, who had a perfect blond ponytail and spotty skin, came to take the bill and the money my father had laid out. She said, "Can I get you anything else?" in a tone that meant she hoped we would say no. A few more people came into the pizza parlor, a man in a Redskins T-shirt, a woman with a baby, two teenage girls carrying shopping bags. They passed our table and glanced at us, then looked away.

Eighteen

The Night Watch kept up their patrols for another month or so, then gradually people became less afraid—or more used to being afraid—and the pairs of fathers stopped circling the block and went back to watching *Monday Night Football*. Perhaps it was the excitement around Mr. Green's arrest; it satisfied everyone to have someone arrested, even if he turned out to be the wrong person.

Now when neighbors got together to drink coffee or sip iced tea they were more likely to talk about George McGovern or the Watergate break-in or foreign affairs. Although it seems to me that our neighbors never again visited one another as frequently as they had before the murder. After those first few weeks of frantic interest, people stopped asking each other if they had heard anything new. All of Mrs. Lauder's bake-sale signs eventually disappeared, to be replaced here and there by campaign placards. Boyd Ellison himself was growing more and more indistinct, until after a

while he simply faded into his name. Even I got tired of counting over the meager facts I knew. He was a short blond boy
with a square head. He once asked to wear my glasses. He sat
in our basement tying knots. He tortured an insect with a
pocketknife.

I was there, I whispered to myself. *I knew him.*

His parents moved to Virginia, and gradually I stopped circling past their house, with its red Japanese maple in the front
yard and pulled window blinds.

Mrs. Sperling made Mr. Sperling put locks on the downstairs windows and took to answering the door by first looking
through the newly installed peephole. The Lauders put up a
stockade fence around their backyard. The Reades bought a
German shepherd. And the Morrises died, one after the
other.

By then we had moved away.

Not long ago I asked a lawyer at the Justice Department, a
friend of a friend, if he could find out if the police ever caught
the man who murdered Boyd Ellison. He said he would call
someone he knew at the F.B.I. A few days later he phoned me
to say the case was still open. Apparently every time a child is
murdered in a wooded area, the Montgomery County police
see if they can link it to Boyd Ellison's murder. They're still
looking for a pattern, he told me. Even after twenty-five
years.

"Couldn't it have been an isolated incident?" I said.

My friend's friend thought not. "No one has the impulse to

do something like that just once," he said. "It's like a guy who cheats on his wife. Once he's done it and gotten away with it, he's going to do it again."

I said it didn't seem like the same thing to me at all, but I thanked him and hung up.

These days whenever I drive through my old neighborhood, which isn't often, I always note that it hasn't changed much. Spring Hill is almost exactly as I remember it, a quiet green place in the summertime, full of neat lawns and hedges and shaggy maples that shade the sidewalks. The houses look a little older and smaller, and more established; trees I remember as saplings are now two stories tall, and in some cases ivy has completely covered a wall or a fence. But children still ride their bicycles back and forth or teeter by on Rollerblades. Men and women who look like the children's parents weed their flower beds or wash their cars. It looks like a safe enough place, even a hopeful place. A few weeks ago when I drove by on my way to visit a client I saw election bumper stickers and a couple of lawn signs. It's that time again.

Our old house no longer belongs to the people we sold it to, or even to the people who bought it from them. When I last passed it, a couple about my age was standing on the lawn with two little boys; the woman had red hair and a disagreeable mouth, but her chubby blond husband had a nice face and he was smiling as one of the little boys tugged at the grass with a toy rake. For some reason, they had decided to paint the house chocolate brown—perhaps a heat-saving measure?—which has given it a squat brooding look. Next door, the Lauders' house still looks the same, although someone has torn out most of the front yard and put down asphalt. Four cars were parked there when I last went by. The Morrises', the Sperlings', and the Reades' houses have all undergone a renovation or two—a set of sliding glass doors, a breezeway, a new garage—without altering their original appearance much. Even the Ellisons' house isn't really different from what I remember; it could be just another three-bedroom split-level on a quarter acre.

Oddly enough, of all the houses in the neighborhood only Mr. Green's house, what was so briefly his house, has really changed. A second floor has been added, and a mansard roof. The marigolds are gone, replaced by an ambitious attempt at a Japanese garden, complete with mossy rocks, a tiny cement goldfish pond, and a little black iron pagoda near where he used to set his sprinkler. And that enormous old copper beech in his backyard is no longer there, dead from some blight or fungus or chopped down by the new owners, who seem intent on small-scale landscaping.

I was surprised at how much I missed that copper beech. You never quite expect a tree to disappear, especially such a big one. It was probably over a hundred and fifty years old, maybe the last tree left from when Spring Hill was simply a hill, and malls and subdivisions hadn't been dreamed up yet. I remember how wide its canopy used to seem, and the bright color the leaves turned in the fall. The whole street seemed slightly unbalanced by its absence, like a row of books when one in the middle has been pulled out. Every time I drive by, I expect to see it. And every time I have to realize again that it's gone.

Once I actually stopped and parked for a few minutes across the street from Mr. Green's house. For years, I could keep myself awake at night simply by picturing the way he had looked that summer morning when he came back from the police station, gripping his briefcase, the outline of his undershirt showing through his wrinkled white shirt. Every time I thought of him I would feel a kind of hot suffocating panic that made me sit up and throw off my blankets, and only after turning on the lights and reading magazines for a while could I push him back south to wherever it was he went.

My life seemed bound to his in a way I couldn't explain and didn't want to. The closest I could come was the feeling that somehow what I'd done to him had made me *his* child, and that one of these days he would figure it out and come back for me.

Yet eventually all that guilty fear was replaced by something quieter, until as I sat in the car by myself that afternoon, staring at a house that could never have been his, I could honestly say I wished him well. I hope he found a nice place to live somewhere in the country. I can almost see him tending a vegetable patch in back of a little wooden house, weeding around his melons and tomatoes, wearing a straw hat, although he must be an old man by now. Sometimes I imagine myself driving down south, to Tennessee or Georgia, and just by accident finding his house. He would be in the yard leaning on his hoe, wiping his pink face with a faded blue bandanna. For a minute or so we would stare at each other, as you do with people you recognize but can't name, then he would give me a short nod.

But whenever I carry this fantasy much further it begins to get tangled up with explanations from my therapist and my own excuses, and Mr. Green and his hoe disappear along with everything I meant to tell him.

Two days after he met us at the pizza parlor, my father drove to Cleveland, his hometown, where the brother of a cousin's husband gave him work in an insurance company. In a funny way, I never expected him to stay in town. Which didn't mean I was glad to see him leave again, only that I wasn't surprised by it. He called us once a week that first fall, usually on Sundays; he was lonely, I think. Then slowly he called less frequently, until we heard from him only around our birthdays and on Christmas and Thanksgiving, or when something in particular made him think of us. Usually we went to visit him for a week or two in the summer. It wasn't the best way to conduct a relationship, but it wasn't as bad as some I've heard about. He put all three of us through college.

Ada came back that September as well, but like my father she didn't stay long. All we heard from her was a single note to my mother, scratched in pencil on the back of an old receipt, slipped through the letter slot one afternoon when no one was home. It said: "I'll call you."

But instead she went to Milwaukee to stay in Aunt Fran's big brick Tudor near the lake. According to Aunt Fran and Aunt Claire, Ada spent most of her time sleeping on the living-room sofa. As I passed through our kitchen one afternoon that fall, just before we moved to the house we would be renting in College Park, I heard the familiar sound of my mother defending Ada on the phone.

"You know Ada, she's always had a different metabolism than the rest of us," she was saying, slapping the phone cord rhythmically against the floor. "Well, maybe she's sleeping so much because she has the flu."

But that very afternoon, Ada woke up from a long nap, threw some clothes into a paper grocery sack, and walked out Aunt Fran's front door. She walked straight to the bus station, bought a ticket to San Francisco, and for the next two years or so, vanished.

No one heard a word from her. Aunt Fran and Aunt Claire hired a private detective. They took out small advertisements in five California newspapers: ADA. WHERE ARE YOU? MUCH LOVE. Although they were furious that Ada had left so theatrically, without even a note—like a child, they said, or a crazy woman. "You know Ada," they repeated to each other, but now in a questioning tone, because clearly neither of them did.

When they heard from Ada again, it was by Christmas card in 1974, a woodcut of a nude Madonna with lopsided breasts sitting on a tree stump; she sent one to each sister. By then she was living in Mendocino, up on the northern California coast. She had married a carpenter, who built a little frame house for them not far from the ocean, and she had her own tailgate business making macramé handbags and plant holders, which she said wasn't "Art," but she could sell them to tourists.

"I often think of you," Ada wrote in lavender ink to my mother.

And perhaps she still does, although that was years ago and I don't believe my mother ever wrote back to her. Or maybe she did write back and decided to keep whatever answers she got to herself. That would be like my mother. But as far as I'm concerned, Ada has disappeared. People can do that. I think that's the worst thing I have had to face as I head into middle age, the years when disappearance begins to be commonplace, when it's no longer such a dramatic thing to lose someone. "I haven't heard from him in years," we say. "She died a while ago. We had fallen out of touch."

But to lose a child—I don't know how anyone would ever get used to that. I don't think you are supposed to get used to it. Years go by and I forget about Boyd Ellison, but then something will remind me and there it is, that hillside in July, afternoon sunlight hanging in the humid air like yellow gauze. It was so hot that day. It was such an ordinary day. Until that little cry reached a tired florist about to get into her car.

Once I've let myself venture that far I can't help but start wondering all over again. What if she had moved two steps to the left? What if she had worn her glasses that afternoon? What if she had listened harder, not been so preoccupied. I wonder if the florist herself still retraces those few minutes, if after all these years she still dreams of climbing the hillside, wading through broken bottles, locust husks, and creeper vines. Could she have done things differently? Could she?

But it wasn't until I found this notebook the other day, helping my mother move some old boxes out of the basement of her apartment building, that I started to wonder what had become of Boyd's parents. All I really know is that they moved to Virginia. Like Mr. Green, they got out fast, but not before they'd had to live through his arrest. Not before they'd had to live through thinking their son's murderer had been caught, that they might actually see the man who had taken everything from them, see that he was real, human, maybe even get to ask him the question that as the years went on must have haunted them—"Why?" they would ask, why? why?—only to find out that it was the wrong man, that their killer was still out there. I should have known all that. And yet until tonight, as I sat here turning the pages of this old notebook, I'd never realized how I must have hurt them, too.

It's funny, after all these years I'm still fascinated by how people hurt each other, why it happens, and by what makes people need to be cruel. But I'm afraid my interest nowadays has become practical. When I was a child, I was curious about the mechanics of pain. Now I want to understand for reasons of security. "Watch yourself"—it's still the best advice anyone ever gave me. Pain is always about to happen somewhere to someone I know and at times it seems that the best I can hope for is not to be the cause of it. In this way I guess I am a product of my generation, most of us anxious pragmatists and skeptics, who are less interested in the mysteries of human pain and cruelty than in how to avoid them.

Which is why, in a curious way, I've come to feel grateful to Mr. Green. Because when you have watched yourself do the worst thing you can imagine doing to another person, at least you know what you're capable of. At least you have the rest of your life to be more careful.

A child's body on a hillside in July. A woman reading magazines in the dark. A man standing alone in an empty street. Like images from a flickering projector, they appear, disappear, but they are always there. I don't want to be melodramatic, but they are what I have.

One of the last times I spoke to my father on the phone, not long before he died last May, I said: "I just want you to know. I don't hold anything against you."

He sounded genuinely surprised when he answered, "Why should you hold anything against me?" Then, as if suddenly recollecting, he said, "It's been a long time, Marsha. I don't know how long you're supposed to hold onto something like that."

"For as long as you don't understand it," I shot back.

"I always loved you," he said softly, breathing onto the phone receiver.

"Then why did you leave me?" I asked. And there it was. I had finally asked. I hadn't even known how much I wanted to ask him that question until I had done it, until that question whistled out of me like a cry. *Why did you leave me?*

For quite a while he didn't say anything. I listened to him breathe hoarsely onto the phone and imagined him sitting alone in his little Cleveland apartment in his recliner, the window closed and locked beside him, one hand drifting through his thin gray hair. Outside, evening would be coming on, sharp light slanting along the sidewalk. At last he said regretfully, "I don't know. I'm sorry. I can't remember that well anymore."

"That's all right," I said, ashamed to find myself relieved. "Maybe we'll talk about it some other time." But of course there wasn't another time. He died a couple months later, of a heart attack that nobody predicted. He was only sixty-seven.

I wasn't prepared for how it would be when he died. I had been living without my father for nearly a quarter of a century and yet when Julie called to tell me that he was dead, suddenly there I was, ten years old all over again, and he had just left me, and the world was a wide place in the dark, and right then I understood as if for the very first time that nothing in my life would ever feel safe.

Acknowledgments

I would like to thank the National Endowment for the Arts and the Massachusetts Cultural Council for their generous support. I am very grateful as well to Marcie Hershman, Eileen Pollack, Marjorie Sandor, Alex Johnson, Jodi Daynard, Jessica Treadway, Phil Press, and especially Maxine Rodburg —all of whom read drafts of this novel and offered encouragement and advice. Many thanks, also, to my agent, Colleen Mohyde, and to my editor, Shannon Ravenel.